KV-576-252

INTRODUCTION

In *Hawbuck Grange* Robert Smith Surtees unashamedly confirms that one side of his personality was cantankerous and intolerant. He declines in this novel to fit in with any of the demands of heroic sporting fiction.

The reader is not to be rewarded by soaring and exciting accounts of hunting days beyond the dreams of the most ardent follower of the Chase.

Perversely, Surtees chooses to inform, to tease and to amuse us by recording the happenings in an exceptionally poor hunting season, that of 1846–7.

Much of *Hawbuck Grange* is clearly autobiographical. As a widely travelled hunting correspondent, Surtees had experienced most of the sporting trials and tribulations which befall his central character, an unexceptional sportsman, Tom Scott, who travels from his home, Hawbuck Grange, to sample sport in other hunting countries.

Surtees had already published his marvellous Jorrocks novel *Handley Cross*, in 1843, and *Hillingdon Hall* two years later.

The glories of *Mr Sponge, Mr Facey Romford* and other superb works were still to come. Yet in 1847, when he was 43, Surtees clearly had the confidence to indulge his most deeply felt prejudices in *Hawbuck Grange*. Romantic interest and subsidiary plot are meagre. Instead, Surtees boldly uses his story line to expound his controversial views on the conduct of hunting, the character of some who take part, and occasional flaws in the sporting environment.

Whatever the novel's faults, Surtees succeeds in holding our interest, and entertaining us vastly, because of his genius for satire, and his immense gifts for descriptive prose.

With what relish he delineates the shortcomings of a truly bad inn: The Goldtrap Arms. Surtees knew only too well the abominations of a slovenly hostelry in early Victorian

England. He gives the food and the service baleful attention, and is equally scathing about the stabling. The ostler is described as attending Tom Scott's mare with "the usual chilling, temper-trying, fistling and fumbling of the slovenly stableman."

Even the inn's poor cuckoo clock gets a Surteesian lambasting. This particular form of time-keeping was another pet hate: "Who would keep a cuckoo clock that didn't wish to be driven mad? This was the slowest, prosiest, most unlike a cuckoo, cuckoo clock that ever was heard ..." And so on, for a lengthy paragraph of cuckoo clock ridicule.

Surtees releases further acid from his pen in the direction of one of his favourite targets: minor aristocracy running country houses, and Hunts, with feckless disregard for punctuality and efficiency.

It has to be recorded, however, that the Surtees brand of acid is not malicious; it is heavily laced with fun. The story teller remains of deadpan visage; the reader is permitted to smile.

Lord Lionel Lazytongs of Dawdle Court is the principal example of less than perfect aristocracy lampooned in *Hawbuck Grange.*

His Lordship irritates by his pretentious "banging on" about foxhunting exploits up and down the land in an after dinner monologue. Yet next morning he offends by being horribly late for the meet. Hounds had found immediately, and been away with their fox at least ten minutes when Lazytongs and his guest, Tom Scott, arrive.

Such a dire crime even excused a rare lack of manliness in this Surtees hero: "Poor Tom was never so vexed in his life. He could have cried, if no one had been there."

The message throughout *Hawbuck Grange* is that pretension and "fashion" sit ill in the hunting field, or indeed in any other sphere known to Surtees. Chapter titles such as "Doubtful Days", "The Bad Meet" and "The Blank Day" confirm the writer's endeavour to demonstrate that it is perfectly possible to make the best of a bad job – that hunting does not depend for its ultimate enjoyment on galloping wildly across country.

He dares to start his season with "the worst hunting November that perhaps was ever known. It was more like a bad March than the glorious, sloppy, burning scent sort of weather peculiar to that month."

All the emphasis on hound work, and not break-neck riding, appeared in *Hawbuck Grange* at a time when the legend of Leicestershire style sport was enjoying its first heyday, having been born out of Hugo Meynell's discovery that the great swathe of grass from Nottingham down to Market Harborough was a perfect setting for hunting in the open at top pace. It was not Meynell, but his growing band of youthful followers who made hunting an excuse for the constant leaping of obstacles.

Although a competent horseman, Surtees was never a thruster in the hunting field, and could not forbear to ridicule harshly and unfairly that great Leicestershire scribe, Nimrod (Charles James Apperley) who rode so ardently with the first rank.

Surtees in *Hawbuck Grange* spells out his views succinctly: "Some people fancy hard riding an indispensable quality for a sportsman, but we believe if we were to canvass the sporting world, we should find that the real lovers of hunting are anything but a hard-riding set. Fond of seeing hounds work, they use their horses as a sort of auxiliary to their legs, and having got a lift across a field they are all the abler to compete with a hedge when they take one, which they feel they would have had to take, even on foot."

Surtees uses the device of comparing foxhunting with hare hunting as a means of emphasising the virtues of hound work. His description of a day with The Goose and Dumpling Hunt is a gem of sporting prose; perhaps the best thing in *Hawbuck Grange*.

The followers of this unpretentious pack of harriers firmly decline to leap anything in following their beloved hounds: "... if there isn't a gap where they want to be over, why they make one."

Their joy and pride in the prowess of their hounds shines

through the masterly description of their day's sport.

Surtees rivals Dickens in his ability to recreate the sort of conviviality of a thoroughly English, masculine dinner party, which the harrier hunters hold after their sport, partaking liberally of the main course which gives the Hunt its name, accompanied by top-class home produced beer. Surtees praises this above mere French wines: "we are quite sure we have tasted bottled ale that would be priced above champagne if it was only as dear."

The day's foxhunting which receives the most enthusiastic attention from Surtees in *Hawbuck Grange* is the least fashionable imaginable: the Stout-as-Steel hounds are a hill and moorland pack, followed by a Master and hunt servants mounted on mules!

But Surtees concentrates on the excellent performance of the hounds, "bright-coloured, wiry-haired, rough muzzled animals, combining the power, mettle and endurance of the fox hound, with the hard bitten pertinacity of the terrier."

In this deeply prejudiced account of a bad hunting season, there is so much to learn, so much to enjoy.

The intricacies of plot, the rascally characters, to be found later in *Sponge* and *Romford* are missing here. *Hawbuck Grange* is a lesser star in the Surteesian galaxy, but it has an honourable and worthwhile place in his creative output. Its self indulgence is surely one more sign of the confidence and enjoyment which Surtees derived from authorship.

Greater works were yet to be penned, and their advent is presaged in *Hawbuck Grange* by Surtees' self-mocking admission that he finds "writing ... something like snuffing or smoking – men get into the way of it, and can't well leave it off."

MICHAEL CLAYTON

Horse and Hound
King's Reach Tower
London S.E.1
January 1988

HAWBUCK GRANGE.

Hawbuck Grange as seen from the South

HAWBUCK GRANGE;

OR, THE

SPORTING ADVENTURES OF THOMAS SCOTT, ESQ.

BY THE AUTHOR OF

" HANDLEY CROSS; OR, THE SPA HUNT,"

&c.

WITH EIGHT ILLUSTRATIONS BY PHIZ.

THE R. S. SURTEES SOCIETY

PREFACE.

ALL we have got to say in the way of a preface to this work is, that our friend Tom Scott, seeing his Adventures advertised as the sporting adventures of " Thomas Scott, Esquire," wrote to us to say that he calls himself *Mister* — Mr. Thomas Scott, and that he has " THOMAS SCOTT, FARMER, HAWBUCK GRANGE," in honest parliamentary-sized letters, without flourish or eye-mystifying gewgaw, on the back of his dog-cart, as any one who likes to inspect it may see.

London,
October, 1847.

CONTENTS.

———✦———

ENGRAVINGS ON STEEL.

LIST OF VIGNETTES.

EXTRA ILLUSTRATIONS.

———◆———

HAWBUCK GRANGE,

ETC.

COLD-BROOK GORSE.

CHAPTER I.

CUB-HUNTING.

"Sport in fox hunting cannot be said to begin before October, but in the two preceding months a pack is either made or marred."— BECKFORD.

"IT *was* the horn I heard," said Scott, as the old mare again cocked her ears to the wind. " It *was* the horn I heard, as I came over Addington Hill, though the country looks so green and gay that I never thought of such a thing as hunting."

This exclamation was elicited as, on a fine bright September day, a month in which, according to the usual course of English summers, harvest operations would be about commencing in many parts, Mr. Thomas Scott the hero of this work, whose "pedigree and performances" must work themselves out as we proceed, was taking a quiet ride "across country" to hear how things were going on at the kennel.

The kennel is a grand summer lounge. One is sure to fall in with somebody to talk to ; either the huntsman ingratiating himself with his entry, the whip sweeping the yards, or the feeder filling his boiler or scalding his troughs. It is privileged easiness—not idleness, but easiness—for the huntsman can " make off " a pup quite as well in the presence of a stranger as when alone, and the whip is not likely to be put off his work by answering "interrogatories," as our friend Bigbag of the Chancery bar calls his questions, nor the boiler turned from his purpose by listening to our rigmarole. Therefore a man goes to the kennel with the certainty of a smiling reception and a gossip, instead of a gruff " Well, what do you want ? " or the " I'm particularly busy just now," of the man who, seeing one's approach from his window, mutters to himself, " Here's that confounded Tom Scott coming to bother me with his infernal nonsense. I wish he was ——. Ah, Tom, my dear fellow, how are you ? " &c.

Tom was riding his favourite old roan mare, that has carried him safely for ten good seasons, and who knows just as well what she goes out for as he does. She had gone stepping along, with the snaffle bridle rein dangling carelessly on her neck, when, on reaching the summit of the aforementioned hill, she suddenly pricked her ears, giving certain indications of gaiety quite incompatible with the sober steadiness of pace she had been pursuing.

Mr. Scott no more thought of hearing the horn in September than he did of picking gooseberries at Christmas, or of having a snowball romp in August. Indeed, how should he ? Take the summer or no summer of 1845 as a "precedent," as Bigbag

would say, and what was he doing in September ?   Shearing a
bit of barley—beginning with the wheat, perhaps and the
"tartars" standing so ridiculously green as to look for all the
world like next year's crop.   The summers of 1845 and 1846
were not in the least like the same thing, neither were the
winters.   Some masters hardly got any cub-hunting at all in
1845, so late and protracted was the harvest.   But, when they
did begin hunting, what a season they had !   Almost a surfeit
—to the short stud ones, certainly a surfeit.   We had not had
such an early season as the one of 1846, since "Plenipo's"
year, when we remember seeing a buck ride up Doncaster
High-street in scarlet and boots on the Leger day.   The summer
was a roaster; but what a winter followed !   That, however, we
will deal with as we go on.

Well, old Barbara was right.   At a second blast, her small
pointed ears almost touched, and she stood stock still.   The
spot she chose was worthy the eye of a painter.   It was the
angle of a road, commanding as well the deep-ribbed Gothic
arches of an old stone bridge, as the bend of the rapid river
above, whose rocky sides were fringed with stately trees of
various sorts, in all the motley beauty of autumnal leaf.   The
hounds *were* out.   Mr. Scott had not stood many seconds, ere
the well known "Get away !" of the whip, on the one side, and
the horn of the huntsman on the other, proclaimed that they had
drawn the banks.

Presently he saw a scarlet — a purple, rather — then
another, and shortly after a small cavalcade, among which
he distinctly recognised the flaunting of a couple of habits,
emerged from the wooded waterside and made for the grass
field above.

The horn again twanged, and the whips cracked loud and
heavily on the clear crisp atmosphere, sounding over the far
country like guns.

"I'm in luck," said Mr. Scott, pretending to tickle old
Barbara's sides with his spurless shooting shoe-heel.   The old

mare, however, wanted no persuasion. Having satisfied herself
what was going on, she forthwith gathered herself together,
and began showing her big black knees below her nose, as she
trotted away in the line.

She knew the way as well as Scott did—in at the bridle-gate
by Squire Ramrod's keeper's, across the lawn, through the
brook, and at the back of Mr. Hacker's farm buildings, then
a long trot along the banks, and another bridle-gate at the
top lets her into the field where the hounds were. She had
often gone that line, but never so early in the year—at least
never for the purpose of hunting.

We have often doubted whether masters of hounds like seeing
people out cub-hunting or not, and we have about settled the
question in our own mind as follows, viz. that huntsmen or
masters who go out early—at day-break, for instance—are glad
to see people, because they are sure that none but sportsmen
will come ; whereas the midday or afternoon performance
favours all the idle, yammering, bothersome, chance-medley
customers of the country.

Take to-day's field as a sample. There were the Misses
Ogleby, beautiful girls, and full of chatter ; and in their train
the great Mr. Tarquinius Muff, dressed like a dancing-
master, and his brother Blatheremskite Muff, who come after
the girls instead of after the hounds. Then there was little
Dr. Podgers, the union doctor, on his black pony, who fell
in with the hounds at Gunton Gate, and is deluding himself
into the idea that he is hunting ; Drippinghead, the butcher's
boy, with his greasy blue coat, and apron tucked round his
waist, who is stealing his hour to the detriment of his
unfortunate nag, who will have to gallop all the way home ;
an unknown gentleman in gambadoes, with an umbrella under
his arm ; Tom Muzroll, the horsebreaker, who is instructing a
four-year-old at the expense of the pack ; and two weed-
riding, be-trousered, be-whiskered young gentlemen from the

"GET TO HIM, ARROGANT," SCREAMED JOE.

To face page 4.

neighbouring town of Scrapetin, who just may be anything
or anybody.

But Scott approaches the field. Hark to old Muff! Tarquinius, that's to say. "Halloo, Mr. Scott!" exclaims he,
with all the consequence of the great Mr. O'Toole, the toast-
master himself. "Halloo, Mr. Scott, you are getting slack in
your old age. What! only coming out now! You've lost the
most *beau*tiful thing that ever was seen—found half-a-dozen
most *beau*tiful foxes all huddled together, and had the most
charming hunt that can possibly be imagined. Hadn't we,
Miss Amelia?" asks he, appealing to the younger of the
sisters.

"O dear! thuch a delightful hunt!" lisps the beauty,
repressing her jet black hair beneath her smart black Malay
cock-feathered hat. "My pony took *thuch* a jump!"
added she, raising herself up in the saddle, as if to show
how it was done, sousing down an uncommonly neat *embon-
point* figure.

Muff is Scott's abomination. Had he ever thought of meeting him, he would have gone "t'other way." Muff knows he
despises him, and calls him a "humbug," but cannot resist the
opportunity of showing off before the ladies by pretending to
be a great sportsman. They don't know that he isn't, and he
thinks by carrying matters with a high hand to prevent Scott
exposing him.

Just as Scott had undergone the Muffs, and made his salutations to the "ladies," who received him in the sort of way
young ladies generally receive incorrigible fox-hunting, not
particularly young or overgilt bachelors—just as Scott had
undergone and performed all this we say, Arrogant, who had
been making the banks echo with her name, at last con-
descended to creep through the wood-fence, and make for the
pack in the hurried way peculiar to disobedient hounds with an
irate whipper-in at their sterns.

"*Get to him, Arrogant!*" screamed Joe, the second whip,

galloping and cracking his whip, as though he would cut her
in two.

Mr. Neville, who had been sitting patiently waiting Arrogant's appearance, to say a few words to the juvenile delin-
quent, and parrying Blatheremskite Muff's importunities to
know when he would begin "advertising," was just turning
his horse to move on when Mr. Scott's appearance attracted
his attention.

"Ah, Tom, my boy!" exclaimed he, his handsome face
brightening up with a smile, "*I was just thinking of you.* I
was just looking at that ugly turnstile, and thinking of the
confounded cropper you got over it on the first day of the
season. By Jove that's twenty years since," added he, with
a shake of the head, and a significant glance of his bright
eye.

"*Three and twenty*, Sir," replied Tom, for so we will take the
liberty of calling him too.

"By Jove, you're right," rejoined Mr. Neville. "*Quite
right, I do declare*," with an emphasis, and a dig of his hunting-whip end on his thigh. "It was the fifteenth season of
my hunting the country, and now I'm in my thirty-eighth—
time flies."

"It passes lightly over you, Sir, though," observed
Tom.

"Middling," replied he, cheerfully. "Middling—can't complain. What do you think of the young hounds? That's a
nice lot," said he, pointing to some yellow pied ones who came
frisking forward as he called them by name; "Marksman!
Merlin! Messmate! Midnight! Myrtle! by old Marmion
out of Marcia," added he, his eyes sparkling as he looked
at them. "Marmion was by Sir Bellingham Graham's
Marmion, you know; and Marcia was by Lord Lonsdale's
Monarch out of Modish;" and so he went on through his
entry.

Mr. Neville is one of the last of the old school of sportsmen;

of men who made fox-hunting their study, instead of mixing it
up with half-a-dozen other pursuits. Everything connected
with his establishment is ordered with the regularity of the
army, and conducted with the precision of a regiment. Cub-
hunting :—Undress ; men in hats, last year's coats, boots,
breeches, and whips, riding, exercising horses ; master in a
sort of costume combining the varieties of the shooter, the
hare-hunter, and the farmer—white hat, green cut-away,
striped cravat and waistcoat, drab breeches, with cloth
caps to his boots, and a pair of heavy-looking spurs ; horse,
a hack ; saddle and bridle, last year's ones, whip ditto ;
and there's the cub-hunting turn-out. Year after year has
seen him in the same ; and so rapidly have they passed, that
the first time appears but as last year. Nor has the hand of
time marked its lapse more strongly on his person. His hair
may be a shade greyer, whiter rather ; but his figure retains its
pristine lightness and neatness, he sits well into his saddle, and
looks like what he is—a gentleman and a sportsman. How
unlike the Muffs with their ringlets, and chains, and brooches,
and gew-gaws—their registered paletots, satin cravats, white
leather trousers, and varnished, heel-spurred boots! They look
more like Hyde Park than the hunting-field.

"This is our *first* day," observed the squire. "Indeed, I
didn't think of going ; but it was so fine, and the Misses
Ogleby persuaded me."

The fact was, the Muffs had bothered him so that he went
to the kennel to get rid of them ; and finding they followed,
he took out the hounds. "We killed a cub in Clifton
Dean," continued he ; "and found a litter in the banks,
and now we are going to Cold-brook Gorse : *we've plenty
of foxes*, and there is a litter there wants disturbing." So
saying he gave the signal to old Ben, the huntsman,
who forthwith tickled his nag in the flank, and, preceded
by Tom, the whip, took a line of bridle gates for Cold-brook
Gorse.

The country was not quite clear of corn ; indeed, they came
upon a field of oats they were shearing, across a corner of which
the route lay.

" Come on, Sir—come on, Sir ! " cried the farmer, from
amidst his workpeople, seeing the squire was turning away to
avoid the damage of the hounds through the standing corn.
" You're quite welcome, Sir !—you're quite welcome, Sir ! "
repeated he, as he held open the gate into the field.   This put
the horsemen into single file ; and as they jogged on, Tom
thus began to ruminate :—

" Cub-hunting is only poor sport to any but the immediately
interested," said he.   " It resembles the tuning of the instruments for a grand let off of a concert, all of which is very
right, necessary, and proper, but a sort of thing that the public
care very little to hear.   To the master, however, it is everything.   It is the rehearsal of the performance of the season,
and upon which much of his credit and comfort depends.   Still
it has more the air of the foreign *chasse* about it than the go-
along clear-the-stage devil-take-the-hindmost-sort of affair of
an English fox-hunt.   It is like a play, with the principal
character omitted—a kill without a run, or the intention of a
run."

Despite the sneer and smile of contempt it may raise on the
features of our friends, we will candidly state that we agree
with Mr. Scott and are not cub-hunters.   We have no taste for
killing foxes " while they suck," as the old huntsman said to
the young one, who was boasting of the number of noses he
reckoned on the kennel door.

Cub-hunting is like the noise and prattle of children, all very
delightful to the parents, but very uninteresting to strangers.
If you get up in the middle of the night to start with the light,
though you avoid the Muffs, you have not the excitement that
attends the same performance in the spring of the year, when
you go to drag up to a wild flying fox.   In the latter case, you
have the hopes of a gallant run over a boundless extent of

country, while, with the cubs, it is all up and down, backwards and forwards, heading and tally-hoing back. Hunting is hunting, no doubt, and the cry of hounds is very delightful— far better than Jullien's or any other body's band—and the cry of hounds is most beautiful in a wood, but a great part of the joyful excitement is lost by the knowledge that the fading dying notes outside, so quickly following "Tally-ho! a-w-a-y!" will not be heard. "Tally-ho! back! Tally-ho! back!" is only a poor cry.

In short, cub-hunting is neither one thing nor another, to any one save the master and his men. There is neither the joyous wide-awake uncertainty and excitement peculiar to the real thing, nor the quiet, staid, take-it-easy, game-at-chess-sort of labyrinth unwinding of hare-hunting. Cub-hunting is good for the ladies and men like the Muffs, who come out for appetites and to kill time. They can take up positions on hills and view commanding spots, join the chiding of hounds with the charms of the landscape, and trot away when they have had enough of either ; but the man who wants his gallop, and to see hounds work, had better take a turn with the harriers. It is bad enough laming a horse with harriers at the beginning of the season, but infinitely worse stubbing or staking one in cub-hunting. Moreover, the ground is generally so desperately hard in autumn, that it shakes and shatters the often not over sound legs and feet of the old hunter. Many a horse is perfectly sound in November, that makes a very pottering shamble of it over the hard ground in September or October. But we are only stating what everybody knows.

The hounds soon arrived at Cold-brook Gorse ; and a fine, large, close, healthy cover it was. Bush swelled above bush, like undulations of the sea, or like cauliflower heads ; and the rising ground of the north side commanded a view of the whole. A belt of now bright yellow horse-chestnuts, broken, weather-beaten, and bent, formed a sort of shelter on that side.

There were eight or ten acres of it altogether, and we hold that one cover of eight or ten acres is worth eight or ten covers of two or three acres.

The low end we should add was bounded by Cold-brook, a very uninviting, sedgy, rotten-banked looking burn, of great reputed coldness of water, as frequently tested in the course of each season.

The hounds were soon in the cover.

The compact gorse began to shake, and in less than two minutes the place was alive with their melody.

They had found no end of foxes ! The scared blackbirds flew in all directions ; rabbits popped in and out ; and every now and then a great golden-throppled cock-pheasant or dusky-coloured hen rose with boisterous clamour, as if furiously indignant at such unwonted intrusion.

Up and down, and round about, the whips rode, hooping, and hallooing, and cracking their whips ; but it is weary work hallooing to hounds with a good scent in a close gorse.

*   *   *   *   *

At last a cub slipped out at the low corner with Marksman, Merlin, and Midnight after him.

" Oh ! pray turn those hounds, Mr. Muff ! " hallooed Mr. Neville from the junction of the rides in the centre of the gorse.

Tarquinius Muff, when thus appealed to, was in the middle of a long dissertation on shirt frills, on which he particularly prides himself, being generally set off in front like a pouter pigeon ; and thinking the appeal to him for assistance complimentary to his sporting skill, he immediately gathered his horse together, and with a touch of his large brass heel spurs, proceeded to show off before the ladies by giving chase to the fugitives.

The horse seemed to like the fun, and went off so resolutely

that Muff never saw the brook until just in time to pull the
horse in, which he did most skilfully, blobbing right over head
in the middle of it!

We are ashamed to say the ladies laughed, as their dripping
friend came spluttering ashore.

With that sorry exploit we will conclude Tom Scott's first
day of a bad season.

TARQUINIUS MUFF'S MISHAP.

CHAPTER II.

THE GOOSE AND DUMPLING HUNT.

"Harriers, to be good, like all other hounds, must be kept to their own game; if you run fox with them, you spoil them; hounds cannot be perfect unless used to one scent and one style of hunting. Harriers run fox in so different a style from hare, that it is of great disservice to them when they return to hare again; it makes them wild, and teaches them to skirt. The high scent which a fox leaves, the straightness of his running, the eagerness of the pursuit, and the noise that generally accompanies it, all contribute to spoil harriers."—BECKFORD.

MR. SCOTT was debating whether to go to Holbrook Fair, or take his dogs and gun and stroll up to the ten-acre piece they were draining, when the short harsh bark of Snap at the door, and the clink of the German catch at the side gate, announced somebody coming.

It was Joe Stumps, Mr. Trumper of Jolly-rise's man, whose trot and bustling air, with the portentous display of a ponderous hunting-whip, bespoke no common errand.

Tom went to the porch to meet him—

"Meazster's compliments and hooundes be out," said Joe, with which laconic speech he was turning his horse's head to go away without deigning to say where "hooundes" were.

"*Where are they, Joe?*" hallooed Scott.

"Stockenchurch Hill, *to be sure!*" replied Joe, as if it was not possible for them to be anywhere else. The man of few words then trotted away, leaving Tom in contemplation of his enormous disk and the hind quarters of his short-legged, well-actioned bay dray-horse-looking nag, whose sides were covered with the flowing laps of Joe's green frock coat.

Mr. Trumper took Stumps on account of his silent qualities (a great recommendation for harriers), a silence nearly reduced to muteness, by Joe's leaving out as many words in the few sentences he does utter as he possibly can, according to the approved fashion of his native wolds. In other respects he is very like the hare-hunter—heavy, patient, 'cute, and cunning, a good rider for a heavy man, careful of his horse and chary of damage. He is perfectly satisfied that there is not a more important personage under the sun than his master, and that he himself is the next greatest man going.

Mr. Scott, availing himself of Mr. Trumper's politeness, enables us to introduce the hunt to our readers.

There is one advantage of harriers—you always know where to find them, and can cut in for a game at romps, just as a dowager does for a hand at whist.

Sleekpow the groom had anticipated Scott's movements; for when he went to the stable, he found the "Wilkinson and Kid" astride of the hay crib, and the well-polished bridle hanging on the hook between the stalls.

"Just put the saddle on old Barbara," said Tom, in the *negligée* sort of way that may mean anything—anything, at least, except fox-hunting.

"Hare-hunting certainly ought not to be made a business of. It should just be taken when one's in the humour." Nevertheless, we don't subscribe to Beckford's doctrine—that a ride to the sixth milestone and back would be as good as hare-hunting; for we think, taken quietly, that hare-hunting is the next best sport to fox-hunting. But to make hare-hunting enjoyable a man should live in a good country for it—in a country where he can just turn out within a mile or two of home, and not have to trash away to a distant one. The hounds, too, should be harriers, and not dwarf foxhounds, that burst a hare in ten minutes where there is anything like a scent. A vicious desire for speed, and of making one thing serve two purposes, has gone far to annihilate the old, respect-

able, slow, and steady "well-hunted good dogs!"—harrier
packs of former days. Instead of the "squire," or a few
substantial farmers, keeping their ten or twelve couple of
harriers, we have a sort of bastard fox-hunt clubs that run
amuck at everything, except the game licence.

The two sports—hare-hunting and fox-hunting—do not
differ more in their nature than the relative expenses of each
differ.

Hare-hunting requires neither state, machinery, nor preparation ; nobody expects to see anything but a lot of merry-
looking little animals wriggling and jumping about, attended,
perhaps, by a man on foot with the couples, or an elderly
servant on an elderly horse ; but an establishment, calling
itself a fox-hunt, is a very different thing, and raises very
different expectations.

There must be a couple of men at the least, with three or
four horses that can both gallop and jump. These two men,
and these three or four horses, trifling as they appear upon
paper, make a considerable item at the end of the year ; and if
the country is at all hollow, which most countries are fast
becoming, from the quantity of draining going on, the expense
of "stopping" alone, comes to as much as the whole annual
expense of the merry harriers. Then the promoters have recourse to all sorts of screwing and scraping, applying to
members of Parliament, and people who don't hunt, and go
running open-mouthed at every chance person that comes out,
to support the rickety concern, which is generally a disgrace to
fox-hunting, and a nuisance to the country they haunt, not
hunt.

Fox-hunting should be done handsomely ! There is something about the noble animal that forbids our treating him
slightingly. He should be hunted like a gentleman. What
chance have a lot of trencher-fed, milk-fattened, street-scouring
beggars with a good high-couraged, clean-feeding, well-con-
ditioned flyer ? None whatever ! The further they go the

THE DELIGHTED MR. TRUMPER PICKS UP HIS HARE.

[To face page 14.

further they are left behind, till the lagging sportsmen have the satisfaction of seeing them struggling in fits, or sinking exhausted in the furrows. Then the talk and noise they make on a kill shows how unusual a thing it is with them. Nothing can be more pitiable than the half-rigged turn out of an ill-supported pretension to a fox-hunt. The boosey-looking huntsman (generally the saddler or publican)—the wretched broken-kneed, over-worked leg-weary job horse—the jaded half jockey, half huntsman-looking caps—the seedy, misfitting, Holywell-street-looking coats—the unclean boots and filthy breeches—with the lamentable apologies for saddles and bridles. We never see a Tom-and-Jerry-looking "scarlet" without thinking how much more respectable the wearer would look in black. We never see a country-scouring, fence-flattening field without thinking how much better they would be with a pack of harriers. But to the hunt.

Mr. Scott reached Stockenchurch Hill just in time to see the delighted Mr. Trumper pick up his hare before the baying pack on the moor-edge side of the country.

Puss had made a wide circuit of the whole, and was run into a small enclosure, whose crop of oats still stood in stook upon the ground.

It was a fine view. Three parts of the hill are encircled with fertile pastures and productive corn fields, while the fourth stretches away, far as the eye can reach, in undulating and occasionally broken moorland ground. The fertile patches irrigating the whole were dotted over with little black-faced sheep, while from the then browning heather the wild and sacred muir-fowl rose in noisy clamour, winging their ways to quieter regions in the distance.

The day was clear and bright, good both for hearing and seeing, and occasional fitful gleams of sunshine fell upon the distant landscape, lighting up the green patches, or disclosing rocky hill-sides, which, but for the sun, would have been lost in the general dimness of the scene.

The field was small, none but members of the hunt being out ; indeed, they don't encourage any other, and Mr. Scott looked upon it as no small compliment their asking him. It was composed of Giles Gosling, of Goose Green Farm, who pays tax for three couple of hounds, and, after Mr. Trumper, is the chief supporter of the hunt ; Harry Beanstack, of Ricot ; Michael and Thomas Hobbletrot, of Lingfield Green ; Simon Driblets, of Loxley Hill Farm ; his cousin, Ben Bragg, of the Waterdown ; and the chaplain, the Reverend Timothy Goodman, rector of Swillingford.

They were all in a similar state of elation to the master, indeed, Mr. Trumper might be taken as a prototype of the whole, for, making allowance for the difference of size, they were all as like each other as peas. This similarity arose a good deal from the sameness of their costume and the singularity of its cut—extremely lo,ng loose, bed-gown sort of bottle-green frock-coats, with laps reaching nearly down to their spurs, and great pewter plate-looking buttons set extremely wide apart behind.

There is nothing makes a person look so queer as an extremely long frock or great-coat ; and our friends making " Guys " of themselves arising a good deal from a spirit of covetousness—unworthy of the generous pursuit they follow— we trust this mention of their foible may have the effect of rectifying it, and of saving the expenditure of much good cloth, which they are always tearing or leaving behind on the fences, or, more properly speaking, gaps. The fact is, the hunt always keep a web of cloth in common, and one man having got his coat a little longer than the others on a former occasion, it set the rest agog, and they have gone on, web after web, stealing a march upon each other, till every man puts on as much sail as ever he can carry. They all turn out in things like dressing-gowns, with huge flapped pockets on the sides, each pocket being capable of carrying a hare. Their waistcoats and breeches bear the same affinity—the former small striped toilanettes, the latter large, deep-ribbed, fallow-field looking, patent cords ; and the great mahogany tops were evidently the production of the same hand, and made without regard to "right or left." Between them and the breeches good warm grey or white lambs'-wool stockings may be seen. On this day, each man clutched a ponderous iron hammer-headed whip, that looked for all the world like flails, they, too, having been bought in stock, and apportioned out to them like swords to yeomanry. Their hats are broad-brimmed, dog-hairy looking things, rather inclined to oval at the crown.

Living in a retired part of the country, away from towns and even railways, the members of the "Goose and Dumpling Hunt," as they called it, from the members dining off goose and apple puddings at each other's houses after the first day's hunting in each week — the members of the Goose and Dumpling Hunt we say—have fully satisfied themselves that they are the finest, primest, heartiest cocks in the kingdom, and their hounds the best that ever were seen.

Indeed, the hounds are as good as can be, and have been in existence nearly forty years, during the whole of which time the greatest care and attention have been paid to their breeding.

Long and solemn have been the consultations and arguments respecting the crosses, and deep the consideration as to the propriety of introducing fresh blood.

These have all been faithfully chronicled by the chaplain and secretary, Mr. Goodman, as also the days of meeting and parties composing each dinner.

The members of the hunt are all real sportsmen, men who love hunting innately, but who take no pleasure in leaping. Indeed, to tell the truth, since Beanstack broke his collar-bone by landing on a donkey instead of "*terra firma*," on the far side of an unsurveyed fence, the members have declined "extra risk," as the insurance offices say, and if there isn't a gap where they want to be over, why they make one.

Some people fancy hard riding an indispensable quality for

a sportsman ; but we believe, if we were to canvass the sporting world, we should find that the real lovers of hunting are anything but a hard-riding set. Fond of seeing hounds work, they use their horses as a sort of auxiliary to their legs, and having got a good lift across a field, they are all the abler to compete with a hedge, when they come to one, which they feel they would have had to take, even if on foot.

Our friends of the hunt we are describing are all of this sort. Mr. Trumper, who stands six feet high, and turns the scale on eighteen stone, never pretends to ride over anything. He thinks if his great bay horse Golumpus can carry him handsomely over the heavy, he is entitled to all the ease he can give him at his leaps ; and if in the early part of the season, when the old gaps are not well re-established, or a place has grown over during the summer, Mr. Trumper never attempts to break them through with his horse, but dismounting, and taking a bed-gown lap over each arm, he pushes backwards through, and clears the way for his horse. So the field take it in turns to clear the course for each other.

We should add that their breeches are all seated with leather, most probably with an eye to these prickly performances.

The hounds are of a breed now seldom seen—long, low, mealy reddish, whole-coloured hounds, inclining to a brownish grey along the back. They are fine-headed, fine-coated, and fine-sterned animals, with light musical tongues, and power and pace quite equal to, but not an over-match for, the best and wildest of their moor-edge hares. They look like harriers, and are very much of the colour of the hare herself.

Not being great hands at riding, the object of the members of the hunt has been to keep down the pace of the pack, rather than to increase it, and they oftener draft at the head than the tail. Indeed, one of the rules of the hunt is, that no man is to ride over a leap that can by any possibility be avoided. When

BEANSTACK LANDING ON A DONKEY.

[*To face page* 20.

anything in the shape of a poser intervenes, such as Narrowdell-brook or a moor-edge boundary wall, what craning and holding, and leaning over is there.—" Now, Mr. Trumper," says Harry Beanstack, "I'll hold your nag till you get over ; " and Trumper, knowing the impossibility of clearing the brook on foot, just slides down the bank into the water, and wobbles through ; then comes the old nag, who takes it quite naturally, and begins eating as soon as he lands. Beanstack follows in similar style, and a roar of laughter bursts forth as Giles Gosling disappears under water after a valiant attempt to clear the brook on foot, which checks the ardour of all the rest, who just stump through as Mr. Trumper did, trusting to the strength and honesty of their boots for not taking the wet in.

But we will suppose Mr. Scott joining the hunt.

"Halloo, Mr. Scott," exclaims Mr. Trumper, who had just paid the last obsequies to poor Puss, who was then nodding her head out of one end of Joe Stumps's hare case ; " Halloo, Mr. Scott, *you are half an hour too late ! you are half an hour too late !* missed the finest thing that ever was seen ! three-quarters of an hour with only a slight check at Littleton cross roads, and ran into her in view." (It had been a good twenty minutes.) "Didn't Joe tell you where we were ? " inquired he.

"Oh yes," replied Scott ; " but I waited for my letters, and then came leisurely along, trusting to chance for falling in with you before you found, or in the course of the run."

"You should never trust to chance with our hounds," retorted Trumper, somewhat nettled at the unfortunate speech. "If a thing's worth coming to at all, it's worth coming to in time," with which somewhat irately-delivered remark, he began to hoist himself on to a great sixteen hands horse that looked for all the world like a pony under him.

"It's not often," observed he, as he dangled for his stirrup, " that we trouble you fine fox-hunting gentlemen ; for, to tell you the truth, most of you make far too much noise, and press far too close upon hounds for our taste ; but, as I know *you* can hold your tongue, and as the Squire hasn't begun advertising yet, I thought I'd just let you know, you know."

"Much obliged," replied Scott, "much obliged ; you may rely upon it, I won't do any mischief."

"Ay, but you may do mischief by riding as well as by shouting," observed Trumper, who had had his wheat desperately damaged on a former occasion by some of the flyers. "Your wild fox-hunters are all for cramming and ramming wherever hounds go, without ever considering that, by standing still, p'raps you'll see a deal more of the hunt. But you must just follow me," added he, putting his great horse before Barbara, "and *I'll* show you what to do."

"Let's be doing then," added he, slipping a small bugle into his bed-gown pocket mouth, which disappeared like a rabbit down a boa constrictor's throat.

The dismounted heavies then clambered on to their horses, and the now refreshed pack began baying and frolicking with delight, making the bright sunshiny scene merry with their presence.

Good humour reigning o'er all the currant-jelly mugs with the glorious find and kill, they proceeded to some fresh ground in the neighbourhood that had not been touched upon in the previous run.

There was no bother or fuss about gathering or restraining the hounds ; they just followed on as they liked ; and first one and then another claimed the admiration of our sportsmen as they passed.

It was quite clear that our harrier masters were not ashamed of their turn-out, and indeed both hounds, horses, and men had a most substantial, yeomanlike, unpretending appearance. The hounds we have already described, and for the horses, we may say that their general stamp was extreme strength and activity on remarkably short legs. They had all square docks, otherwise the ponderous carcases of many of the riders would have made them look more like ponies or cobs than full-sized hunters, which they were.

Before Scott had finished his mental valuation of the whole, he was interrupted by Mr. Trumper hallooing out to his whip, who was a little behind, " Which way now, Joe ? "

" Bray doikes," replied Joe ; and accordingly the field separated, each man taking his own hedge-row.

These they began flopping and beating with their flail-like whips, while Trumper and Joe drew the hounds across and across the fallows and enclosures.

*   *   *   *   *

Hares were not very plentiful, and half an hour elapsed ere Simon Driblets telegraphed a find.

Unlike a fox, the hare puts no one in a fluster or hurry about a start. She is generally so accommodating as to wait till she is set a-going by some one turning her out of her form.

So it was in this case.

Mr. Driblets having seen Trumper and Joe's backs turned across the field again with the hounds in their wake, just started her quietly, and let her steal away at her leisure.

All was on the silent system. No views, no hallooing, no heads staring up in the air. The hounds were never taken off their noses.

Mr. Trumper just drew them across the line, and, as if by magic, they struck the scent ; after a wild scream of delight, that thrilled through the field, the hounds went away at score.

Puss, though far ahead, was still within hearing distance, and having had a round with them before, mended her pace, and pressed away for the open.

The field had now got gathered together from their respective beats, and each man was hugging his horse as though he were bent on destruction.

Mr. Trumper rode first, and they all fell into places, like a troop of horse, the chaplain and Joe bringing up the rear.

" *This way, young man !* " cried Trumper to Scott, seeing he was going to take the line of the hounds, instead of following a field road through a line of gates that rather bent away from them. "This way," said he, pointing with his whip, " she'll turn at yon pasture end and skirt the turnips, said he, " and we shall catch them up at the cowshed in the field but one beyond."

Trumper was right. The hounds ran to the very point he predicted, and came out into Newsell's-lane by the cowshed— all busy and bustling like bees.

"You never saw better hounds than those ! " observed Mr. Trumper, *sotto voce*, pointing to them in ecstasy.

"No," said Joe, who happened to be within hearing.

Presently the pace mended, and the trot that had been pertinaciously maintained was converted into a canter, some of the fatties standing up in their stirrups as if for the purpose of easing their horses, though as yet they had done nothing.

Still they kept the lanes and field roads, which appeared to turn up most accommodatingly whatever way puss pointed.

Sometimes, indeed, they seemed to turn their backs on the hounds, and to be riding away from them altogether ; but it was only momentary, and they presently found themselves at some pet gap or friendly rail, which, succumbing to the heavy-hammered whips, set them on the line again.

So they went on, from lane to field, and from field to lane, for some time, the pace being occasionally good, but never great—the music beautiful.

Having run the length of Green-pasture Valley, and crossed Stockenchurch Hill, near the village or hamlet, a cur dog had got sufficiently near puss's quarters to cause her serious uneasiness for her safety, and had forced her off her line, to the astonishment of the field, who, not knowing what had happened were calculating upon Maddingly Common as a certainty   Indeed, Michael Hobbletrot had cut away for the common at once on reaching the village, instead of turning short to the left at the blacksmith's, as the others did, Michael not being quite sure that the gap by the pond had been opened out, and reckoning he would save time by riding a little about instead of waiting his turn in case the gap had to be re-established. We believe we may add that Michael is rather given to "nicking."

Well, great was the astonishment of the field, when, after a short check, where the hounds over-ran the line, Twister, with something between a note and a yell, struck the scent down a newly built wall pointing direct for the moors.

"Great heavens! She can't have gone for the hills!" ejaculated Tom Hobbletrot, with a lively recollection of a deep bog he had been in on the moors.

Towler, Lovely, Ruffler, Cottager, Guider, all the unerring ones of the pack, however, confirmed the surmise, and that, too, with an energy leaving no room for doubt.

The scent had improved, and they went away at score. They packed beautifully—close as turnips.

"We shall be in trouble," ejaculated Hobbletrot, as he got half way down the side of the next field, and saw that Coldbrook Burn was inevitable.

A brook is the only thing in the list of hunting obstacles that admits of neither hope nor palliation. It is a regular "take it, or leave it" affair, and Coldbrook Burn is one of the deepest, nastiest, and most twisting in the country—it seems to be everywhere.

Moreover, the horrors of a brook are materially increased by a previous acquaintance with it ; for a bold leader will frequently entice a funking field over a place when it comes unexpectedly in chase, at which many would crane and measure, and measure and crane, and ultimately turn away, if encountered in crossing from cover to cover. A brook is a thing at which no man can do anything for another—unlike a wall, or a rail, or a hedge, or a locked gate, the brook stands boldly on its own merits, as big a leap to the last comer as to the first, nay, sometimes bigger, for rotten undermined banks are apt to give way under the weight of horses. Brooks being formidable customers at all times, we need hardly say that they were considerably aggravated by the autumnal rains ; indeed, places that in summer well-nigh suspend payment altogether, begin running and roaring and behaving in the most riotous manner imaginable. Coldbrook Burn may be mentioned as a particular instance of a refractory streamlet ; for its course being deep, and its bank sedgy, it is well calculated for holding an uncommon quantity, and when Mr. Trumper reached it this day, he pronounced it a bumper. Scott observed, however, that Trumper didn't seem a bit put out on coming to it. On the contrary, he was more intent on his hounds, who had thrown up on the bank, and were trying for the scent up and down.

" Yooi over, good dog ! " hallooed he to Risker in delight, as his dark head and back rose above the stream. Gleamer, Guider, Rachael quickly followed, and then went the body of the pack. " *Yooi over*, all on you ! " hallooed Trumper, hat in hand, trying to get the young ones to follow.

The field sat in mute attention, watching the proceedings on the opposite side.

Risker first snatched the scent, and there was a rare splashing and scrambling among those in the brook to get at him. "Now you wild fox-hunters," said Mr. Trumper, turning to Scott as he sat eyeing the hounds shaking themselves on the opposite side, " would try to leap that burn. Now I'll show you what us hare-hunters do," continued he, seeing the hounds putting their heads for the moors ; saying which he gathered his reins, touched his horse with the spur, and bustled away to Bewdley wooden bridge, about a mile off, followed by the whole of the field as hard as ever they could lay legs to the ground.

     *   *   *   *   *

"That's far better nor gettin a wet shirt!" exclaimed Trumper, as his ponderous horse clattered over the wooden fabric, making it shake again with his weight.

"But we've lost the hounds!" observed Scott.

"Fiddle-te-dee!" exclaimed he; "I know where they'll be to a nicety. Come up, horse!" cried he, as his nag began shying at the stone-steps, at the taking-off end of the foot-bridge.

Having effected a landing, he forthwith gathered his reins, and, tickling Golumpus freely with the spur, set off at a good round pace, the old nag indulging in a sort of make-believe kick in his canter.

They were now upon the moors, with nothing to fear but bogs and holes, and ruts, things that did not seem to be included in the list of casualties of the Goose and Dumpling Hunt, for all the members began charging abreast instead of following in the goose fashion they had been pursuing before.

The hounds were long out of sight; indeed, they had run up a ravine, from which the *détour* by Bewdley Bridge had interposed a hill; but the fatties saw by the staring of the sheep the line they had taken, and the field jogged on in high exultation at the splendour of the run, and delighted at the idea of astonishing the stranger.

Presently they got within sight of where sheep were still running, or rather wheeling about, and then a shepherd's hat on the sky line of a far-off hill announced where they were.

The riding was only awkward, the heather hiding both stones and holes, and the turf on the bare places, particularly on the hill-side, being extremely slippery. Nevertheless they clattered on, trusting entirely to their horses for safety.

Presently they heard the cry of hounds.

"Hold hard!" exclaimed Mr. Trumper, "they are coming towards us. Hark!" exclaimed he (pulling up short, and holding up his hand)—"now, Mr. Scott, if you'll come here, I'll show you the hare," said he.

Accordingly, Scott followed him through a narrow defile to the left, and, looking over a hollow in the rocky hill upon the country below, he saw poor puss dribbling along in a listening sort of canter.

The field followed to partake of the treat.

"Oh, she's a fine un!" exclaimed Mr. Trumper, his eyes sparkling as he spoke ; " but she's pretty well beat," added he ; " she'll most likely begin to play some of her tricks : these things have far more cunning nor foxes," added he. "Now this is the time," continued he, addressing himself seriously to Scott, " that you wild fox-hunters would take advantage of, for the purpose of cutting short the diversion, by mobbing, and shouting, and taking every advantage of him ; but we do the thing differently. *We* let our hounds hunt ; and if they can't kill a hare fairly, why they lose her."

The hounds had now descended from the hills and turned the corner of the last angle that shut them out from view. They were working a middling scent, which they caught and lost and lost and caught alternately.

Puss heard them, and regulated her pace by theirs.

Presently she began the tricks Mr. Trumper anticipated. Having got into a small fallow, she dribbled up a furrow above which her back was scarcely visible, and having run the length of it, she deliberately returned the same way, and with a mighty spring landed in a thick hedge-row.

"That'll puzzle them," said Mr. Trumper, " for the scent is but cold at best, and the wet of yon furrow won't improve what little there is."

"But you'll let them hunt it of course ?" observed Scott, thinking Mr. Trumper was paving the way to a little assistance.

"*Undoubtedly,*" replied Trumper, with a deep sideway inclination of the head—"undoubtedly," repeated Trumper, " *We'd scorn to take an unfair advantage* of her. But look how they hunt!" added he, " Did you ever see hounds work better:

no babblers, no skirters, no do-nothing gentlemen here ; twelve couple, and all workers ; *we* keep no cats that don't catch mice, Mr. Scott. Oh, but they're beauties ! " added he in ecstasy, as they came hunting her as true as an arrow.

When they got upon the fallow it certainly was not propitious. There wasn't a hound that could speak to the scent, and Twister and Towler alone guided them on the line.

" Those hounds are worth two hundred thousand pounds apiece to Prince Albert, or any of the royal family who really know what hunting is," whispered Mr. Trumper. " See what confidence they all have in them. Hark ! Cottager threw his tongue. That's the first time he's spoke since he came into the field, but he's had the scent the whole way. Oh ! hare-hunting is beautiful sport, the most delightful amusement under the sun," added he. " There's nothing to compare to it. Is there, Beaney ? " continued he, looking over his shoulder to our friend Beanstack, who with the rest of the field were now clustered behind in ardent admiration of their darlings.

"*Nothing ! nothing ! nothing !* " was vociferated by all.

The hounds had now got to the end of the double, and several of the young ones dashed beyond. Not so Twister and Towler, who cast a small semicircle in advance, and then returned to the spot.

" *That's hunting now !* " exclaimed Mr. Trumper, " your wild fox-dogs would have been half over the next parish by this time, but those hounds won't move an inch without a scent. See how they hunt it back. That's something like, now. Far better than getting a hold of them and pretending to tell *them* what you keep them to tell you, *which way the hare went.*"

" Ah, that's all very well," observed Scott, " with the hare sitting in the hedge-row ; but a fox, you know, keeps travelling on. There's no time for dawdling with him."

" You don't know but that hare may be in Jollyrise township by this time," snapped Mr. Trumper ; " it doesn't follow because she took the hedge-row, that she's there still. But we are in no hurry. Fair play's the universal motto of hare-hunters. We even have it on our buttons," added he, turning up a great pewter-plate-looking thing with a hare and the words "Fair play" underneath.

"The gentleman doesn't seem to understand much about the thing, I think," observed Michael Hobbletrot, who had got dribbled up from his *détour* by Maddingly Common, after a most enjoyable ride of the line.

"Fox-hunters seldom do," rejoined Simon Driblet.

"More at home at a steeple hunt, p'raps," suggested Gosling.

The currant jelleyers were getting personal, and there is no saying to what lengths they might have gone in the wild moor-land region in which they now had their unhappy victim, had not Twister fortunately obtruded his nose so near puss's hind quarters as to cause her to bound out of the hedge, to the gal-vanisation of the pack, who, with heads in the air, struck up a strain that set the now freshened horses a-frisking. Away they went in view.

"*Yonder she goes! Yonder she goes! Yonder she goes!*"
"Lauk, what a dog is that Twister!" with which exclama-tions the bed-gown wearers began climbing on to their horses much in the style that *Punch* represented the old French King climbing on to "Artful Dodge."

Fairly and coolly down the hill-side now they went "*who-a-ing*" and "*gent-ly-ing*" to their horses as they unravelled the zig-zag mysteries of the track.

The pack, meanwhile, were screaming and streaming away in the distance.

When they had all landed at the bottom and shaken them-selves, and those who had "led down" re-mounted, the hounds were fairly out of sight; but Mr. Trumper, nothing daunted, tickled Golumpus into a canter, and putting his head the re-verse way of what Scott had seen the hounds going, cut down a long slip of grass land lying between the rocky hills and the

Hold hard!

enclosures, and taking a sudden twist to the left by the corner
of a turf fence, shot away like a meteor to the north, through a
long line of white field gates, whose pleasing perspective opened
in the distance.

Where these would have ultimately led to we know not, for
when they had got through about half a dozen of them, Mr.
Trumper suddenly stopped short as if shot—an evolution so
quickly followed by the rest of the cavalry, as to have the effect
of shooting several of the loose riders on to the pommels of their
saddles.

Trumper saw the hare! Indeed they all saw her; but
Trumper saw her first.

She was bearing right down upon them, in a style that would
most inevitably have led to a collision, had they not pulled up.
Full of what was going on behind, she never thought of looking
ahead, and nearly ran into them. Poor thing! She came so
close, that they distinctly saw the curl of warmth on her soiled
fur, and the big heaving of her anxious breast.

A hare is a curious mixture of cleverness and stupidity. We
see them lobbing and staring along as if they hadn't an idea in
their heads, and then all at once they perform tricks worthy of
a wizard.

"She's a fine un," observed Mr. Trumper, *sotto voce*, as he
sat, whip erect, staring her out of countenance.

The noise he made had the effect of awaking her to a sense
of their presence, and caused her to pop through a meuse in
the hedge.

"She's about done," observed he, eyeing the performance,
for Trumper can calculate the amount of "goment" left to a
nicety; Tom Hobbletrot then pulled out a great turnip of a
watch from his fob, of which having made a good open ex-
posure, he shut it up, with the observation that "it was about
time."

"Domplins be ready, ars warned," said Stumps, feeling the
effects of hunger himself.

The hounds now came towling and picking along with the weak scent of the sinking animal.

Just as Twister and Towler were again eliciting the admiration of the field at the way in which they unravelled the line, a loud shrill *hoop! hoop! hoop!* from the rising ground in the next field but one, got up the hounds' heads, and caused them to work their ways through the high hedge to get at the halloo.

Great was the horror and perturbation of the field, as the hounds flew away, and greater still their disgust at seeing a great fat man in white leather trousers, and bright heel spurs, with a gold-banded blue cap, and a registered paletot, capping them away at a canter.

" Hold hard, Sir," " hold hard, Sir," " God bless you, hold hard, Sir ! " " God d—n you, hold hard, Sir ! " were shouted and vociferated by the indignant field, now rendered perfectly furious by not being able to get at him, unless they either charged a tolerably-sized fence that looked to them like an impregnable barrier, or rode two hundred yards " t'other way," to get through at the old established gap.

In vain Trumper, having dived into the bottom of his bed-gown, fished up the little bugle—in vain he blew, in vain he screamed, in vain he imprecated. There wasn't an evil or an adverse element that Trumper didn't wish the stranger visited with.

The hounds topped the hill, and were out of sight in no time.

Fury, unspeakeable fury, was depicted on the faces of the field ; nor was it diminished by seeing the hunted hare pop out of the hedge, as they moved away to ride for the gap.

Moreover, she accompanied them as far as their joint lines lay, in the direction of the hills, almost as it would seem for the purpose of deriding them. As they pounded and clattered down the stoney, rutty field-road, she kept working her way up a furrow, about twenty yards to their left, in the next field. Doleful were the looks our friends cast on her as they passed on the alteration of their lines.

"She couldn't have stood two minutes before them," sighed Tom Hobbletrot, who was next in rotation for a hare.

"Who *could* it be?" gasped Parson Goodman, who was riding a still pulling four-year old, and had had something else to do than stare about.

"*I know*," responded Trumper; "*I'll sarve him out*," added he, bringing his ponderous hunting whip crack down his boot.

"Most infamous thing that ever was done!" exclaimed Giles Gosling.

"So like those wild fox-hunting fools," muttered Trumper, leaning over his horse's shoulder to open a gate. "Never happy but when they're galloping," added he, throwing it open, and striking into a gallop himself.

He presently reached the eminence over which they had seen the hounds disappear, from whence Trumper was horrified at seeing "white leathers" absolutely casting the pack! casting the hounds that Trumper deemed it next to high treason for any one to speak to but himself.

There was the stranger in the middle of a twenty-acre turnip field, riding about, tasselled cap in hand, describing a circle, which he kept enlarging each time round, after a fashion of his own.

Trumper turned deadly pale at the sight. If there is one thing in the world that he hates more than another, it is a pair of white breeches, and his detestation seemed to increase by the length of the present articles.

"*Mister Muff! Mister Muff!*" gasped he, as if in the last agony of a stomach-ache. "Mister Muff!" repeated he; but Mr. Muff was deaf to the cry. "*He's mad! he's mad!* he *must* be mad!" continued Trumper, eyeing Tarquinius's manœuvres among the turnips, who, regardless of Trumper's imprecations, continued his career to the damage of the turnips and the danger of the hounds.

Trumper then put on all steam, and charged down hill, followed by the train-band, bold.

Tarquinius, full of his own importance, not only as a first-class swell, but a fox-hunter, held up his hand as he saw them coming, exclaiming most importantly, "*Hold hard*, gentlemen, hold hard! *Pray* hold hard!" continued he, seeing the exhortation was disregarded; adding, "*I know* how far they brought her."

"*You* know how far they brought her?" grinned Trumper, in agony, as he leaned fumbling the chain of the gate opening into the field where they were. "*You* know how far they brought her? I wish I knew how far I might take you to hang you." "I never *did* ride over turnips in my life," observed he to himself as he got the gate open, "but I'll have a shy at them to-day."

So saying, he stuck spurs into Golumpus, and went pounding and smashing through the middle of them.

If it hadn't been for the hounds, we believe Trumper would have charged Tarquinius full tilt. Luckily, some of the beauties popping above the turnips, which being guano sown were uncommonly forward, caused Trumper to get his horse more in hand, and ultimately to pull up a little short of assaulting distance.

"Oh, Mr. Trumper, it's *you*, is it?" observed Muff, in the most patronising way to our gasping and perspiring sportsman. "I thought it must be a heavy-weight pack, as none of you were up with them."

"Up with them!" gasped Trumper, "I wish you would ride about your business, and leave our hounds to themselves."

"Why, my good fellow," replied Muff, turning his horse to the now assembled field, "I was doing you an absolute service. I viewed the hare, and laid your beagles on to her."

" *Beggles!* " vociferated Trumper, " Beggles," repeated he, as if he was going to be sick ; " Where the deuce do you use any *beggles* here ? "

"Them's harriers," observed Hobbletrot, with the utmost contempt, muttering something about "d—d frenchified" something that sounded rather like " fool."

" Well, but my good fellow, let me make my cast perfect, at all events," continued Muff, who had been studying Mr. Smith's patent "all-round-my-hat " cast in the " Diary of a Huntsman " that morning.

" *You* know I know something about hunting, Tom Scott," continued he, appealing to our friend with the familiar "Tom," instead of the distant "Mr." he uses on ordinary occasions, when he is coming it grand.

" *Indeed I don't*," replied Tom, nettled at his meanness, and unable to resist the temptation of having a shy at him too.

" That's right, Mr. Scott ! Speak your mind like a man ! " exclaimed Trumper, slapping his whip down his boot.

" Not about fox-hunting, at all events," continued Scott, thinking to qualify his answer.

" And I'm sure he knows nothing about hare-hunting," ejaculated Tom Hobbletrot, determined not to let Muff off.

" But, my good men," minced Muff, with the greatest effrontery, throwing back his registered paletot, and showing a profusion of trinkets appended to his glittering watch chain, at the same time sticking out a great leather-covered leg—"my good men," repeated he, " at all events, you must admit, that but for me you would have seen no more of your hare ; your little dogs could hardly own the scent when I capped them away close at her scut."

" D—n you and your capping," roared Tom Hobbletrot, unable to restrain himself at hearing Muff take credit to himself for losing him his hare ; " you've *lost* us our hare, Sir, instead of helping us to catch her."

"That's because you interrupted me when I was making my cast," retorted Muff.

"Cast!" screamed Trumper, "you hallooed us away to a fresh hare."

"Fresh hare!" sneered Muff—"fresh hare," repeated he, shrugging up his shoulders, and throwing out a primrose-coloured kid-gloved hand, "my *good* fellow, do you *suppose* I'm such a fool as not to know a fresh hare from a hunted one?"

"Yes, ar do," roared Tom; "I don't think you know nothin about one except you see her in the soup plate."

"Silly man! silly man!" simpered Muff. "If this is not the hunted hare, I'm——"

"Well, Mr. Muff, it don't argufy a bit," interrupted Trumper, whose choler had been subsiding as the other's had been getting up; "it don't argufy a bit, Sir," repeated he; "the hunted hare is *back*. I saw her make for the hills as we came to your halloo. I tell you how it is, Sir! I tell you how it is, Sir!" his anger rising again as he spoke, "You are a fox-hunter, Sir —no objection at all to fox-hunters, Sir—none whatever; Mr. Neville's an excellent man, Sir—can't be a better—always most civil to me when I go out with *his* hounds, Sir; but I never presume to halloo, Sir. If I see a fox, Sir, I hold up my hat, Sir; *never* think of hunting the hounds, Sir. Glad to see Mr. Neville, or any of his gentlemen out, Sir, with *our* hounds, Sir, but I hope they'll do the same when they come, Sir—*hope they'll do the same when they come, Sir*. Now, Sir, you've lost us our hare, Sir," continued he, "so I'll bid you good morning, Sir—I'll bid you good morning, Sir, and we'll go home to dinner, Sir—we'll go home to dinner, Sir."

So saying, Mr. Trumper made Mr. Muff a bow, and diving into his bed-gown pocket for the horn, gave it a twang, and, having gathered his hounds, retraced his way through the turnips.

*   *   *   *   *

"He'll cut his stick now," observed Mr. Trumper, looking over his shoulder as he got to the gate to see where Muff was.

"We'll just try and see if we can recover the hunted hare," added he, looking at his watch, and seeing it was a little past one.

"That Mr. Muff," continued he, jogging on, half to himself and half to any one that would listen to him, "is the most disagreeable man I know; he's eternally teaching somebody something. He thinks, because he rides in scarlet, that he's fit for a huntsman, whereas, saving Mr. Scott's presence," said he, looking at Scott, I really believe there are more fools in scarlet than in any other colour. I'd rather have laid in bed all day —a thing I detest after sunrise," continued Trumper, "than have asked him to join our hunt, for he's *certain* to make a mess if he comes. He's just one of those sort of daft bodies that can't hold their tongues, and must always be doing. Gently, Cottager—good dog," added he ; " I know where she *is* better than that," continued he to Cottager, who was feathering on the grassy side of the road. "If that stupid man had hallooed them fox dogs away," continued Trumper, " as he did ours, there'd have been an end of the thing ; but there's one great advantage of hare-hunting, that you need never give her up—never as long as a hound can own the scent."

"And when they can't, you begin to prick her, don't you ?" asked Scott.

"*That's as may be*," replied Mr. Trumper; "*We never dig her out, at all events !* "

"She doesn't give you a chance," replied Scott, as Trumper hastened to conclude the dialogue by getting out of hearing.

They soon reached the fallow where puss and they had parted company, and certainly it seemed a most unpromising speculation trying to recover her. Even the redoubtable Twister and Towler could make nothing of it, though she was plain enough to prick where the water had left a sandy wash on the furrow ends of the poor, undrained land.

Trumper's keen eye saw these plainly enough, though his paternal affection made him anxious to transfer the credit of the feat to the noses of the now mute pack.

*   *   *   *   *

At length even pricking failed.

Puss, with a tact often displayed by hunted animals, had selected an enclosure so cold, so bleak, so barren that nothing but a few water-weeds grew upon it, and of those there were only barely sufficient to hide her track.

Trumper pulled up as the hounds got upon it, feeling quite incompetent to form the least opinion as to whether she was on, or sideways, or back, or down, or where.

Twister, however, thought she was on, and a greenish spot of land on the rising ground, towards the middle of the enclosure, yielding something that acted upon his frame like a scent, Mr. Trumper moved forward, and Twister spoke to her at the hedge-row.

They were now again upon a large fallow, and Trumper felt the difficulty of picking the cold scent with the danger of starting a fresh hare. However, he went on, eyes well down, in hopes of seeing something.

The day, having changed for the worse, was now getting raw, and the ceremony of hunting by inches, though very interesting to masters, is anything but exhilarating to strangers : at last, having come to about a dead lock—not a hound being able to own the scent, or to carry it a bit further —Scott ventured to suggest that it was all " U. P."

" Gad, now do you know, I thought you'd be saying that," replied Trumper, starting round. " I never saw a fox-hunter yet that didn't think it was time to shut up as soon as they were run out of scent."

" We've been *walked* out," replied Scott.

"Very true," retorted Mr. Trumper, "very true," repeated he, "and that makes me think she won't be far off; Gad, sir, she's under your horse's nose at this moment!" added he, "*Hold hard!* while I draw the hounds off, or they'll spoil her."

Trumper then drew the hounds away, and looking a little ahead Scott saw what at first looked like a clod, but which, on closer observation, proved to be poor puss.

"To be, or not to be," was the question,—a live hare or a dead one.

"*Save her!*" whispered Scott, "save her! she's a good-un, and will give us a gallop another day. Mercy's all that's wanting to make the day's sport perfect."

"Nay then!" rejoined Trumper in astonishment, as he still kept drawing the hounds off, "I thought you fox-hunters were all for blood."

"So we are," said Scott, "so we are—but not *hares'* blood."

"Well, then, I'll humour you," said Trumper, "and let her live; but you must allow she was well hunted."

"Never saw any thing better in my life!" exclaimed our friend. "It was a most wonderful performance."

"Wide difference between fox-hunting and hare-hunting, you see," observed Trumper, fishing the bugle from the bottom of the bed-gown pocket, and giving it a twang.

"Come away, good dogs! come away!" hallooed he, as if he was giving the game up for lost.

"You should never give a hare up," said he, "when you come to those sort of solemn stops, for, ten to one, she's not far off. A fox *would* be far off, and the longer you persevere, the further you're left behind; but come," continued he, briskly, "we've had a good day's sport. You lost the first run, to be sure, which was an uncommon good one, as good a one as ever was seen; but this hasn't been a bad-un, and now, suppose you finish the day by dining with us."

" With all my heart," replied Scott.

" Goose and dumplings," observed Trumper ; "goose and dumplings : suppose you can dine off them ? "

" Nothing better," said Scott, " nothing better."

" Lots of onions ! " added Trumper, " lots of onions ! "

" That's your ticket," replied Scott, " that's your ticket."

*　　*　　*　　*　　*

They soon got upon the Edge-hill Road, and the longer they travelled the smaller the pack became, one hound cutting off at a stile, another at a gate, a third at the cross-roads, all making for their respective homes.

There are two things in this world that there is seldom any mistake about—the smell of a fox and the smell of roast goose. Even the most unsophisticated in sporting matters, though they may not think it prudent to exclaim " I smell a fox," as the peculiar odour crosses their noses on the pure air of a hunting morning, yet never assign the effluvia to any other thing ; while in the matter of roast goose, the veriest igno-ramus has no hesitation about it.

It so happened that Mr. Scott winded the savoury bird ere he viewed the buildings at the back of Jollyrise Farm, which are shut out from view at the back approach by a row of gigantic hollies, then in the full luxuriance of the deepest green and the reddest berries.

" I smell goose ! " exclaimed Scott, at the turn of the road.

" You may say that," replied Trumper, "*four* on 'em, I expect."

" You go the whole hog in the goose way," observed Scott.

" A goose to two's the allowance," replied Trumper ; "there'll hardly be that to-day ; but you needn't make yourself uneasy on that score, there'll be plenty for us all."

The out-buildings, forming an ample square at the back of Jollyrise House, were like Mr. Trumper himself—large, roomy, and substantial. The beasts in the fold-yards revelled in the cleanest straw, and if there was the slightest smell of any sort, it was entirely overpowered by that of roast goose.

What surprised Mr. Scott most was some half dozen gigs and dog-carts, all drawn up under a shed on entering.

"What do you do with so many gigs, Mr. Trumper?" asked he. Before, however, he had time to get an answer, the trampling of the horses' feet drew out as many attendant clowns, who forthwith assisted their masters to alight. They had brought their "drinking carts," as they call them, in exchange for their hunters.

After a bucket of gruel a-piece, the latter took their departures home. Trumper, having boxed Golumpus, proceeded to cast an eye round the buildings to see that all was right.

*   *   *   *   *

"Come, Tom, come!" exclaimed Mrs. Trumper from the long staircase window commanding the landing and angle of the staircase, in which she now appeared full length, in a black silk gown and cherry-coloured ribbons to her cap, looking most blooming and buxom. "Come, Tom, come!" repeated she, as she saw her husband wandering from filly to foal and from heifer to cow.

They all then made for the back kitchen, where towels and basons, and boot-jacks and slippers waited their pleasure, superintended by a nice fresh-looking maid, in a blue cotton gown, with crisp cork-screw ringlets dangling down the sides of her merry healthy cheeks.

The party were presently divested of their tops, and now appeared in most comfortable woollens and slippers. After running the joint stock comb through the lightish crops of straggling hair, they waddled into the parlour, where they were greeted by the "missis."

This was a low wainscoted room, situate on the right of the front door on entering, with one window looking to the south

and the other to the east, the latter commanding a view of the
twisting Auborn water, and the well-wooded Greyridge Hills
beyond. The walls were profusely decorated with rare hunts
in every stage and variation of the sport, from the turn out
from the kennels down to " *Who whoop!* " There were hares
sitting, and hares running, and hounds finding their own hares,
and people finding the hares for them, and hounds hunting,
and hounds viewing, and hounds at fault, and hounds hitting
her off again, and hounds running into her, and hounds catching her, and hounds baying her.

Then there were stuffed hares in cases on the mantel-piece
and about the broad skirting boards of the walls, with inscrip-
tions detailing the exploits of each, and sometimes the names
of the favoured few who were out. Long before Scott had
made the circuit of the room, however, the well roasted geese
came hissing in hot from the spit, and each man paired off with
a partner for one.

The Rev. Timothy Goodman having said grace, they all
set to with the most rapacious and vigorous determination.

For people who are fond of goose (and who is not ?) a greater
treat could not be devised. There was no taking the edge of
the appetite off with soup, or fish, or patties, or cutlets, or side
dishes of any sort ; but they sat down to dine off the one thing
they expected. This, too, was done in the fairest, most
equitable way imaginable ; for instead of a favoured few getting
the breast and tit-bits, leaving nothing but gristly drumsticks
for late comers, each man had his own half goose, and could
take whatever part he liked first, without eating in haste and
fear that the next favoured cut would be gone ere he could get
at it again. All, too, dining off goose, and eating most profusely of stuffing, none could reproach the other with " smelling
of onions."

Silence appeared to be the order of the day both morning
and evening, for with the exception of a voice occasionally
hallooing out " *Beer!* " scarce a word passed, until the dishes

presented a most beggarly account of bones. Beer they might call it, and beer it might look like, being both light and bright, but it was uncommonly strong and heady to take.

Let the French talk of their *vin ordinaire* or pure St. Julien claret, with considerable body, at 28s. a dozen : what is it when compared with the *vin ordinaire*, the malt and hops wine of old England ?—a quart of Trumper's beer would sew up the best Frenchman that ever was seen. We are quite sure we have tasted bottled ale that would be prized before champagne if it was only as dear. How few people appreciate still champagne ! It is the fiz, the pop, and the cream that makes sparkling champagne such a favourite, and good bottled ale has all those concomitants.

Trumper, having made a most exemplary onslaught on his half goose, and washed it down with many potations of malt liquor, at last threw himself back in his semicircular chair, and bellowed out the word " BRANDY." Mrs. Trumper immediately dived into her pocket, and beckoning to the maid, gave her the key of a cupboard formed of one corner of the room, from whence she produced a most liberal sized blue glass spirit stand with the names, " HOLLANDS," " RUM," " BRANDY," in gilt letters round the bottle necks.

" Take a thimbleful of brandy, Mr. Scott, after your goose," said Trumper, appealing to our friend ; and forthwith the little maid brought him a large wine glass on a *papier mâché* stand with a hare painted on the bottom, and proceeded to help him. " Stop ! " exclaimed Scott, when she had got it half filled.

" NAY," roared Trumper in disgust, " what's the top of the glass made for, d'ye think ?—*fill it up, woman* "—and the woman did fill it up.

" I drink to you," said Trumper, tossing off a like quantity with the most perfect ease.

" Mild as milk," observed he, smacking his lips as he put down the glass.

The floodgates of conversation now began to be loosened, and each man having drunk to his goose partner, began asking his neighbour to take a drop—so the drops went round.

The dumplings now came rolling in—ten dumplings on ten dishes and five boats full of sauce. Apple dumplings are the order of the day, but the apple crop having failed they had recourse to currant dumplings, approaching very near to plum.

Cheese followed these, and then they cleared the old oak table and drew it towards the fire. The party ranged round : biscuits and filberts constituted the dessert, and "glasses" formed the beverage. Mrs. Trumper stood in for a tumbler of something and water, and when she retired, the little maid again appeared, and diving into the cupboard, produced sundry clay pipes, a large tobacco box with a hare hunt on the lid, and several little round boxes with sand in the bottom, which she distributed among the party.

"You don't object to baccy, I suppose?" observed Mr. Trumper, filling his pipe.

"Not a bit," replied Scott, taking a pipe and doing the like.

A solemn reverie followed, each man smoking and apparently either thinking or dreaming.

"I did wrong in leaving her," at last said Trumper, breaking silence, at the same time knocking the ashes out of his pipe.

Thereupon they all began to throw their tongues, and they hunted that hare over again.

Then Timothy Goodman reminded them of a similar run they had had twenty years before, when they killed at Little Gaddesden, after having "all but" given her up. Then Harry Beanstack recalled another, and Ben Bragg a third. More hot water was then called for, and brought. More cold also—more sugar ; and then more brandy—more rum ; and the hollands being exhausted, its patrons had recourse to gin. They then began to get noisy—one talked of his horse, another of his hound, a third of himself, a fourth of his farm, and Gosling, who had lately married for the third time, talked of his "bran

"THERE'S NOTHING CAN COMPARE."

[*To face page* 44.

new wife." Then they would drink her health, and some one
proposed "all the honours," which being duly responded to,
some of them found that resuming their seats was rather a
difficult matter. Toasting, having begun, went on briskly,
and then singing commenced. The songs were various, but all
in honour of the hare. The one that gave most satisfaction
had for a chorus—

> " There's nothing can compare
> To hunting of the hare,"

which they kept hammering away at, laying the emphasis on
to the nothing can,

> " There's NOTHING CAN compare,"

till they got it so high that no type could convey an idea of the
din, save the great capitals used by some of the " He-who-runs-
may-read " advertising wine or " Reform-your-tailor's-bills "
fraternity.

Suffice it to say, that our friend Scott felt the fumes of the
spirit for three whole days after, and the ghost of—

> " There's NOTHING CAN compare
> To hunting of the hare "—

haunts him still.

CHAPTER III.

A CHOKER.

Mr. Scott's noble friend—for, like most rustics, he has one noble acquaintance, whom he dignifies with that title when he is coming it strong—Mr. Scott's noble friend, Lord Lionel Lazytongs, son of the Marquis of Fender and Fireirons, says that when Lady Lazytongs' maid calls him on a hunting morning, and he halloos out to know " what sort of a day it is," the invariable answer he gets is " A bad morning and *very cold.*"

The question seems superfluous ; for few men, let alone a tender delicate maid, are capable of forming an opinion whether the weather is favourable for hunting or not.

We never ask any questions, but somehow there are certain indications that give us an idea as to what sort of a day it is before we get to the finishing touch of the toilette. One's razors give the first indication of a raw ungenial atmosphere ; and an eye into the fields or towards the road shows how the country people are clad. If the carters have their duffle coats on, and the poor turnip pullers their thick shawls wrapped across their breasts, it is a sure sign of a raw unkindly atmosphere—an atmosphere warranting the warm-backed waistcoat, if not the lambswool and fleecy-hosiery also.

The November of 1846, to which season the following adventures of our friend Mr. Scott are confined, was the worst hunting November that perhaps ever was known. It was more like a bad March than the glorious, sloppy, burning scent sort of weather peculiar to that month. November is generally the freshest, greenest spot on memory's hunting waste, but the one in question will be remembered more as a nasty, harsh, windy, mutton-broth, cold-in-the-head, shivering-shaking sort of affair, than for the sterling qualities associated—in a sportsman's mind at least—with November's existence.

The fact is, the year 1846 was a month in advance of itself all the way through, and we had November in October.

There was very good hunting in October in many counties —that is to say, the huntsmen and whips had very good hunting.

We will describe a November day of 1846, for the benefit of posterity, should the plates save our work from the trunk-maker or butter-man.

On Monday, the 16th, Mr. Neville's hounds met at Horndean Toll-bar, midway between the towns of Scrapetin and Skinflint, and having scarcely recovered from a half-suppressed, half-cured, agueish sort of cold, which had prevented his taking the field before, Mr. Scott was anything but pleased at the dull, unblooming look of the clipped horse's coat, when he went into the stable, confirming the suspicions he had indulged in while dressing, of its being a nasty cold day.

When he got upon the road he found his worst fears confirmed, for the mudscrapings were dry on the north side, and the whole surface of the turnpike gave indications of its being a cold drying day.

The horse didn't like it, and champed the bit, and set up his back, as though anxious to warm himself with a gallop.

There are some days of so dubious undefined a character, that one may ring the changes with the people we meet between a "fine day" and a "bad day" with the probable chance of success with each, but it would have required an extremely complaisant person to agree that this was a pleasant day—a nice day, or a day deserving any of the various forms of phraseology denoting approval of the weather   It was an arid drying day, with just sufficient wind to send the cold cutting air through one's carcase. Even fox-hunters—of all men the most merciful and least hasty in condemning a day—could only observe "that it *might* be better than it looked." A day certainly may be so bad as to be good for nothing but fox-hunting, but these are generally of the sloppy order, not your withering, dust-raising sort of days. Moreover such a day in November is perfectly discreditable, for the least one can expect is to come home with one's feet well wet up to the ankles, from the slushiness of the ground.

A scarlet coat is generally considered a better specific against cold than the stoutest double-milled broad-cloth or extra strong Saxony ; but on this day its charms were gone. Mr. Scott shivered as he went along. The few men he overtook were flopping their arms, or had their mouths tied up in shawls or cravats, as though they were coming from the dentist's. The greetings were of the desponding order, as if each thought he would be better at home. If Tom had been ordered by the Horse Guards, the Admiralty, the Home Secretary, or any one in authority, to turn out on such a day, how he would have grumbled ! What a pretty kick up he'd have made. Nevertheless, there he was, trotting along, trying to delude himself into the belief that it was pleasure.

It must be a marvellous day, or a wonderful country, when the advertisement of a regularly established pack of fox-hounds fails to bring some one. When he got to the toll-bar, Tim Bilk, the collector, had half filled his white apron pocket with coppers, and it was gratifying to see some one looking happy. The hounds did not, neither did the horses, while the quick movement, and the thumping of hands against thighs, plainly told how cold it was. A drop hung to old Ben the huntsman's nose, which, as he chased it away with his worsted mitten, was quickly succeeded by another. Still many people did not seem to think it so cold as it was, simply, we believe, because it was early in the month of November. Had it been about Christmas.

they would have exclaimed against waiting, and showered blessings on the heads of all late-comers. Mr. Neville, we may
observe, did not even send a horse on ; and there we think
he showed he had not hunted so many years for nothing. In
the absence of the Master a Regent is generally appointed, and
some time was consumed by old Ben in expectation of some one
either appointing himself or being appointed by the field. As,
however, a Regency imposes the propriety of staying with the
hounds till the end of the day, it did not seem in request, and
at last they put into cover without one.

The only drawback to Horndean is its proximity to the
towns of Scrapetin and Skinflint. These at times pour forth
rather a troublesome population. As a harbour for foxes, as a
good place to get away from, and as a cover commanding a
run, if a fox does but get clear, it is second to none in the
country. Had it been a moderate sort of meet Scott would not
have troubled it, but there is no such thing as staying away
from Horndean. The cover is about a mile long, with all sorts
of lying, timber, plantation, underwood, gorse, broom, fern,
every accommodation, as the lodging-house keepers say. The
deepest and strongest part is at the end where they meet, the
whole hill, or rather precipice side, being covered with gorse in
every stage of health and every variety of growth, open here close
there, middling elsewhere, with occasional slides of bluish slate
or bare patches of ground, giving the occupants on the opposite
side a fine panoramic view of Reynard's peregrinations. The
bunnies, too, are plentiful, and many a capering yard wand
goes home on his "three and sixpence a side," with the full
conviction that one of these dotting, popping, burrowing little
beggars, is *the* animal he has hired his horse to come out to
see hunted.

"*Tallyho!*" exclaimed Tom Scott. "I declare there he is,
bounding out of yon thick patch of gorse, straggling up to the
hill-top ; and now he comes banging down the side like a
rocket. *Tallyho! Tallyho!* Confounded old fool that I am!

I declare I am just as keen about seeing him as I was the first time out, and that's a quarter of a century ago," added our friend to himself.

What commotion the hunt has created in the lately untenanted valley ! The hills are clustered with spectators, and the few leafless ashes by the road-side are crowded with boys. All are agog with excitement, all straining their-eyeballs, in the hopes of seeing him, and most of them looking the wrong way. Even Bilk has left the gate in charge of his niece, and stolen away to see the find.

" There's a better scent than I thought," said Scott, eyeing the pack flying together. Now they pour down the steep hillside, right on the line bold Reynard has taken. What a crash ! what a melody ! The old gorse bushes snap under their weight, and the green masses shake and tremble with their bustling. "They'll have him out before long," said Tom, and then he began hugging himself for coming. "Never does to stay at home because the morning doesn't look well," said he, cocking up a leg and drawing his girths : "shouldn't wonder if we have a run ; and then, how vexed all the fellows will be that haven't come ! "

And now " hats off" further up, shows that Reynard is viewed, but the second whip being there prevents any noisy ebullition of delight. The hounds are working on the line and will soon be at the spot. He's *on*, by Jove ! horses' heads turn to the west, and rising shoulders bob above the opposite wall to where Scott is—he cuts away through the old established gaps on his side of the dean, for there never was a fox cover yet without its regular way all round, though few people care to learn more than one side.

What a clatter the roadsters make on the opposite side ! and how they hurry on regardless of the hounds !—yon gentleman in the linen trowsers on the runaway chestnut is going at score.

In vain the huntsman shouts, in vain the whip imprecates—

THE GENTLEMAN ON THE RUNAWAY CHESTNUT.

To face page 52.

on, on, he goes, like Gilpin, and, in all probability, with a similar
result.

They say that every woman has one chance of being
married, and every fox one chance of breaking cover, and
we believe this fox had every intention of going, if it
hadn't been for this genius. There is a narrow gully near
the west end of the dean that nine flying foxes out of ten
emerge by, facing as fine a tract of open country, chiefly
pasture, as eye can traverse, but the chestnut got there first,
and Reynard declined following. A fox, like a sovereign,
must be first or nowhere. It's all nonsense depriving him of
his precedence—people who go out hunting must make up their
minds to let the fox go first.

A cold east wind shivered a chill of disappointment, as the
field, on turning their horses' heads to the now baffled hounds,
met it careering up the valley. The warmth of excitement
seemed to die out all at once. The hounds even seemed disappointed, and came lagging along, now on the scent, now off,
in a far different style to what they had flown with the first
outburst of joy, produced by a close proximity to the brush.
Who doesn't know the result of such a mishap as this? Who
doesn't know the blighting influence such a catastrophe has on
the spirits of the field? how what might have been the finest
day that ever was seen, becomes tainted with the title we have
placed at the head of our paper?

The sportsmen were presently all back in their places, just
like people who had gone out of a French theatre between acts.
There was old Ben with a fresh drop on his nose, yoicking his
hounds, himself and his horse embedded in gorse—there was
the second whip again standing erect in his stirrups, looking
out for a view—and Tom, the first whip, was back on our
friend Scott's side of the dean, ready to attend Reynard away
should he be inclined for a trip to the south.

Up and down, and round about, the hounds worked him,
the scent getting weaker, and the ground getting worse, the

more it was foiled. Now they'd give it up, and now they wouldn't ; now Ben viewed him, and now Joe, but Tom and Mr. Scott, who sat on the opposite side, saw that the chance of getting him away again grew worse and worse.

" Some may call this fox a coward," said Scott to himself, as he sat eyeing the proceedings, and ruminating on the mutabilities of the chase, " but he certainly has no right to that title for both his performances this day. According to the common doctrine of courage, he who flies at once is a coward, and viewed in that light, Reynard would be censured for doing what we want him. He started away at once, and if the linen leggings interposed, that was no fault of his, nor should he be blamed for keeping where they do not come. I'm not sure," continued he, " but it requires more courage to stand the efforts of those two-and-twenty couple of slapping hounds in that small hill, than to fly the country, and take the chance of sheltering hedge-rows, friendly woods, and other contingencies. Yet we call the fox a coward for not running away. The doctrine of fox courage is not clearly defined. The doctrine of *cold* is, though ; " continued he, sneezing and shrugging up his shoulders as the keen wind took him across the back.

" Thank God ! there's old Ben putting his horn to his mouth at last," exclaimed he, and the clear shrill noise sounded through the country. The willing hounds gladly left the unkindly gorse, and came straggling up to Ben's horse's heels.

" If it wasn't that I have broken into the day, and shouldn't be able to settle to anything after, I'd go home," said Scott to himself ; " for there's no sure find within four miles of this, and the day is getting colder, and the wind higher." Moreover the day, without being absolutely stormy, was just boisterous enough to prevent hounds hearing, and consequently bad enough to prevent hunting.

The choice now lay between Hunter's Oak Spinney and Kenley Gorse—the one being in Scott's way home, the other

out of it. Of course they chose the one out of it, and after
four miles, trot, trot, bump, bump, at that most uncomfortable
postboy pace that hounds jog from cover to cover, they
arrived at the gorse just in time to see two shooters emerge
from it.

We need hardly say they drew it blank; indeed, after so
much gorse work, we were only surprised that Ben drew it at
all; but huntsmen must make out a day somehow when
master is absent, and that with as little unnecessary disturb-
ance of country as possible.

Farmer Buckwheat then came up, and assured Ben that he
had seen a fox an hour before rolling on his neighbour Rush's
fallow,—a piece of intelligence that Ben eagerly availed himself
of, and drew the hounds across and across as though he really
expected to find him.

That performance being over, and eleven red-coats remaining,
nine of whom lived to the north, Ben announced his intention
of drawing Parkham Bush Dean, a most impracticable cover,
to the south—impracticable at least in as far as getting foxes
away is concerned—an intimation that acted like lightning
upon the field, causing the red-coats to stop short, those who
had comforters in their pockets to tie up their mouths, those
who had warm gloves to produce them from their horses' girths,
and all to make preparations for cutting home,—declaring that
they had had enough, and that it was the most beastly day they
had ever been out in.

Cold, dejected, cheerless, dispirited, and chilled, our friend
sought his solitary home, and having got rid of an hour in the
stable, at last found himself in the old red morocco chair with
cane sides, that has grown old, and tattered, and shabby in
his service. There, as he dozed over the fire, with the
melancholy light of a pair of mutton fats, he reviewed the flight
of life, and glanced at the prospect of the future.

"Hunting," said he, "has been the balm and charm of my
youth—it has solaced the seclusion of my summers, and de-

lighted the retirement of my winters ; but, hang it, if this November is to be taken as a sample of what's to come, it's precious little use persevering in the line."

Thereupon he gave a tremendous sneeze.

" What a fool I was to go out on such a day ! " continued he, burying his face in a capacious bandana, "*far* more likely to increase a cold than to cure one." *A-whitz—a-whitz—a-whitz*—" regularly in for it, and nobody to nurse one. Poor Lydia Clifton ! If it hadn't been for this hunting I'd have married you long since." *A-whitz — a-whitz — a-whitz.* " James ! " hallooed he to the boy he now heard fistling in the passage, " take a foot-bath full of hot water up-stairs directly —*boiling !* d'ye hear ? I really think I'll give up hunting and marry her still," added Tom, rising from the morocco chair, " for it's no use keeping horses for such work as this." So saying, he stumped up-stairs, to parboil his feet and think over the pro's and con's of matrimony.

CHAPTER IV.

A CHEERER.

" A chosen few alone the sport enjoy ! "

AN UNGENIAL DAY.

HE next day was so deuced overcast and bad that our friend didn't venture further than the stable, or we really believe he would have ridden over to Snailswell, and ended a nine years' courtship with an offer. As it was he lay at earth, watching the rows of drops stringing themselves together like illumination lamps on the window frames, the raw drizzling rain gliding down the panes, and the heavy spongy clouds rolling themselves like bed hangings round the opposite hills. A more ungenial day, perhaps, was never seen. Even in the country it was scarcely light, and what those poor benighted folks who live in towns must have suffered "baffles the comprehension." The glass had run itself down to nothing, and everybody said they were in for "weather." The wind rose towards night, and dashed the now swelling drops against the casement with redoubled fury.

Scott fully made up his mind, as he turned into bed, to be done with hunting, and to settle quietly down to matrimony. " It's no use persevering in a sport when one hasn't weather to enjoy it in," argued he, considering what he should do with his horses. " She's a nice little creature," continued he, pulling the bedclothes up to his snuffling nose, " and although she hasn't much money, yet she's so careful that her management would be quite as good as a fortune." So saying, he dozed away to sleep, and dreamt of bells ringing, ribbons flaunting, beer flowing, fiddles scraping, girls dancing, farmers feasting, " three times three and one cheer more ! "

How different everything looked the next morning. The dreary, foggy, water-charged clouds had cleared away, and been succeeded by bright, smiling, sunshiny weather.

The landscape was just like a newly cleaned picture. What yesterday was all blotch, mystery, and confusion, to-day stood forth most luminously distinct. Nay, beauties appeared, that a stranger would have said had been added—Oakhope spire, the herd's white cottage on the Compton Hills, and the sky-line breaking fringe of beech, crowning the summit of Blackdown Moor. All nature seemed to rejoice in the change. The cattle grazed freely in the fields instead of sheltering behind trees and hedge-rows, the labourers doffed their jackets to their work, children played bareheaded about the cottages, and the horses in the stable had acquired a silky gloss on their late dull unkindly coats.

The hounds met at Hollyburn Green, twelve miles by the road, nine by the " crow." Our friend certainly had no intention of hunting when he went to bed—none whatever ; indeed he had fully determined, if his cold was well enough, to ride

over to Snailswell ; but we must add that he did not anticipate
so fine a day.

"Saddle old Barbara," said he to Will Sleekpow, who was
preparing for exercise, "and you ride the colt on as far as
Ratchburn Mill, and then take the fields for Hollyburn Green,
till I overtake you ; " with which directions Tom hurried back
to dress and breakfast.

Will seemed rather surprised, but, like a sensible servant, he
proceeded to do what he was told,—a very indispensable quality
for a person calling himself a servant.

What a different sort of day it was to the last ! Instead of
a drying, pinching, hide-bound sort of feeling, it had all the
soft, fresh, bland luxuriance of spring. Quite a day for
taking the creases out of one's face. The ground was well
saturated with wet, and the old mare went snorting, and
bounding, and trotting along as if in equal enjoyment with
her rider.

The observation is as old as the hills, that we seldom appreciate anything till we lose it, and the truism holds good with
hunting as well as with other things. The two previous days
had been so wretchedly bad, and the glass had given such little
indication of amendment, that few of the field had looked upon
hunting this day with any sort of confidence. Indeed the
boisterous night had well-nigh quenched the hopes of even the
most sanguine, and few had thought of giving any hunting
orders on going to bed. Tarquinius Muff had turned in, at
eleven, without a word on the subject ; Blatheremskite had done
the same at twelve, having taken an hour's snooze in his arm-
chair after his brother was gone, and all the " easy ones " had
gone off in a similar way.

The consequence of all this was, that though they didn't
muster so strong as they would have done had the previous
weather been fine, yet those who did come were mostly of the
right sort, and all were in the high glee of joyous excitement
and expectation. Perhaps a slight cause of exultation might

arise at the circumstance of there being so many absentees ;
for though fox-hunters are all most desperately loving and
sociable when together, yet there are very few who can't put up
with the absence of a cocktail—nay, there are some who even
like to have a crow over a comrade. There was what might be
called a good field ; numerous enough to be pleasant, and not
overcrowded. No fox-headers by profession, no linen-trowsered
young gentlemen, with yard-wands for whip-sticks, no grooms
on rearers, no horse-breakers on kickers, no young farmers on
runaways : there might be fifteen scarlets and a dozen blacks.
For the real pleasure of hunting we hold that to be quite
enough. When you have just the cream of a hunt, people
settle into places in a run quite naturally, without the jostling,
sorting, and winnowing incident to a crowd. Old Mr. Neville
came bustling along almost first, as if his absence on the last
day had set the razor of his keenness on edge. Old Ben's features as he trotted up the green, with the spicy, blooming,
bitch-pack at his chestnut horse's heels, had relaxed all the
keen rigidity of muscle that contracted them on the Horndean
day, and he was now swelled out to his natural size, looking like
an elderly cherub on horseback.

Tom Scott overtook Sleekpow between Ratchburn Mill and
the meet, and got the young horse in a very cool and collected
state ; nor was his equanimity disturbed by the sight of Scott's
red coat, nor yet by the cantering and splashing past of Tom
Muffinmouth and his cousin, Bill Bullfinch, on their cover
hacks. When Scott mounted he felt wiry and strong under
him, light and pleasant in hand, and altogether as if he would
go. It is a great thing for rider and horse to start pleasantly
together. Another great advantage is, not having time to
quarrel between the start and the meet. This is one of the
great advantages of a cover hack. When a man rides his own
horse " on," a difference of opinion is very apt to arise on the
road, particularly on that most important of all points, whether
he shall walk or trot ; and as it is painfully true that a man

TOM SCOTT AND THE "YOUNG 'UN" ON THE WAY TO THE MEET.

[*To face page* 60.

may see too much of his best friend, so it is equally so that he
may have too much of his best horse. Though quite a man for
the morning, and always at cover as soon as the groom, Scott
likes sending on, not only as a great saving of valuable temper,
but also as a certain means of getting two horses well exercised.

But to the sport, for the field are on fire, and eager for the
fray.

The eager hounds would scarcely wait for the dismissing
cheer and wave of old Ben's hand, as they approached the
accustomed corner of Heatherside Plantation, and disdaining
all make-believe drawing, dashed on to the thick of the lying
on the projecting banks, from whence they had so often un-
kennelled the "varmint." Old Columbine's deep tongue,
which no rate or whip crack ever followed, infused joy into the
field, and hats were fastened down and pressed firmly on the
brow, and reins gathered up, ere three whimpers had escaped
her. *Hoic! Hoic!* cheered old Ben, kicking and jagging the
chestnut through the brushwood of the cover ; but the pack
needed no monition—the old bitch's tongue was quite enough
to draw them to her like lightning. Master Reynard was on
the alert, and had left his sheltered couch at the cheer
following the second note, being strongly of opinion that
the noise he heard was very like what had disturbed him
about three weeks before, when he had deemed it prudent
to visit the distant cover of Neverbreak Forest, whence
indeed he had only lately returned, finding, greatly to his
discomfort, that his earth had been usurped by a badger in
his absence.

Tremendous was the outburst of melody as the pack reached
the now vacated kennel, and powerful the scent that its late
occupant left, as he brushed through the faded fern and browning heather of his dry warm quarters. If he had any doubts at
all as to what was going on, they were speedily dispelled by a
loud, clear, full "TALLY-HO ! *gone away!* " from the far end of

the cover, proclaiming that, having run its utmost limits, he
had taken his departure.

"*It's the old boy!*" exclaimed Tom Bowles, the first
whip, whose halloo had just been heard—he broke at the
very same place he did before, and crossed the field at the
same spot.

"Yonder he goes!" added he, viewing the fox travelling
evenly away over the opposite hill.

The pack tied on the scent, and went away in a style that
would have funked the directors of an insurance office, if they
had done a policy on Reynard's life. There was mischief in
the cry. "Hold hard, gentlemen! for *one* minute," exclaimed
Ben, pulling up short to get the hounds well away; and that
minute being freely accorded, he started off at a canter, and all
did the same.

There wasn't a fence worth speaking of for the first five or
six fields, so that the riders had time to get their horses well in
hand and settled in their stride before business began.

A fallow field brought Tom Scott's five-year-old to his bit,
and having once dropped upon it, he went as steadily and collectedly as possible.

"He's a hundred guineas' worth," exclaimed Scott, as he
shot over a flight of hurdles like an arrow; and that was
putting sixty pounds on at once, for the only time he had
ridden him before he was so crazy and "tail first" at his leaps,
that he would have taken forty for him—forty! even though
he had bred him, and no one ever breeds a horse that isn't
occasionally worth a hundred. Hundreds are easily talked of,
but difficult to realise out of a dealer's yard. But this is no
time for a dissertation on dealing; for the hounds, after racing
past Dewlish and over the large open fields of Risborough Lordship, are now making the wooded banks of the Brentwater echo
with their melody.

"Hold hard, gentlemen!" halloos Mr. Neville, from behind,
adding, as the obedient field pulled to the summons, "I've seen

more foxes headed at that point than at almost any other in the country."

"Tallyho! Yonder he goes!" added he, viewing him from the rising ground on which he had stationed himself.

Another minute, and the hounds were out also, the scent not being quite so good in cover as it was in the open.

"Now he's away for Neverbreak Forest!" screamed Mr. Neville, shortening his reins, "and let those catch 'im who can!"

So fair an invitation, so sportingly given, caused every man to settle himself in his saddle, and to hug his horse by the head as though he were bent on destruction.

The bitch-pack are terribly fast, and take a deal of catching at most times. This day seemed likely to put something extra to their pace.

A cloud that had overcast the sky cleared away at the moment the fox broke from the end of the belt of wood at the water side, shedding a halo o'er the scene, and disclosing to those who had time to look ahead the dreaded Neverbreak Forest in the extreme distance. It could not be less than six miles in a straight line—a mere trifle to stag-hunters, who know nothing under twenty, but a space admitting of many pleasing variations in the up and down life of matter-of-fact fox-hunters. To heighten the interest of the scene, the line to the forest seemed to lie up the broad green valley of Grassmere, a valley as famous for fattening oxen as it is favourable to scent. The pollard willows through the centre indicated the "presence" of water, as the chemists say, even if the sun had not lit up the broad patches of it here and there, and shown the white bridges at the foot crossings. The mere mention of the forest acted as a stopper on some of the field, so famous is it in the fox-hunting history of the country for tremendous runs, heavy fencing, deep galloping, desperate swimming, confounded cramming—all the funking fireside attributes of hunting—as if there were not big places in all countries, if people only look out for them. If the forest had been such a regular " kill bull," Old Ben must have died of it long ago, for he's been riding towards it and from it once a month at the least during the season, for the last thirty years ; and when Scott saw him slide down a steep bank, and turn the corner of a flight of rails, that appeared to him impassable, he thought, as he followed him, that he was very likely to ride a good many more.

The bruisers and would-be bruisers, of course, kept up the bottom with the hounds, and when great Captain Rasher, with a mouthful of moustache, came to the first sedgy watercut dividing the meadows, and saw the valley was not the smooth-sailing race-course he expected, he would have had no objection to turn back, if Tom Muffinmouth hadn't come up full tilt, causing his second charger hunter to blob right in, where he was immediately joined by Muffinmouth and his horse, the whole stirring up the black bog earth like a gigantic mash.

" It's very odd," said Old Ben, who was now careering along the sound bank through the familiar line of gaps, " that gentlemen always *will* ride into those bogs. I dare say I've seen a hundred horses floundering in them, first and last, and yet we never come this way without some one trying them. *Forrard! forrard!* " continued he, cheering on his hounds, notwithstanding they were beating him as it was. " Forrarding " with huntsmen, and "hissing " with grooms, are things they get so into the way of, that many of them can't help themselves.

If *extreme* pace lasts, a run can't last. That is a truism worth remembering by pullers-up and people fancying themselves about to be beat by the pace. Up the Grassmere Water Meadows the pace certainly was extremely good—so good that the hounds ran nearly mute ; but as they neared the neck where the meadows run up into a ravine, some few found time and wind to throw their tongues ; and most welcome were the

notes, borne back on the soft light breeze. A momentary
check at the top let in the successful followers on either side of
the valley, while a mixed tail of blacks and reds dotted the line
of country over which they had come. The lathered horses
now stood panting and blowing, and shaking their tails, after
their exertions, whilst the red-faced, perspiring sportsmen durst
not dismount to ease them. "Bless us, what a pace!" "Did
you see Muffinmouth in the bog?" "Who was t'other
chap?" "Where's my groom?" "You've lost a shoe."
"Have I, by Jove? It's all dickey with me, then!"
were the exclamations that burst forth, while Ben bustled
away to the well-accustomed point, to get the pack on with
their game.

Up the steep dean-side then they scrambled, and after
squeezing through a stiff and very scratch-my-face fence, they
found themselves in a large fallow, with the hounds lob,
lob, lobbing across, now mute, now dropping a note, but
pointing for the forest, now a conspicuous object in the rising
foreground.

Old Ben began kicking the chestnut into a canter to get the
hounds across the fallow as quickly as possible, well knowing
the importance of killing the fox in the open. Not that he
ever expresses a doubt of catching him in cover, but he prefers
the publicity of the plain. He is all for fair play, especially
when there's a burning scent.

The rivalry of riding was now about over, all being satisfied
that if their horses got into the deep rides of the forest, they
would want all the "go" they could save for them, and trotting,
and holding, and easing, and furrow-seeking, and headland-
riding, became the order of the day.

Mr. Swillbut, the brewer's, great gaunt brown horse
Molasses, who had given indications of a stiff neck down
below, had been so fairly pumped out by clambering up the
rough brushwoody dean, that he lay down on the fallow just
outside the stiff fence, and so awkwardly did he repose

himself, that the few horses behind had to leap over him, or force a fresh breach through the lofty, newly switched, almost impenetrable fence.

Still the desire to save their horses was outweighed by anxiety to kill the fox in the open, and nobody regretted to hear the light musical notes of the bitches again swelling to cry as they got upon a large, rushy, old pasture, causing the field to get their horses by the head, and urge them again into a canter.

The thing had now got so select that there would be honour and glory enough for them all, consequently, those who "*never* open gates," and *never* "pull down fences," now began to do both, and those who always open and pull down, now did so the more.

So what with one, and what with another, they about dispensed with leaping altogether. It was, "I'll get off if you'll hold my horse! that's a good fellow; I'll do it next time," or "You'd better get off and lift it," as Tom Bowles was fumbling at a chained gate.

This, however, is all under the rose, the stiffest fencing and the hardest riding being always, by courtesy, supposed to come last.

So they went on from field to field rejoicing.

*   *   *   *   *

After skirting Birkshaw coppice, and taking a look at Cranfield farm buildings, Reynard did not find such accommodation as induced him to desert his original point for the forest; but a colley dog chasing him, pumped out the little balance of wind he had left; to recruit which he shortly after lay up in a hedge-row, from whence, after the usual flash forward and feathering flourish of the pack, he was soon elevated in the arms of Old Ben before the admiring eyes of "glorious seven," each trying who could WHO-HOOP loudest.

The following may be taken as a sample of the usual varied accounts that attend a good run :—

Real distance, eight miles.
Real time, forty-five minutes.
Checks, one.
Heavies up, four.
Lights, three.

Telling distance, fourteen.
Telling time, one hour.
Checks, none.

The result of our friend **Tom's** ride was, that he repriced the young 'un at 150*l.*

CHASED BY A COLLEY.

CHAPTER V.

LORD LIONEL LAZYTONGS.

DELIGHTED with his day with Mr. Neville, pleased with the performance of the five-year old, in love with all the world, particularly with his sweet charmer Lydia Clifton, our friend gave his horse to Sleekpow, with an intimation that he should want Rough Robin the next afternoon, being fully determined to ride over to Snailswell, and finish the matter off-hand, whether he gave up hunting or not.

"It's time I was married," said he, stamping the conglomerated mud off his soaked boots, and casting an eye downwards on the stained and spattered cords.

"It doesn't follow," continued he, as he opened the back door, and hurried into the house, "that I need give up hunting the first year at all events, or perhaps not even the second, or yet the third;" and if anything was wanting to clench his determination about matrimony, it would have been the fact of his stumbling over one of those abominable tape-women's baskets that had been left in the passage, while the owner carried on the usual promiscuous barter with the females—ribbons for rabbits' skins, shawls for suet, tape for tea, and so on.

It's very odd, but bachelors always use twice as much tea as married people ; at least they pay for twice as much.

A letter with a large seal lay on the entrance table— a seal so large that, had it been in black, Tom would have thought all the crowned heads in Europe had demised together.

"Who can this be from?" exclaimed he, eyeing the spreading-many-quartered shield and crests, surmounted by a coronet. He broke it and read as follows :—

" DAWDLE COURT.

"DEAR MR. SCOTT,—*The Tear Devil Hounds meet at Ecclesford Green, near here, on Tuesday next, and we shall be glad if it will suit your convenience to come on Monday and stay till Wednesday, with*

" Yours, very truly,

"LIONEL LAZYTONGS.

"To THOMAS SCOTT, ESQ., Hawbuck Grange."

"What the deuce can have come over him now?" exclaimed Tom, as he read it ; "his lordship has been living at Dawdle Court these three seasons, and never got further than a card, or a call, or a hope that I'd come to him at that most undefined period 'some time,' and now he breaks out in a downright invitation to stay."

No man is more keenly alive to the extreme absurdity of people visiting out of their own station of life, or censures it more severely in their neighbours than Tom does ; after which our readers will not be surprised to learn that he looked out his best boots, &c., and wrote to say he would go.

*   *   *   *   *
*   *   *   *   *

The premature closing of a winter's day, but little aided by the slender horn-like circle of the young and rising moon, saw him before the massive pile of Dawdle Court, whose heavy outline, he, however, forsook in favour of the stables, into whose spacious yard he rode with an "at home" sort of air.

It is not every man that can face the silk-stocking smartness and lace-daubed splendour of a front-door entrance ; but between the denizen of the stable and the fox-hunter, there is a something in common that prevents the latter feeling *distrait.* Though our walk in life has not been either lofty or extensive, we are free to confess that we have seen lackeys who looked quite as much like gentlemen as their masters. "Small blame to their masters for keeping them," as Paddy would say ; but it is inconvenient for a stranger to scrape and bow to the servant : equally disagreeable to take the lord for a lackey. We, therefore, like the stable. We like to ride quietly in and ask the groom, or coachman, or the postilion, or the anybody connected with horses that we see moving about, if Sir John, or Sir George, or my lady are at home, and then, if we get an answer in the negative, we just ask them to take charge of our cards ; and if they say " yes," why we see our horse put up ourself, and so save old Patepowder, the porter, the wickedness of the oaths he might let fall as he hobbled away with him from the front door. Seeing the horse housed oneself, also, gives one time to rectify any little derangement of dress incurred on the road, stamp off the mud sparks, pull up one's collars, comb out one's whiskers—all extremely proper and allowable, but which a modest man would feel a delicacy in doing at a front door, with all the eye windows of the house full upon him, and no saying how many pair of bright roguish eyes within, criticising his movements. We do not know a more nervous situation for a shy man than to place himself in the pillory of public observation, before a large house full of company in the country— luncheon time, say—when all the ladies are together, giving a loose to their tongues and their appetites. Unfortunate young man ! Should you be accused of sweethearting anyone, how they would pull you to pieces, especially if you were " booked." There wouldn't be a feature but what they would condemn, or a sin in the whole catalogue of crime but what they would lay to your charge.

There is an advantage in riding direct to the stables, when one goes to stay all night, even though the shades of night would protect one from idle curiosity. One sees what sort of

accommodation one's horse gets ; sees what sort of screws they
keep of their own ; and so while away an hour that might be
very heavy in the house. The best ginger beer that ever was
bottled won't fiz above a certain time.

Well, Tom Scott rode into the yard, as we said, with a "rest,
soldier rest," sort of feeling, and also with the pleasing conviction that in the course of his ride he had earned an enormous
appetite.

It was four o'clock, stable hour, and the horses, after being
stripped, strapped, and watered, were now in the full enjoyment of their corn, standing up to their bellies in clean
wheat straw, as shown by numerous lanthorns hanging from
ceilings.

The trampling of his horse's feet drew a shirt-sleeved helper
or two to the doors, and one more venturesome and less afraid
of fresh air than the rest, keeping his head out sufficiently long
to receive the shot of a question, Tom ventured to ask "where
his stable was ? "

"We don't take in osses ere, old boy : it ain't a livery
stable," replied the man, taking our friend for a groom.

"Hush ! " exclaimed a voice behind, pulling the speaker
back, "it'll be Mr. Scott ; I've just sent his servant on."

A very orthodox, roundabout, stud groom, then came forward with a lanthorn, and casting the light over Tom,
lest he might compromise his consequence by misplaced
politeness, observed, with a touch of the hat, " Mr. Scott, I
believe ? "

"Yes," replied Tom, adding, " would you have the kindness
to show me my stable."

"I sent a helper on with your servant, not half an hour
since," replied the groom, " and he's not returned yet ; but I'll
endeavour to get some one to take this," continued he, ringing
a small bell.

"Don't you take in horses?" asked Tom, as the little tinkler
ceased sounding.

"Why—no—yes—no—not exactly here," hesitated the groom; "at the Lazytong Arms, close by, just outside the park. Excellent accommodation—kept by an old coachman of ours—Esau Broadback—two-year old oats—sweetest hay that ever was smelt."

"But if the park is as wide that way as it is the one I've come," replied Tom, "it will be a precious distance, and how am I to manage for want of a servant? I have only a groom."

"Oh, Mr. Lampoil, the groom of the chamber, will manage all that for you, sir," replied he, at the same time turning to a group of helpers, whom his ring had drawn together; he inquired of one, whom he designated Mat, "What he was doing?" and receiving the usual answer, "Nothing," he ordered him to saddle Usurper, and "lead this ere orse over to the Arms."

"But if it's close by, what's the use of taking out a horse?" asked Tom.

"He'll be none the worse of a little exercise," replied the groom.

"Nor Mat, either, perhaps," observed Tom.

Not being quite satisfied about the locality of the Arms, and the moon now giving a more available light, Tom thought he might as well consume part of the two hours and a half that still separated him from dinner, by riding the old mare to her quarters; accordingly he set off, accompanied by Mat on Usurper, a thorough-bred hack with a bang tail down to the hocks.

It was not without a longing look that Tom took leave of the Dawdle Court stables, feeling satisfied that, however good the "Arms'" ones might be, they could not beat the "Court."

Taking in horses has almost become the sole perquisite of the poor, at least those that the world call "poor," though they often have more to spend than those that the world call "rich."

Men in our friend Tom Scott's class of life, never think of separating " man and horse." If they can't take in both, they send word, clearly showing that " not " taking in, is the exception.

There are some places of such convenient distance that they stretch or contract like telescopes, according to the wishes of the party. We have known the same place both two miles and four in the mouth of the same person. The Scotch talk of their miles and a bittick ; but their miles and a bittick are not a bit more undefinable than an Englishman's " close by."

Although enlivened by Mat's agreeable conversation, who, not having heard the groom's orders to take over Tom's mare, concluded by Tom going that he was a fellow servant, was both inquisitive and communicative, informing Tom, " what he had," and anxious to know Tom's wages ; our friend found the " close by," a long way. When one expects to arrive at a journey's end every minute, distance stretches out amazingly. Even on an ordinary beaten road, travelling the last mile is often the longest. The meanderings of the road through the park seemed as if they would never end, and views and vistas, that might be very beautiful by day, were anything but inter-esting on a winter night, illumined only by the fitful gleams of a crescent moon.

At last Tom and his conductor reached the noble lodge, and following the turnpike road upon which they now got, the creaking of the glittering sign containing the Fender and Fire-iron Arms, as it swung to and fro in the little garden before the house, at last proclaimed Tom's journey done.

Following Mat, he presently found himself in the soft bedding of a farm yard, the little panes of glass for windows in the encircling buildings, emitting gleams of light indicative of occupants within.

" Have you bespoke a stable ? " asked Mat, halting in the middle of the straw yard.

"No," replied Tom : "I thought his lordship took in horses."

"I fear you'll come badly on, then," said Mat, "for they've only six decent stalls, and they seem to be all full."

"Holloa!" exclaimed he, giving a loud, shrill, shilling gallery sort of whistle, which had the effect of awakening a man in an open-doored building to a sense of their presence, who, on coming forward, proved to be Sleekpow. This worthy was in the usual state of mental depression, of a groom who hasn't got the best stable. "He was sure he didn't know what they should do. The stable wasn't fit to put a dog horse in, let alone such horses as *ours;* " and after divers lamentations he led the way into a sort of a cross between a stable and a cowhouse—not very good to be sure, but a place that might have been a great deal worse. The ceiling was very low, and formed of loose rafters for the support of hay ; but that was a deal better than no ceiling, or a roof with holes in it ; and though the stalls were merely formed of swing bars, that is of little consequence with horses that know each other. The stable was warm and dry, and there was plenty of clean straw ; and the hay being last year's (1846), it was almost superfluous smelling it, for it was sure to be good.

However, having humoured Sleekpow by joining in his grumble, and admitting all his objections to be valid, Tom proceeded to worm it out if he knew whose horses were there.

"There's Captain Tipthorn and Mr. Blobditch, Major Tinhead, and a gentleman, whose name he forgot, Squire Muffinhead, or something of that sort.

"The hounds met at Ecclesford Green, but where that was he couldn't tell ; Esau Broadback, the landlord of the Arms, who knew as much about hounds as coachmen generally do, stating it to be two miles, while Major Tinhead's groom declared it was four." However, two or four was no great matter ; so ordering Sleekpow to bring the mare in time for the four, Tom retraced his steps through the park, and was

"WHAT TIME DO WE DINE?" ASKED HE.

[*To face page* 76.

surprised to find himself back at Dawdle Court in "no time."

*   *   *   *   *

"What time do we dine?" asked he of one of the bedizened flunkeys who rushed to his assistance as he entered, and persisted in stripping him as if he hadn't a hand of his own.

"Dinner's *ordered* at seven," replied he, with an emphasis on the "ordered."

Having possessed himself of Tom's hat, gloves, whip-stick, and paletot, he handed him over to a pump and pantaloon gentleman in a cataract of white linen, who guided our friend along a labyrinth of passages, lighted in the true pick-up-a-pin style, to the library.

Here Tom found his noble host, booted and breeched, in the midst of an admiring circle whose peculiar costume indicated sportsmen in *mufti*—cutaway coats, fancy neckcloths, striped vests, cord pantaloons, and so on. They all seemed as if they had come on horseback, and hadn't got the straddle out of their legs yet.

His lordship, who, in addition to boots and breeches, was attired in a smart new pea-green cut-away, was exhibiting his long length before the fire, in the true British style,—a lap over each arm,—detailing for the third time the splendour of a hare hunt he had been engaged in; which narrative he was kind enough to break off—though he had nearly hunted puss to destruction again—as Tom entered, in order that he might edify him with it from the beginning.

"Gad, Mr. Scott," said he, after mutual salutations were over, and he had moved a little to the left to give Tom a smell of the fire, "Gad, Mr. Scott," said he, "d'ye know, I was so pleased with your account of the Goose and Pudding Hunt that I wrote up to Tattersall to buy me a pack of harriers, and I've been out with them to-day for the first time, and I do assure you I never enjoyed anything more. We met at Furzey-

down," continued he, " about three miles and a-half from here,
and found a hare by Clipston Clump, who went as straight as
an arrow to Gatley Coppice, from whence, sinking the wind all
the way, she ran to Silverspring, skirting the plantations at
Stover, then on to Frogley Glen, where there was a slight
check—not more than five minutes, hardly so much—owing to
a flock of sheep ; however, we hit her off again, when the
hounds flew like pigeons over those fine large pastures to
Hackthorn, skirting Rookley Bog, and she was finally killed in
the middle of Broadfield village, just by the blacksmith's shop.
I dare say you know it, Mr. Scott—close to the public-house—
the sign of the Frugal Spinster."

Here Tom managed to intimate that he didn't know the
country.

" Ah, if you don't," continued his lordship, without drawing
breath, " my friend Captain Windeyhash here does,"—as if
Windeyhash's knowing it was the same as Tom ; and on his
lordship went again, talking of hunting, and riding, and foiling,
and casting, and crashing, till the announcement of Colonel
Buckskin again brought him " to."

Having got himself settled among them, much after the
fashion of a lost hound casting up, Buckskin essayed to show
his perfect ease by observing on his lordship's boots and
breeches.

" At it," his lordship went again, beginning with the find at
Clipstone Clump, and hunting the hare, with variations,
through all the places before mentioned, running out into a
long dissertation on the comparative merits of Pelhams and
snaffles, each of which he had been trying on the horses he had
ridden that day. This, too, in defiance of the gong, whose
last boom had long died out, and been succeeded by the light
notes of a musical clock chiming a quarter to seven.

Still his lordship rattled away, talking of scent, and skirting,
and nicking, and babbling, and leaping, and creeping, and
flying, and bruising, and rasping, and racing, and ramming, as

Lord Lionel discourses on hare hunting

if there was no such thing as dinner in the wind, at all events, as if his sporting keenness had completely subdued the keenness of his appetite.

At last Lampoil, the white-breasted gentleman Tom had encountered on entering, appeared at the door, followed by a flunkey with a tray full of flaring wax lights ; which appeared to draw his lordship's attention to the fact of his not having dined, for whisking one up with a flourish that sent the accumulated wax all over his leather breeches, he transferred the rest of the company to Lampoil, and proceeded to show Tom to the " blue room."

"Gad," said his lordship, again sticking his back to the fire, after going through the usual evolution of showing the bell, the boot-jack, &c., " those are capital hounds of mine, and I'm very much obliged to Tattersall for buying me them."

"Suppose we take a turn with them to-morrow," continued he, after a pause.

" We are going out with the Tear Devil hounds, aren't we ?" asked Tom, turning the airing shirt at the fire by way of giving his lordship a hint that they ought to be dressing.

" Ah, true ! " replied he, with an air of a man awaking out of a reverie, " to-morrow the Devils meet at Stallington Hill, nineteen miles from here, but that's nothing with two good hacks."

" Ecclesford Green you told me in your letter, I think," observed Tom.

" Ah, true ! " rejoined his lordship, " Stallington's on Saturday—you're right ; to-morrow is Ecclesford Green, and a deuced bad place it is too."

Just as he gave Tom this pleasing piece of intelligence the tower clock chimed seven, and observing that he " supposed they ought to be dressing," his lordship lounged out of the room, having now enlightened Tom as to the meaning of the footman, in saying that dinner was " ordered " at that hour.

"What a queer bitch it is," said Tom, as his lordship's gaunt figure disappeared through the doorway.

"He seems to be keen about hunting too," continued he, running his proceedings and conversation through his mind; for we should inform the reader, that though we called him "Tom's noble friend" in a former chapter, yet Tom knew very little of him, his acquaintance having commenced by helping him out of a bog at the close of last season, when his lordship had paid Mr. Neville's hounds a flying visit of inspection with a very liberal stud of very fine horses—nearly as many as would have done for hunting a country twice a week.

Not having a confusion of coats to bother him in a choice, Tom was not long at his toilette, thanks to the footman, who had laid all things out for him.

*   *   *   *   *

When he got into the speaious drawing-room, redolent of fragrance and gilt, and decorated to the highest pitch of French art, he found Lady Lazytongs with her lazytongs cocked on the sofa, who gave Tom the sort of distant bend that some ladies give their husbands' friends.

Fortunately Sir George Stiffnecke, a neighbouring knight of immense pretension, had arrived, and was doing the polite in his usual ponderous style, in which effort he was presently aided by Captain Windeyhash, a sort of general hanger-on of the house.

The whole party having at length assembled, and some having looked at their watches more than once, his lordship at last strolled into the room with the air of a man who had had a good luncheon at three, for though the effervescence of the hare hunt was still in full froth when Tom arrived, it had been over about two, and the hounds back in kennel by three.

However remiss his lordship might be about dinner, it was gratifying to see that he was still tenacious of the character of the sportsman, for he was now elaborately got up in the full-dress uniform of the Dazzlegoose Hunt. In the dress department even Lady Lazytongs seemed to take an interest, for she beckoned his lordship towards her, that she might have a nearer view of the richly-braided gold fox with a silver tag on the crimson velvet collar of his beetroot-coloured coat.

Having eyed him up and down, and turned him round, as a child would a doll, she again sunk on the sofa, with the observation that she supposed he "might as well ring for dinner."

His lordship then strutted away in his rose-coloured breeches and white silk stockings, looking uncommonly like a mountebank.

Dinner was shortly after announced.

What pen could do justice to that meal? Who can describe the noble apartment, the ponderous plate, the splendid chandeliers, the glittering sideboard, the light and tasteful confectionery, the crystal-like glass, the snow-like diaper, the beautiful flowers—above all, the sparkling wines and rich and varied dainties?

Not Tom Scott, certainly. Nevertheless, he did pretty fair justice to the victuals, as who would not that had breakfasted at eight and tasted nothing since?

Indeed, to tell the truth, he ate so much, and of such variety, *potage à la comtesse*, or soup made of Countess, *turbot à la Hollandaise*, or Dutch turbot, with sauce we don't know what, "*hors-d'œuvres*" of all sorts that came in the way, to say nothing of two cuts at a leg of mutton basted with devil's tears, followed by a slice of "*dindonneau à la Nelson*" or nautical turkey, a turn at a "*salade de grouse à la Soyer,*" in addition to Nesselrode pudding, *crême à la vanille, Charlotte Russe,* and other trifles, that he was dreadfully afflicted with the nightmare, and fancied that old Louis Philippe and all his sons, with their wives, were squatting on his stomach together. But we anticipate.

When the ladies retired—for there were two or three besides
Lady Lazytongs—they had another burst about hunting from
his lordship, who threw back his beetroot-coloured coat as
though he were going to make a " clean breast of it."

He had all the talk to himself, and never did Scott hear
man run on so about horses and hounds, and the system of
kennel.

" Out upon Nimrod ! " said Tom, who in his swell quarterly
dinner at Melton—and that, too, after a splendid run—tells
us the subject of hunting was never once mentioned.

" Here have I been training myself," continued he, " for
civilised society upon a similar basis, and now I find my Lord
Lionel Lazytongs, son of the Marquis of Fender and Fireirons,
blazing away like an engine."

Tom then tried to get a word in sideways, but the steam of
his lordship's eloquence was still too strong, and he resumed
the position of listener.

Nor was Tom sorry ; for his lordship talked well, and
apparently to the purpose, and having seen hounds and
countries that Tom only knew by name, what he said had the
advantage of novelty, though it might want the charm of
personal participation. What runs he told them of ! What
leaps he described ! What brooks he cleared !

As he went on, he built up places with knives, forks, and
spoons, and introduced finger-glasses and tumblers till he
brought the very places before their eyes. Then he criticised
this master and that—compared one great establishment with
another, and described their respective countries, till Tom almost
regretted not living nearer so great a luminary.

Like all great talkers, however, we are concerned to add that
he did not circulate the liquor.

Had Captain Windeyhash, who most needlessly acted the
part of showman, or trotter out, leading his lordship on to his
stories, and helping him out with the lame ones, devoted himself to the circulation of the bottle instead, it would have been

quite as agreeable to the guests. However, "time and the hour against the longest day," and the same able adversary conquers the longest evening too.

When they got back into the drawing-room, the covey of company was broke, and then for the first time Tom had an opportunity of saying a few words as to the morrow.

The first person he addressed was Major Tinhead, whom he had seen out with Mr. Neville's hounds once or twice.

"Hope you've brought your best horse," said Tinhead, after a common-place or two, "for it's a desperate country—*stiffest in England*, isn't it, Blobbey?" continued he, catching that fat gentleman by the elbow, as he waddled along, coffee-cup in hand, to a sofa.

"Oh, *tre-men-dious* country," replied Blobditch, giving his head a solemn shake. "I always say that the man who can ride across *our* country needn't be afraid of any country in the world!" With which compliment to himself, he proceeded on his journey.

Tom got a similar account from Captain Tipthorn; indeed they all seemed bent on the usual course of frightening the stranger.

Music and cards in the drawing-room, with billiards and naps outside, filled up the evening, till at last it was bedtime, even for my lord.

The ladies had retired shortly after Sir George Stiffnecke took his departure, and wine and water having filled up the interstices of the stomach, Lampoil again made his appearance in front of an illumination.

"Good nights" being exchanged, each man hurried off with his candle.

His lordship's politeness induced him to accompany Tom again to his bed-room, where, having stirred the fire, he established himself in his old position, and again began "harping on his daughter."

He forgot they were going out with the Tear Devil hounds,

and talked of the Currant-jelly dogs as if they were going to
have a turn with them.

"Ah, true," replied his lordship, in answer to Tom's
observation, that it was the Ecclesford Green day. "True, I
forgot. Let me see, then," continued he, ruminating.

"You and I'll breakfast together at half-past nine," said he,
after a pause, "and then we shall be quite independent of
every one. I hate bothering and waiting for a family breakfast on a hunting morning," added he.

"So do I," Tom would have added, but his voluble lordship
did not give him time.

"At half-past nine, then, *precisely*," continued his lordship :
"in Dian's Bower, the room to the left of the library as you
enter."

"So be it," replied Tom.

"I'll tell Lampoil to have breakfast ready *to a minute*," said
he. "How is your time by mine?" asked his lordship, producing a most diminutive "Geneva" watch, about the size of
a half-crown piece, from his waistcoat pocket. "I'm now
half-past twelve," said he, turning its little pale face towards
Scott.

"And I am twenty-five minutes past," said Tom, showing his
grandfather's great gold turnip.

Au revoir, then," said his lordship, extending a brace of
fingers, repeating as he left the room, "Then, MIND, *half-past
nine to a minute!*"

*   *   *   *   *

"Louis Philippe," as we said before, having established
himself and family on Tom's stomach during the night, in
consequence of the miscellaneous dinner he had eaten, Tom
did not require much calling in the morning. Indeed he
heard every hour strike after three, about which time the
heavy monarch and party soused themselves down. He succeeded in dislodging them about four ; but between that hour

and five they returned with redoubled force, and Tom dreamt
that the old fat Queen Mother of Spain actually sat herself
down on his mouth.

So he battled and struggled on till it was light.

It was eight before day was fairly established, and, thinking
it was no use interrupting the house-maids, Tom just lay in
bed until within three-quarters of an hour of the breakfast
time that his lordship had appointed, which he knew would
enable him to be down to the moment.

*   *   *   *   ᴧ

"Is his lordship up ? " asked our friend of the jean-jacketted
lackey who brought him up his hot water.

"I don't know, I'm sure, sir," replied he ; "I've not seen
his lordship's valet yet."

"He'll be *sure* to be up," thought Tom, bounding out of
bed at the recollection of the evening talk and the overnight
injunctions.

"Some men are only punctual in hunting matters," continued Tom, lathering away at his chin.

So he proceeded in his dressing.

Boots certainly don't carry well in saddle-bags, and Tom
never understood the value of the fisherman or bishop's sort
until this morning. You can take and stamp them into
saddle-bags just as you would a pair of dirty stockings, and
they'll unfold as smart and bright as ever ; but woe betide
the tops that have not elbow room to themselves. Tom's
turned out only "so so," when he came to inspect them by
daylight, and he knew it would be worse than useless asking a
six-foot figure footman if he could remedy the little irregulari-
ties of putty powder they presented. Besides, he had not
calculated his time to allow of *recommodes*, as the French say,
so he just pulled them on as they were.

Tom had some difficulty in finding the Hall of Dian ; but
when he did, he found that it was rightly named.

It was a comfortable-sized room, small in comparison with the magnificent entertaining ones he had been in over night, but what would be considered a *very* good room in a moderate-sized house. It was square and lofty, with richly ornamented panelled walls, and full-length portraits in each compartment.

Those who have remarked the various representations of Her Majesty and Prince Albert, or indeed those of any other illustrious individual, will excuse Tom's getting half way through the series before he discovered that they were all Lord Lionel Lazytongs.

Above the richly-carved white marble mantel-piece his lordship stood beside a grey horse in the morning costume of the Dazzlegoose Hunt—bright, apricot-coloured coat, white cravat, striped buff vest with black binding, white cords, and longish top-boots.

Next it, on the left, he appeared in scarlet on a gallant bay, careering over an open country which, with the exception of a couple of swallows, he seemed to have all to himself.

The third represented him about to do a little fantastic toe. Dressed in the evening dress of the Swell-boys' Hunt—lavender-coloured coat, with rose-coloured linings, richly embroidered white satin waistcoat, with white kerseymere shorts and white silk stockings, he stood drawing on a pair of pink kid gloves before an opening door, which disclosed a cut-glass chandelier above sundry satin petticoats, whirling about with white-legged gentlemen.

In a larger piece between the windows he appeared on horseback again. He was in the act of changing a white hack for a black hunter, in the imaginary dress of Master of the Buckhounds, an office he had bespoken for himself on the coming in of the Tories. Scene—Ascot Heath—the Grand Stand crowded with ladies, perfuming the air with their pocket handkerchiefs. Artist—of course, Frank Grant.

On the door-side of the room his lordship appeared in three panels—one clearing such a gate as never was seen, in the brimstone-coloured coat of the Tear Devil Hunt ; another riding like fury at a thing like an arm of the sea ; and a third cantering past the statue of Achilles on his return from a day in the Vale of Aylesbury, with Baron Rothschild's Staggers. This was by Count D'Orsay, and was done to commemorate the feat of his lordship having ridden "all the way there and back." There were a couple of niches vacant on the side opposite the window, one of which will most likely soon be occupied by him in the pea-green cutaway and leathers of the hare hunter.

Altogether it was a regular sporting apartment, and only wanted breakfast, and a little knowledge of hunting on the part of some of the artists. Not but that there were symptoms of breakfast in the shape of a snug round table near the fire, garnished with a profusion of plate, but, as yet, there were no eatables.

Tom took another hasty round of the pictures, but still there was no indication of breakfast.

He then proceeded to stare out of the window to see if he could see anything in the hunting line, and again returned to the fire and began to inspect the polished ivory handle of the bell-pull.

   *   *   *   *   *

It was now a quarter to ten, and he began to be seriously uneasy.

"Surely his lordship, so keen and precise overnight, can't have changed his mind," thought he. And then he began to wish his lordship had let him breakfast with the rest.

"Perhaps there would be no great harm in ringing the bell and asking if breakfast was going on elsewhere," continued he, laying hold of the knob, when just as he was going to turn it down, the well-known "clonk, clonk, clonk," of spurs in the passage arrested his hand, and drew Tom's eyes to the door.

It *was* his long lordship, who now came forward to greet

him, but not in the dress Tom expected at that advanced hour
of the morning.

Instead of the coat and waistcoat of the fox-hunter, he was
enveloped in a long flowing blue and silver brocade *robe de
chambre*, confined at the waist with enormous blue and silver
cords with tassels as big as bell-pulls. He had a heap of letters
in one hand, and the Times, Post, and Morning Chronicle
tucked under his other arm.

"Gad," said he, with a knowing look, "I really think the
ministry won't stand. It's clear there's a split in the
cabinet. Old story — Grey and Palmerston — Grey and
Palmerston — don't like each other — don't like each other.
What do you think, Mr. Scott ? "

"Hang'd if I know," said Tom ; "don't care either, so long
as it don't come a frost."

"Ah, true," replied his lordship. "That reminds me we are
going to hunt ; better have breakfast, perhaps — better have
breakfast, perhaps ; " so saying, he gave our old friend the bell
a hearty peal.

"Well, but," resumed he, taking a dressing-gown lap over
each arm, and placing himself in his favourite position before
the fire, "you're a Tory, ain't you ? "

"Dash'd if I know what I am," said Tom ; "it makes
precious little odds what men like myself are. I *was* a Tory,
or Conservative, or whatever you call it, and joined the
gobemouches in abusing the Whigs, and *hoo*raying Sir Robert ;
but I've thrown up politics, and devote myself to draining, and
d——ning him instead."

"Ah, well," rejoined his lordship, with a smile at the mixed
occupation, "well, but you'd like to see the Whigs out, of
course," eyeing himself in the Master of the Buckhounds picture·

"Not if it was to let Peel in again," replied Tom. "I hate
the sound of his name."

Just then in came Lampoil, followed by no end of footmen,
with tea and coffee, muffins and meat, and eggs and ham, and

potted game, to which Tom had hardly got a fair start before the noisy clock struck ten.

"Is that nine or ten?" asked his lordship, as it was still on the strike.

LORD LIONEL IN HIS FAVOURITE POSITION.

"Ten, my lord," replied Lampoil, who, with two footmen, were doing all but eat their breakfasts for them—handing everything that was within reach, and so on.

"The hounds meet at *eleven*, I presume?" said Tom, trembling for the answer.

"A quarter *to*," replied his lordship; "we're in plenty of time; they're *close by*," saying which he again had recourse to The Post.

A dead silence followed, broken only by the noise of their jaws, as they worked away at the viands.

* * * * *

"I'll be with you in five minutes," at last said his lordship, drawing himself slowly from under the table, and handing Tom the newspapers. "Send for the hacks," said he to Lampoil.

"*Hacks!*" repeated Tom, as his lordship clonked out of the room, "I thought it was close by."

"So it is," replied Lampoil, "at least what his lordship calls close by—four or five miles, perhaps; his lordship thinks nothing of eighteen or twenty—desperate man on the road."

"It's to be hoped he finds hacks for his friends," observed Tom, not relishing the idea of galloping the old mare to cover, and hunting her after.

* * * * *

It was full half-past ten ere his lordship re-appeared, and then he had to get his sherry flask filled and his pocket stuffed with sandwiches and gingerbread nuts.

* * * * *

Just as they were crossing the great hall on their prolonged departure, her ladyship was descending the spacious staircase followed by her youngest child in the nurse's arms.

"Oh, Lionel!" exclaimed she, without taking the slightest notice of poor Tom, "what *have* you got that fright of a neck-cloth on for?"

"*Fright!*" repeated his lordship, "why Jowett sent it down as the newest fashion; he says George Ringlets wears it with the Queen's, Beau Sarsnet with the Duke, and I don't know who else besides."

"Never mind who wears it," snapped her ladyship, "yellow, with black spots, don't become *you*, so pray take it off."

"But I shall be keeping Mr. Scott waiting, my dear," replied his lordship, intimating Tom's presence by laying hold of his arm.

"Oh, Mr. Scott won't mind waiting a minute or two, I'm sure," replied her ladyship, deigning him a sort of bow at last.

* * * * *

"Well, if you wish to have *him* all spotted like a leopard," said her ladyship, with a significant glance and shake of the head, as her spouse still hesitated, "you'll go as you are."

His lordship then commenced a rapid ascent of the staircase, taking three steps at a time.

We don't know whether ladies look upon neck-cloths in the same light as they do their own ribbons—things that can be changed in a minute—but we can assure them neckcloths are much more serious affairs. It was full five minutes ere the clank of his spurs announced his lordship's arrival on the landing in a skyblue satin cravat, instead of the proscribed yellow and black spots ; and though we could have changed in half the time, yet for his lordship we don't think it was long.

"Will *this* do, my dear ? " asked he, buttoning his waistcoat, and adjusting his shirt-collar, as he descended the staircase, and her ladyship having received the parting kiss for her assent, and the child having lisped its " Ta, ta," our sportsmen at last found themselves among the body of the servants in the outer hall.

If they had been two Daniel Lamberts they were going to hoist on to their horses by sheer strength, they could not have required more. Numerous as they were, however, the opening door disclosed more outside.

There was Tom's plummey, over-night friend, the stud-groom, in his brown cut-away, toilinette waistcoat, drab kerseymeres and gaiters, ready to take the cover hack from an attendant in fustians the moment his lordship appeared, and there was a swell groom in leathers and livery, whose gold-laced hat alone would have furnished half an outfit for Sleekpow.

That worthy individual's face showed the displeasure he felt at having been kept three-quarters of an hour on the gravel, his vexation being heightened, perhaps, by numerous little anecdotes he would pick up relative to his lordship's pace on the road, and the distance they had to go.

" It's *five* miles," groaned Sleekpow, handing Tom the mare, with which dread intelligence the clock tolled the quarter.

" We haven't much time to spare," said his lordship, who, having now mounted a prancing grey barb, was

" Provoking the caper that he seemed to chide,"

to the admiration of her ladyship, who was pointing out "Pa's" feats to the child, and also to the edification of sundry house-maids and dolly mops looking out of the windows above.

Having performed in a style that would have done honour to Astley, or to the Champion at a coronation, he at length kissed his kid-gloved hand, and sticking spurs into the barb, dashed off in a gallop.

" D—n the fellow ! How does he ever suppose I can keep pace with him ! " exclaimed Tom, gathering the old mare, who, thoroughly disgusted with her long wait, was now kicking and imitating the feats of the barb.

" You had better get forrard, sir," said the groom, coming up full canter, hands well down, as though he was setting to for a race.

" His lordship rides *very* fast," added he, shooting past.

" Well, this is the most confounded wild-goose chase I ever rode ? " exclaimed Tom, as his lordship charged a flight of rails, followed by the lad, who could now hardly get forward in time to unlock the private park door.

✳   ✳   ✳   ✳   ✳

Having passed this and so cleared the park, they were now
upon the road, a place not at all suited to Tom's old mare's
legs, which, though sound in the soft, are only what Sleekpow
calls rather "crambley" on the hard.

"Gently, old lass," continued Tom, patting her neck, to try
and get her to ease herself down to a trot, "gently, old lass;
it's no use fretting; you are both hack and hunter to-day."

But the old mare's monkey was up, and she clattered and
battered along as if she had two or three sets of legs at home.

Finding he would take as much out in fretting as he saved
in restraining her, Tom at last let her go, and Wideopen Common shortly intervening, he kept his lordship in view, and
sailed away at what would have been called an "excellent
pace," had hounds been running.

After clearing the common, they again got upon the road,
and meeting two or three cover hacks, Tom saw the hounds, at
all events, had come.

In close shaving, either for railway time, or dinner-time, or
fox-hunting time, or indeed almost any time, it is bad policy
stopping to ask questions, for if one is not past time already,
the stoppage may make one so. The only plan is to "keep
moving," and hug oneself at each person one gets past, without hearing, "Ah! the train's gone!" or, that most appalling
sound of all, "*They're away with him!*"

Tom got past three return grooms with a stare from two
and a touch of the hat from the third, and, following his
noble friend with his eye towards the rising ground, up which
their course now lay, we saw him dash among a dark crowd
on the hill-top, dismount, and in the twinkling of an eye
disappear on the other side.

"That's all very well," sighed Tom, "for a man with a
stable full of horses; but I, who ride my own to cover, can't
afford to blow it on the road."

So saying, he eased the old mare down into a trot, and just
jogged up to the group on the hill with as unconcerned a face

as a man in scarlet can assume, when the hounds have gone
away with their fox.

"You're o'er late, sir !" said a kindly-disposed horsebreaker,
with a shake of the head, as he backed his three-year old out
of Tom's way; "they *fund* directly they put in, and have
been away with him this ten minutes."

"The deuce they have !" exclaimed Tom, pulling up in full
panoramic view of the scene—Deep Dean, where they found
him, the end at which he broke, the still open gate through
which the field had passed the bothering brook, the kindly bridge,
and the boundless expanse of noble country over which they
were now careering.

Nothing could be finer.

" 'Tis distance lends enchantment to the view," wrote the
poetic Campbell, speaking of general scenery, and surely it
holds good with fox-hunting scenery too, for distance reduces
the leaps, so as to make all countries look pleasant and practicable. This one did so particularly, and the last brimstone-
coated whip seemed to glide over the plain, as he took on the
tail hounds, as though there was nothing bigger than a water
furrow.

Poor Tom was never so vexed in his life ! He could have
cried, if no one had been there. "All that hanged neck-
cloth !" exclaimed he.

*   *   *   *   *

"There was a gentleman just before me," observed he, as
soon as he recovered his articulation.

"Ah, that's my lord," replied the breaker, with a sneer,
" *You mustn't follow him.*"

"Why not ?" inquired Tom, as his lordship's brimstone-
coloured coat now appeared careering on the line.

"Hoot ! he just rides after anything," replied the man. "All
he cares for's a gallop."

"But he rides hard," observed Tom, looking at his

lordship crashing at a big fence with an open gate close at hand.

" Oh ! he'll ride hard enough," replied the man, with a knowing leer, for there are few better-informed persons in these matters than horsebreakers. " He'll ride hard enough," repeated he, " especially if there are any ladies looking on ; for his great pleasure is in dressing up and showing off ; and he certainly does make as good a turn-out as any nobleman in the land. He had two as fine horses here this morning as ever was seen, the one he's riding, and the one his pad groom's on with ; and last Wednesday he had two horses with these hounds, and two with the Dazzlegoose, and managed to be with both packs without seeing a run with either. He's a rum 'un's my lord."

CRASHING AT A BIG FENCE.

CHAPTER VI.

THE GOLDTRAP ARMS.

" You were out of luck," observed Esau Broadback, Tom's host, or rather his horse's host, as Tom arrived on foot on the morning after the Ecclesford Green day, with the intention of getting his horse to go home.

"Yes," grunted Tom, with the tone of a man who doesn't want to be questioned.

"You might get a day to-morrow," observed Broadback, with the sagacity of an innkeeper towards his own interest. " The Stout-as-steel hounds are within reach."

"Where are they?" inquired Tom.

"At the Bridge of Bevis Mount, about ten miles from here," replied Broadback.

"Ten miles!" hiccuped a drunken voice, "it's more like twenty!"

This was Tom's friend the horsebreaker, who had been drinking ever since they parted, and had got through a half-crown Tom gave him, and several of his own to boot.

"It won't be above fifteen, anyhow," resumed Broadback, amending his geography.

Fifteen's as good as fifty, in Tom's estimation at least, in as far as sending on in the morning is concerned, and if a man has to move his horse from one country inn to another, he may as well be sociable, and go too.

It so happened that our friend Tom had a great desire to see the Stout-as-steel hounds, having heard no little of them in his early days. They were originally a miner's pack, hunting the beautiful but hilly region so favourably known to all tourists and scenery hunters as the Kiss-sky Mountains. The pack has been in existence above a century, not exactly as an advertising one, with a huntsman and whips, but a good useful cry of dogs, never under five, and sometimes as high as ten couple. After towling about the valleys, and the bases, and the middles, and the summits of the mountains, with the usual pony and pedestrian fields of " peep-o'-day packs," they got a piece of vale country, which they gradually extended, and in the course of time came out in type, looking (upon paper) as big as the best. At length they got weaned from the view-hallos and cow-horns of the miners, and under the mastership of Tom's late cousin, Simon Squander, who in the handsomest manner ruined himself by keeping them, they acquired considerable renown.

After his death (which took place some ten years ago, and was caused, as many of our readers will recollect, by his drinking a glass of oxalic acid in mistake for gin, being at the time rather overcome with brandy), the hounds floundered on for some time in the hands of a committee, and at length passed into those of Captain Cashbox : a gentleman, who, we believe, was caught at the " Corner," and most likely adopted on the strength of his name, though, if he was, it has turned out a failure, the captain's talent consisting in walking into other people's cash-boxes, and saving his own.

This little episode will explain why it was that Tom was anxious to see the Stout-as-steel hounds ; an anxiety that caused him to ponder in the stable, and consider whether, now that he had got so far, he had not better go a little further. and gratify his inclination.

The meet, the bridge at Bevis Mount, sounded quite familiar to his ear, or rather, perhaps, looked quite familiar to his eyes— just as familiar as the " Devil's Dyke " or " Telscombe Tye " of the old Brighton or Brookside harriers. look to the eye of a

Sussex squire.   Indeed, the column of " Hunting Appointments " is not the least interesting one in the papers, and
through its medium one establishes a sort of hunting acquaintance with all the packs in the kingdom, assigning to each meet
such a country as we think the name indicates, and not
unfrequently indulging in an imaginary run from it.   If the
mesmerisers would only invent a process for taking off one's
thoughts when half asleep, we could produce some astonishing
runs, far better than anything we can write.

But to our friend Tom.

Having taken a look at the map in the traveller's room of
the Lazytong Arms, and run his eye from the great greasy
thumb-mark denoting the " here we are " of Dawdle Court
into the intricacies of the hills, Scott saw that Bevis Mount
was quite beyond distance for a morning's start ; but observing the town of Sludgington on the line, which he remembered
to have heard his late cousin extol, our independent friend
determined to dispense with the services of Sleekpow, and go
" bags and all," feeling that it would never do to return to
Hawbuck Grange without being able to tell Mr. Neville and
" their chaps " what sort of dogs either the Tear Devil or the
Stout-as-steel ones were.

*   *   *   *   *

That point being settled, he was very soon on the back of
the old mare, and after divers twistings, and turnings, and
crossings, and missings, and askings, the curtailed proportions
of a winter's day found him gazing at the chubby tower of
Sludgington Church.

Having cleared the toll-bar, he presently entered the
town.

It consisted of one long, narrow street, formed of all sorts of
houses, and cottages, and shops, and premises ranged in a most
higgledy-piggledy state of confusion—a good house here, a bad
one there, a dirty cottage next, a public-house after it ; then a

coy freestone-faced mansion, retiring within its own iron rail-
ings, followed by a smithy adjoining a cowshed. The street
was one continued bed of hard, loose whinstone, whose roughness and sharpness was only relieved by a plentiful covering of
cold, bleak-looking mud.

In passing along, Tom could not help thinking, if the old
mare was to fall, what a state her knees and his clothes would
be in. Fortunately no such catastrophe befell Mr. Scott, and
a ragged urchin with a ladder having lighted a glow-worm
sort of oil lamp, a little in advance of where he rode, he
deciphered the words "Goldtrap Arms" below one of those
resplendent shields that indicate the great man of the
country.

In truth the sign was a perfect extinguisher on the house,
making it look like a boy in a man's hat. However, there it
was, and being about the centre of the town, there was no
doubt about its being the head inn, even if Tom's friend with
the ladder had not proclaimed it.

He did more, he rang the bell for the ostler.

There is no saying, if our friend was advertising, in "Grand-
mamma," the Sunday Times, or any of the matrimonial
mediums of communication, what compliments he might pay
to his person, but in this bid of confidence with our numerous
readers we don't care admitting that it isn't everybody that
takes Tom for a gentleman.

So on this occasion Sam Beer, the ostler, answered the
summons in a way that plainly showed he thought our
traveller and he were about equals—at least would be, if the
latter had his Sunday clothes on, instead of a pair of rotten-
looking fustian trousers, a tattered waistcoat, and a *very* dirty
shirt. Top-boots having about devolved entirely upon fox-
hunters and servants, a man perhaps may be excused not
knowing "which is which," without the red-coat; at all events,
Tom consoled himself with that supposition.

"Stop all night?" said Sam, laying hold of the reins, as

Tom rode under the wretched low archway (filled with unwashed gigs, empty barrels and hens) leading into the close contracted passage of a stable-yard.

"Yes," replied Tom, adding, " you've room, 1 suppose ? "

" *Plenty* of room ! " replied the man ; and truly, when Tom fighted on a veteran dung-heap at one stable door, and saw the broken panes and gaping deals of the other, he didn't wonder at it ; and he almost wished he'd brought Sleekpow, when he saw the place, as well to relieve him from the trouble of superintendence as to teach Sleekpow not to grumble unnecessarily in future.

Having loosened the saddle-bags and chucked them over on the far side, in the way that guards and other disinterested parties deal with luggage, Beer gave Tom the mare to hold, while he slunk into the kitchen in search of a candle.

After two unsuccessful attempts to bring it past the draught of the gateway in his hands, he had recourse to an old hat, and at last succeeded in planting it triumphantly against the wall in a holder formed of its own grease.

He then led in the old mare, and commenced the usual chilling, temper-trying, fistling and fumbling of the slovenly slatternly stableman.

We have often thought, when at places of this sort, of Nimrod's account of the metamorphose a pair of boot-trees turning out of his buggy effected in the manners of the landlord and servants of an inn he drove up to in Scotland—Kelso, we think,—during his " Northern tour," and the tip of a scarlet coat-lap peeping out of the corner of the saddle-bags, which we omitted to mention were taken into the kitchen when Beer went for the candle, operated similarly in Tom Scott's favour.

Cornelius Cake, the landlord, having been a gentleman's servant—a *baronet's* we should say—butler to Sir Digby Goldtrap, whose arms his house bears, thought himself a judge of gentlemen ; and, being struck with the cloth, came into the stable to see who had brought it.

Tom saw as plainly as if Cake said it, that he was bothered with his appearance, not knowing whether he was master or man.

He glanced first at Tom's boots, then at his bottle-green cut-

" COULD HUNT A LITTLE, I SHOULD THINK."

away, with bright buttons, and having carried his observations up to his hat, without having come to a satisfactory conclusion, he turned his attention to the old mare.

" Nice nag you've got there," said Cake, in a careless sort of way—" could hunt a little, I should think, that nag."

" *A good deal*," replied Tom, adding, " that's just what I keep her for."

" Indeed ! " replied Cake, with a touch of his hat and a low bow.

" I want to see the Stout-as-steel hounds to-morrow—how far is the Bridge of Bevis Mount from here ? "

" Bridge of Bevis Mount—Bridge of Bevis Mount," muttered Cake quickly, as if he knew the place so well that he quite forgot it. " How far is the Bridge of Bevis Mount from here, Beer ? " asked he of the ostler.

"Bevis M-o-u-n-t, Bevis M-o-u-n-t," drawled the dawdler ; " Bevis M-o-u-n-t ? " repeated he—" W-h-o-y, it'ill be up 'mong hills, l-o-i-k-e, away by Gussingen," wagging a hand in the air as if pointing to it.

" Ah, I know," replied Tom, walking away in search of the saddler.

Having found that functionary, and learned all about it, he was presently stamping the cold, slaty mud off his boots in the doorway, beneath the blazing sign of the Goldtrap Arms.

" *This* way, Sir, if you please," exclaimed Cornelius Cake, rushing out of the little back parlour commanding a view of the entrance, throwing open the black door of the little parlour on the right, in whose pittance of a grate smoked and spluttered some white-ashed, slaty-looking coals.

Though the best room, it was small and low, papered with a tasteless, repulsive-looking, dark-green paper, carried half way down the wall, the part below the skirting-board being white-washed. We sometimes see papers so hideously ugly as to look' as if they had been made for a premium.

On the wall opposite the windows, and above the wooden mantel-piece, which latter was decorated with paper fans, spars, card-racks, china-poodles, and other dust-catching articles, were portraits of Tom's host and hostess—Cornelius and Mrs. Cake.

They were evidently by the same hand, most likely acquired in the usual way of inn portraiture,—some travelling artist painting out his bill. On no other supposition can we account for the wonderful tendency publicans have to "run to portrait."

How hard, and cold, and solemn, and vulgarly like himself, Cornelius looked down upon Tom from his gilt frame !

When he brought in candles, he had brushed up his hair to the picture point, and arrayed himself in the snuff-coloured coat with the velvet collar and black waistcoat of the portrait. He only wanted the amplified neckcloth, with the butterfly brooch, and red cord watch guard, to be perfect.

"I should like to have some dinner," said Tom, after Cake had deposited the candles, and let down the scant drab window curtains, trimmed with red gimp.

"What would you like, sir ?" inquired Cake, with the air of a Lord Mayor's cook.

"What have you in the house ?" replied Tom, anticipating the usual variety—mutton chop, beef steak—beef steak, mutton chop.

"There's soup, sir ; mutton broth, at least. Fish—fish, sir, I'm afraid's not very fresh—not what I could recommend. You could have a fowl or a duck, and a nice little French dish to follow."

"French dish !" exclaimed Tom, as the Dawdle Court banquet, and Louis Philippe night-mare flashed across his mind. "French dish ! what, *you* haven't a French cook, have you ?"

"My lady's a Frenchwoman," replied Cake, speaking of her in the true Debrett style ; "my lady's a Frenchwoman ;" as if that was enough to constitute a cook. The fact was, Cornelius had been butler, and Madame Cake lady's maid to Sir Digby and Lady Goldtrap, and—but our readers will anticipate the rest.

"Well ; I'll have the broth, and a fowl, and a French dish to follow," said Tom.

"Any sweets?" inquired Cake! "Sir Digby always took sweets."

"Yes; you may let me have a nice little French dish of sweets, too," replied Tom. So saying, Cake departed to execute the order.

Tom had revisited the stable, fed the mare, seen his bedroom, opened the window, drawn the stuffy blue check curtains, stared up the street, examined the portrait of Madame Cake, and thought how the light, tasteful spirit of French elegance must have shuddered at the harsh matter-of-fact looking cap and brown silk gown in which she was daubed, ere the bump of the tray against the weak door announced that it was about time to take his seat :—*the oaths* at a dinner of this sort are frequently taken after.

Having deposited the little basin of mutton broth before Tom, Cake, with a napkin-covered thumb, lifted the little delf lid off with the flourish of a man uncovering a glittering tureen of many hundred ounces weight.

"What wine will you please to take, sir?" asked he, giving the hock glass a push against the other two to draw Tom's attention to their presence.

It's a fearful thing when a man's consequence entails a variety of wine-glasses upon him at an inn.

Had Tom brought Sleekpow, he would have attributed the misfortune to him, concluding he had been telling where they had come from. As it was, he was obliged to put it down to the superior refinement of his host over himself. Indeed, we know men who keep servants to teach them what they ought to do.

Tom wouldn't give twopence a gallon for hock, so he humbly replied that he'd take a pint of sherry.

"Some of Sir Digby, I s'pose, sir," replied Cake.

"Of course," said Tom; and away he went for the liquid.

The mutton broth, or pot barley and water, was execrable:

Cake and the Cutlets

and Tom had dropped the spoon in the plate in despair ere
Cake came back rubbing a tiny decanter with a napkin.

" You'll find this very fine wine, sir," said he, holding it up
to the candle, and smacking his lips as though it were most
luscious.

He then helped Tom to three quarters of a glass.

" Sir Digby always calls this my golden particular," added
he, setting it down.

A bad dinner and a loquacious waiter are evils that no man
can stand jointly ; so Tom intimated, by a lateral motion of
the spoon in the plate, that he was ready for the " follow," as
they say at the Clubs.   This was old *Cock-a-doodle-doo !*

If possible, it was worse than the broth, being black,
and hard, and dry, and tough,—a very old chanticleer
indeed.

Cake saw it wouldn't do, and proposed making a grill of it.
" Sir Digby was very fond of grills," said he, as if that was
enough.

Tom didn't care much about it, having an eye to the nice
little French dish that was to follow ; so he said, " Perhaps
you may as well bring in the next dish ? "

" Certainly, sir," replied Cake, whisking away both fowl and
plate.

The precipitancy of the remove made a gap in the
series, and left Tom a little time to speculate on the next
" follow."

He wondered what it would be,—" *Blanquette de veau aux
champignons,*" " *Côté de Bœuf à la Bonne Femme,*" or perhaps
game dressed in some peculiar way—" *Escalopes de Chevreuil,*"
or " *Faisan à la Péregueux.*"

" One wouldn't expect French cookery in a house of this
sort," observed he, looking at the most perfect public-house
appearance of the little parlour and its appurtenances ; but
there's no saying what one may meet with in this world.

Just then somebody threw open the door, and in rushed

Cake with a round vegetable dish, encircled in a napkin, clasped in both hands.

This he set down with a noise betokening the most perfect confidence in its contents.

" Hot plate ! hot plate ! " exclaimed he, as if a moment's delay might be fatal to the feast.

He lifted the lid, and lo ! four great fat, greasy mutton chops, slightly sprinkled over with bread, appeared.

CHAPTER VII.

A MORNING GALLOP.

SED as our friend Tom Scott is to the solitude of his own chair, still there was such an utter un-homishness in the solitude of the Gold-trap Arms, that he could not compose himself to his ac-customed nap after dinner. He was so vexed with the nice little French dish, and also w i t h a great Y o r k s h i r e pud'ding of an omelette that followed, that he would not listen to his host's advice about a bottle of curious old port, that "Sir Digbv greatly commended." He therefore had some hot water and sugar, and took his revenge on the bad sherry by making it into negus before Cake's face ;—the most practical reproof that can be given an innkeeper.

The musical cuckoo clock struck seven as the hot water came in, hinting by its provoking monotony what a long weary evening it would be.

Who would keep a cuckoo clock that didn't wish to be driven mad ?

This was the slowest, prosiest, most unlike a cuckoo, cuckoo clock that ever was heard. It did not seem to travel above four miles an hour. First it began with a shivering sort of jingle among the works as if they were all loose together, and were in a devil of a hurry to be off; then came a jingling tune, followed by a clap caused by the opening of the wooden shutters through which the stupid bird emerged on to its board, shouldering its wings, and beginning " Cuckoo ! " " Cuckoo ! " " Cuckoo ! " " Cuckoo ! " at intervals of a couple of seconds ; so that what with the tune, the noise, the notes, and the striking, the clock was scarcely ever quiet, — *a perfect nuisance.*

Finding he couldn't sleep, Tom began to exercise himself about the little room. Below the portrait of Mr. Cake hung some book-shelves, containing the usual miscellaneous selection, or rather collection, of an inn library—three old copies of " Boyle's Court Guide," " Drysdale's Sermons," many numbers of the " World of Fashion," a monthly magazine of the courts of London and Paris, " Le Cuisinier Royal, ou, l'Art de Faire la Cuisine," " History of New York," " The Courser's Companion." two volumes of the " Gentleman's Magazine," a well-thumbed " Baronetage," and an old " Post Office Directory."

" What dissatisfied mortals men are, to be sure," mused Tom. " Last night, and the night before, I was grumbling and growling (to myself) at the bother of company, and the long-winded stories and hunting eloquence of my noble host, whereas to-night I am fit to cut my throat for want of somebody to speak to. What creatures of impulse we are, too," continued he, adjusting himself in an uneasy easy chair before the fire, and cocking a foot on each hob. " Only last Saturday I fully determined to go over to Snailswell, and make the long-delayed offer to Liddey instead of which I am first tempted to

Dawdle Court, and now, of my own voluntary free will, have
come on this wild-goose chase to Sludgington, to be bored with
the monotony of a cuckoo clock, and wearied with the hum,
pipe-tapping, and distant jollification of the kitchen guests.
Oh, this hunting ! this hunting ! what a deal **it** has to answer
for. It is odd " (continued he) " what a vast of idleness one
can stand at home, and yet how oppressive it is away. At
home, I just chuck myself into the easy chair after dinner, and
fall into a reverie, a hunting, a draining, or a castle-building
speculation, as naturally and easily as possible ; whereas here I
can neither compose myself to sleep, nor to dream, nor to do
anything. If I thought yon repulsive, clotted-looking inkstand had anything but a black bog of ink in it, and a stumped
pen, split up to the feather, I'd take a letter-back and concoct
an offer to Lydia " (continued he) ; " but who ever found both
a pen and ink in an inn inkstand that would write ? " Strange
to say, curiosity tempted him to get up and examine this stand,
and finding that a veterinary surgeon might pass the pen, and
that a few drops of sherry would revive the ink, Tom devoted
that quantity of drink to it, and was presently in possession of
very " go-able " materials.

Our fair readers will doubtless now be anxious for the offer
produced under such inspiriting circumstances ; but, alas ! for
the mutability of a sportsman's intentions ! In sorting his
letter-backs, he pulled out the one containing Lord Lazytongs'
invitation, which operated like the make-believe pills of the
doctors on people who have nothing the matter with them.
Finding he had got something to do he forthwith began trying
to shirk it, and, resuming his seat before the fire, with one leg
up and the other down, returned to the visit at Dawdle Court,
recalling the flow of words that proceeded from his noble host's
lips, and all the wonderful performances he narrated. Ther.
Tom thought how needless an appendage such a man as
Captain Windeyhash was to his lordship, who was so well able
to run himself out ; and at last his thoughts settled into the

channel, that at slower or at faster intervals produced the fol‑ lowing current of ideas :—

"Trot him out," thought Tom ; ay, that's a proceeding adapted to bipeds as well as quadrupeds. "Trot him out again, Joe ! that's to say, show him off, and see if you can't catch a flat. There is just the same sort of thing among Christians, and whether it is done in the palpable way of the horse exhibitor, or the apparently natural though oftentimes studiously arranged *impromptu* depends altogether on the skill of the one party and the docility of the other."

And here, leaving our friend in his arm‑chair for a few minutes, we may say that we " back " the observation. " Trotting him out " is a very common recreation ; and though it requires the fine and delicate hand of the fly‑fisher, yet we frequently see it attempted by the clumsy fist of the mere dredger. In truth, the office of " trotter‑out " requires a con‑ siderable amount of skill, knowledge, and observation ; tact in drawing stealthily on the line of the joke or story, apprising the individual without preparing the party, knowledge of the humour, we might say the caprices, of the " trottee," and observation of the time most appropriate for introducing the subject. What can be worse than a sulky " snub " instead of a " rise," or a still‑born joke shattering itself among a cast‑ iron‑faced company ? Poor old Matthews used to say that if he came on to the stage and saw his friend L—d—'s imper‑ turbable features, and great silver‑rimmed spectacles fixed upon him, it was such a damper that he could hardly raise his spirits to go on with his " At home."

There are two ways of trotting a man out, just as there are two ways of trotting a horse out. There is the trot to display, and the trot to expose. We don't know that many men object to being trotted out for admiration, provided the case is not too palpable, or the audience one before whom the " trottee " has too recently appeared. The " trot‑out " to expose is seldom undertaken by any but ill‑natured fools, fellows with gumption enough to see, but not charity enough to help, the amiable weaknesses of the world—fellows who say, " See how I'll trot old Goodfellow out after dinner ; " and because the kind, meek old man doesn't kick them, they fancy he doesn't see what they are after. We have all some pet story or other that we like telling, and are we to be branded as " twaddlers " because some gentleman has heard us tell it before ? The fault is his for being present again, not ours for telling it.

This, of course, applies to natural, appropriate, impromptu stories, not to your " lug-him-in-neck-and-heels " sort of jokes. These latter fall more in the department of the regular professional, or licensed trotter-out.

A regular licensed trotter-out should keep a day-book, and enter the performances of his Magnus Apollo, registering the stories he tells, the jokes he uses, how they were brought out, and the audience before whom he appeared, so that he may not " trot him out " before the same parties again too soon. A story, like a fox-cover, should be allowed a certain rest before it is disturbed again. In this respect a town trotter-out has a great advantage over a country one, for, with the large and varied field of the metropolis, the same story may be come upon or trotted out very often without running the risk of falling into that dreadful wet blanket, a dead silence, an " I think I've heard that before "—or the still more bearish and unfeeling " That's *meant* for wit, is it ? "

What can be more chilling than a set of hard, dry, matter-of-fact features, contracting into a sneer instead of a snort at a joke ? Blessings on the man, say we, who will help a lame dog of a story over a stile with a laugh. We can forgive anything in furtherance of fun, except the petty larcenist who sells another's jokes or stories, and murders them in the telling. Silvester Blubberhead is a great hand at this. Most families keep a sort of first and second class company, into which bachelors are thrust indiscriminately, just as it suits the convenience of the table ; but Blubberhead, tying a better neck-cloth, if anything, than our funny friend Tom Sparks, and wearing both studs and rings, has rather the " call " of him, as they say at the " Corner," and Tom frequently follows in the second class train, picking up the scraps and remnants of his own good stories, just like a cook after a crockery crash.

Blubberhead, however, comes more under the denomination of a proser or a twaddler than a trotter-out.   Joe Slowman may be classed under the same head.   Joe will swear a man to a secret that he swore him to twelve months before, and that most likely a secret not worth knowing.

Still, " trotting out " is worthy of cultivation as a liberal science, and is capable of utilitarian as well as of mirthful application.   For instance, a host and hostess at either end of a long table, with a Birnham Wood of an epergne or a round of ship beef between them, screening not only themselves but shutting out half the company from a knowledge of what their respective " pieces of resistance " are, may usefully trot each other out thus :—

Mr. Blowout. " What have you got there, my love ? "

Mrs. Blowout. " Ten chickens and a tongue my dear. What have you down there ? "

Mr. Blowout. " Round of beef, my love."

So champagne " stinters " might invent a " trot out " instead of that horrible holding of the bottle to the light : but that being an unworthy application of the art, we shall leave them to contrive a form for themselves.

Trotters-out for admiration are generally kind, obliging sort of people.   With no great talents themselves, or perhaps with an over modest estimate of what they have, they yet lend themselves to the amusement of society, by showing off others who they think have more.   Those who are in the secret may see a professed trotter-out " touting," as it were, for a story laying the bait, during the progress of the soup, that is to

bring in the rich " guffaw " of a laugh after the first glass of
champagne. London party-givers understand the doctrine of
" trotting-out " so well that they never think of separating a
joker and his accoucheur. Indeed, the professed punster
wouldn't stand it. Have me, have my friend, Orlando Burst-
sides.

It is derogatory to a wit to act the part of a retriever.

We have seen this sort of cut-and-dried trotting-out attempted in the country, but it is not adapted for general use,
and this reminds us that we are taking—if not the words out
of Tom's mouth—at all events the thoughts out of his
head, who the obliging reader will have the kindness to
consider as still dozing in his arm-chair, with much the
same thoughts passing through his head that we have been
detailing.

The most flagrant case of premeditated " trotting-out " I
ever witnessed, thought Tom, beginning to grapple with partic-
ulars, was that of poor Jerry Goldfinch, of Bumpkin Lodge.
Jerry had the vanity to marry the daughter of a dilapidated
baronet, and having nothing but her pedigree to regale on, she
is extremely tenacious of maintaining her dignity ; and awful
were the rages she used to get into when her claims were not
recognised and allowed. When she first came into the county
she spoilt two or three dinner parties by declaring she had the
cramp in her stomach when she was not taken out first, and
monopolised all the hot plates to apply them to it, instead of
letting people get their victuals upon them. All this, of
course, was visited on poor Jerry's head when he got home.
" Poor spiritless wretch, to see his wife used so ; " " not fit to be
called a man," and so on. By-and-bye, Jerry, who had been
bred to the bar, started what he would call a " beautiful fiction," a sort of " leader of the gallop," or " trotter-out." This
was a sneaking, grinning, wriggling, old bachelor, of the name
of Rufus Slackbags, who goes the round of country parties just
as an organ-grinder's hat goes the round of street ones. The

following was their mode of proceeding ; it is much in the style of the old thimble-riggers :—

The company being assembled, Jerry and Slackbags would get together in the thick of the covey, and start a controversy respecting the date of some real or imaginary baronetage, which Jerry would carry on in the loud argumentative style so distinctive of the lower order of the bar ; while Slackbags, on his part, maintained his position with a greater degree of tenacity than is usually shown by gentlemen fishing for dinners. He would say, that " Sir Mark was a baronet of yesterday, a baronet of yesterday—yes, a baronet of yesterday ; " speaking as if he held new baronets in the utmost contempt. Cunning Jerry would then take the other side, and maintain the antiquity of the title ; and so they would wrangle and battle on till they got general attention drawn to themselves,—a thing not at all difficult to do, just before dinner, especially in the country. " Well, but my good friend," Jerry would rejoin, *sotto voce*, as if his delicacy rather made him shy of proclaiming it before company, —" well, but my good friend," he would repeat, his voice rising as he saw the plot ripen, " I *know* you are wrong, and I'll tell you why. In the first place," continued he, applying the forefinger of his right hand with a flourish to the palm of his left —" in the first place, I MARRIED THE DAUGHTER OF A BARONET. My wife, Mrs. Goo-o-o-oldfinch,"—for he puts no end of o's in—" my wife, Mrs. Goo-o-o-oldfinch, is the sixth DAUGHTER OF SIR MARTIN MOONSHINE, OF SUNBEAM-COURT, IN SOMERSETSHIRE, AND "—" Please, sir, dinner's *sarved !* " exclaims old Berlins, throwing open the door ; and away goes the happy, smiling, smirking, Mrs. Goldfinch, with the host, minus the cramp in her stomach.

I'm sure, thought Tom, draining his tumbler of negus, I saw that " cross " come off half-a-dozen times, till Mrs. Goldfinch got her precedence fairly established.

The greatest " sell " I ever heard in the way of a " trot-out," continued Tom, as he brewed himself another, was that by my

old friend Mr. Trumper, of Jollyrise, of the great Mr. Tarquinius Muff, of Muff Hall. Trumper doesn't like Muff—
never did, indeed. Long before Tarquinius hallooed him on to
the fresh hare, and insulted his harriers by calling them beagles
(or beggles, as Trumper pronounces it), he used to fight shy,
and talk of him as "that man Muff," "Noodle Muff," and so
on.

Somehow, Muff doesn't see it, or doesn't fancy it possible for
any one to be insensible of the importance of his acquaintance,
and he patronises Trumper extensively. He thought to show
him off to his friend Major Tinhead, of Blocksby, at the last
meeting of the Stumpwicket Cricket Club.

At the previous meeting Mr. Trumper had been discussing
the merits of Mr. Neville's and the Teardevil countries, when
he entered into a very long and interesting discussion, showing
how by the omission of certain great woodlands in one, and the
drainage of certain great tracts in the other, an excellent country might be formed of the two ; to all of which "Muff" said
"ditto," as though most thoroughly appreciating and approving
the doctrine. Trumper then favoured us with some of his
"hunting reminiscences,"—what he did long, long ago, much
in the style of Nimrod's popular work of that name ; and
altogether the party spent a most agreeable and instructive
evening, as the newspaper reporters would say. Well, the
next meeting being the last, and consequently the best,
each member had the privilege of feeding a friend, and
the strangers being placed next their hosts in the seats of
honour at the top of the table, our thinker sported Trumper,
and Tarquinius brought Tinhead, the couples sitting opposite
each other.

Tarquinius having "wined" with Mr. Trumper, and done all
that a gentleman in diamond studs could be expected to do by
an old drab-breeched farmer, tried to trot him out during
dinner, beginning with the subject that had brought him out
before. Trumper kept snorting and tucking in his dinner,

giving monosyllabic answers and most likely angry looks, varied occasionally by a kick of Tom's shins under the table, just as if he were spurring a horse to get away from a humbug out hunting. Tarquinius, however, was too dense to see anything of the sort, and attributed Trumper's indifference to devotion to his dinner ; and after the usual loyal and patriotic toasts had gone the rounds, and the tight-lacedness of eloquence had dissolved into the freedom of a circle round the fire, Muff began again before the now diminished audience. Never was such a man set to tickle a trout as Muff ! His action was just like the ungainly gambol of a cow compared to the smooth glide of the race-horse. Instead of getting something fresh and 'ticeing him up another stream, he tried the old bait that Trumper had already refused to nibble at. He went out of his way in the most forced, self-evident manner, and interrupted an argument on draining to lug in that of hunting. And he *would* have it in, too, despite the efforts of the Rev. Timothy Goodman, the chaplain of the Goose and Dumpling Hunt, who, seeing the perplexity of his great patron, tried hard to restore the current of conversation to its former channel.

"Don't you think, Mr. Trumper," asked Tarquinius, appealing directly to our friend, "that Neverbreak woods are a great drawback to Mr. Neville's country ? "

"Well, but if a two-foot drain will carry," interposed Goodman.

"At all events, don't you think we could easily afford to give them to the——? "

"The Elkington system of draining," again interposed the parson.

"Well, but now there's no man knows more about hunting or the country than you do, Mr. Trumper," observed Muff, throwing out an arm, and raising his voice high above that of the chaplain, "and I'm sure there's no one whose opinion we all respect more : might I ask now, for the sake of information,

what is your opinion of the general character of this country as
a hunting one ? "

That was a point-blank question, and put so forcibly and

" THINK OF THE COUNTRY—ARLE BOG ! "

publicly that Muff hugged himself at having at length pinned
him, and thought how his promise to Tinhead of trotting out
Trumper was about to be fulfilled.   He was, however, reckoning
without his host.   Trumper, who had had recourse to a pipe by
way of parrying Muff's importunities, sat some seconds after

the question was put, with his keen eye glistening, and a smile on his countenance, which Tarquinius construed into an arrangement of thoughts, and expected the same extensive observation and luminous discussion he had listened to before, showing how the Grassmere vale was very fine, and the Roxley Hills very heavy, and the Tew Woods very troublesome, and so on, all of which he thought would impress Tinhead with a due sense of his (Muff's) great importance as a sporting character.

Instead of this Trumper sat "*whif, whif, whiffing,*" until silence could no longer be maintained without rudeness, when knocking the top ashes out of his pipe on the hob, as if he were going to begin, he looked Muff in the face, and uttered these words, "Think of the country—*arle bog!*" amid the outrageous laughter of the party.

"And yet Trumper will trot when he's properly handled," mused our friend Tom, still sipping at the tumbler.

"A great deal," continued he, "depends on the skill of the leader in the matter of a trot-out. A man will trot quite freely with one person and yet be perfectly restive in the hands of another. Nay, I have seen men trot themselves out who would "shut up" directly if the trot was attempted by another. Trumper may be quoted as an instance of this sort. He has a joke that has laughed off half the waistcoat strings in the country, which he lies in ambush for with the most perfect *malice prepense* that ever was witnessed. It is the chorus of a hunting song, not the old—

> " There's nothing CAN compare
> To hunting of the hare ! "

but a regular ballad, built by the local bard of the country in honour and glory of Trumper himself, descriptive of his superlative qualities, his keenness—his gameness—the worth of his hounds, with the usual flourish about his love of the poor and all that sort of thing, the chorus of which is—

> " May Trumper live a thousand years, a thousand years,
> May Trumper live a thousand years,
> And I be there to see."

This is the stock song of a certain set in our country ; the farmers sing it, the ale-houses roar with it—it comes belching out of the beer-shop doors—the clods hum it at the smithy, and altogether it is just as well known as the cross in the market-place. If I have heard it sung once in Trumper's presence, I have heard it sung fifty times, and have often wished for the pencil of Thackeray to sketch the delightful complacency with which he sits listening to all the handsome things that are said of him. But richer far is the twinkle of his eye and the sly chuckle of his face as he prepares to let off the well-accustomed joke. It is a fine piece of acting. The first time over he merely puts on a wise face and cocks his ear as if surprised at the proposition, and considering whether if he is to take a lease certain, he may not as well ask for twelve or fifteen hundred years. Then he listens while the song recites the stoutness of his horses and the mettle of his hounds, when he begins fidgeting his great patent cords about in the arm-chair, as if unable to sustain the idea of separating from the darlings at any time ; but when the chorus again bursts forth, limiting him to a paltry

" THOUSAND YEARS,"

his feelings quite overcome him, and starting from his seat, he exclaims at the top of his voice.

" I DON'T LIKE TO BE STINTED ! "

amidst the uproarious plaudits of the delighted company. Hooray ! hooray ! hooray ! hooray ! Reader ! what say you to " One cheer more for old Trumper ! " HOORAY !

" Confound it," continued Tom, rousing up with the excitement produced by this last recollection, " I'll be hanged if I won't put these thoughts upon paper—make an article for Bell's Life, the Quarterly Review, or some of the periodicals." So saying, he snuffed the thick-wicked cauliflower-headed candles, stirred the fire, arranged his paper, and when he had got all ready he found his thoughts had taken flight and he could not catch any of them.

He therefore went to bed instead.

CHAPTER VIII.

THE STOUT-AS-STEEL HOUNDS.

PEOPLE who fancy all the dirt and discomforts of life are centered in large towns, have only to visit the small one of Sludgington to satisfy themselves of their error. One would think that a place through which a two-horse coach can barely pay its way thrice a week, would be tolerably free from the noise and din of bustling places ; but not even the "White Horse" in Fetter-lane, or the old "Bull and Mouth," in their noisiest, dirtiest, most coaching times, could surpass the disquiet of the Goldtrap Arms. Long before daylight Mr. Scott was aroused by the roll of carts, and the most unearthly yells proceeding from the drivers to their horses ; a sort of guttural sound, that seemed to come up from their very stomachs, much like what one hears aboard a steam packet. Having once commenced, the nuisance was repeated every half-hour or so, either at the front or the side of the house, both of which passages his bedroom commanded, until it seemed as if all the carts in the world were grinding about the Goldtrap Arms. Sleep with such a noise was impossible ; even if his old friend the cuckoo clock had not kept jingling, clattering, and chiming, in the intervals unoccupied by the carters. He was curious to see what could cause such commotion, and availed himself of the first dawn of day to look out of the window to see what sort of a morning it was, and look what the carts were loaded with. Of course they then suspended operations for a time ; and having tired of staring at the closed shutters of the chemist's opposite, and the sign of "Isabella Jenkins, licensed dealer in tea, coffee, tobacco and snuff," at the side, he again crept into bed, thinking the transit was past, and he might yet sleep off the head-achey discomforts of the night. No such thing, however. Just as he was dropping into a doze, *jingle, jingle, jingle*, went the works of the old cuckoo clock, bang flew the doors, out pounced the bird, and cuckoo! cuckoo! cuckoo! sounded with the most provokingly prolonged monotony. When it ceased, two cats on the top of Isabella Jenkins' house commenced a serenade that was enough to disturb the whole town.

"Flesh and blood can't stand this!" cried Tom, turning deliberately out of bed and groping for his razor. "I'll abate two nuisances at once;" so, stealing quietly on to the staircase where the clock was, he very soon returned with its weights in his hand, leaving the cuckoo to flounder itself down it its leisure.

Up then went the window, and *bang! bang!* went the weights at the cats, causing them to start in the midst of a most uproarious frolic, and run helter skelter over the pantiles in contrary directions.

Singular as it may seem, notwithstanding the constant noise the thing kept up in the house, neither Cake nor Madame missed it; at least Scott heard nothing about it, and the house is too small to allow of any commotion without it being heard "all over." He heard no observation about the cuckoo clock having suspended payment—no sudden exclamation, "Law me! what's got the cuckoo clock weights?" nothing, in fact, to indicate anything "out of the common." Nor was there anything in the bill, though it had almost every imaginable item printed, from pipes and baccey down to ginger beer.

When one gets into a place, how it magnifies, and how one feels part and parcel of it! Though there never was a more contemptible place than Sludgington, still, like a vapouring bully, it had forced itself into something like importance; and it was only when three or four strides of the old mare took

Scott clean out of it up the road towards the hills, that he was satisfied what a regular " cock-o'-my-thumb " place it was.

*   *   *   *   *

" FLESH AND BLOOD CAN'T STAND THIS ! "

How beautiful everything looked—magnificent, we might say,—the noble mountains, in all their pure and placid grandeur, swelling over each other till the snow-clad points of the highest seemed to touch the very sky. The goats and sheep

browsing on the sides looked like mere specks ; while the bells
of the cattle lower down kept up a lively jingle, as each motion
in feeding set them agoing. The road was well calculated for
showing off the scenery ; now winding round the hill bases,
now past some stupendous steep, with naught but stunted trees
starving in the rocky desolation around ; now skirting some
gentle slope up which the plough had ventured as high as the
depth of soil would carry ; now past some wooded dell at the
base of adjoining hills, down whose rugged course the mountain
torrent flowed in gentle, sparkling streams. All about was so
pure and healthy—such a contrast to little cramped Sludgington.   The white farm-houses, the rose-twined, heather-
thatched cottages, the rustic bridges, the very rustics themselves, all had a clean wholesome look, far different to the
frowsy ostler and people Scott had left at the Goldtrap Arms.
The incompatibility—to make use of a fine term—of combining
real romantic scenery with first-rate hunting, is, perhaps, the
only drawback to the chase, and certainly the two have hitherto
been denied to all countries we have seen. Those wags of all
wags, "the Warwickshire wags," as the song calls them, used
to boast of the picturesque beauties of their "shire ; " and
" picturesque " is a very proper term to apply to them, being
chiefly of the tame tractable order suited to a picture—beauties
that look better in a picture perhaps than in reality.   But the
grand mountain scenery of the Welsh side of our island, where
the sagacious reader will of course see our friend's travels
lie, defies the power of the artist ; and however good their
pictures may be for recalling the scene, they fail of conveying
an idea of the bold realities of the land to parties who have not
been there.

     But we are turning artist instead of sticking to our text—
the Stout-as-Steel Hounds.   Scott had penetrated some five or
six miles (according to time, for they don't sport milestones)
into the bowels of the mountains ere he saw any indication of
hunting. Having pulled up at a cross road a little beyond a

small row of white cottages, to try and decipher a washed-out finger-post, a halloo and a wave of a hand to the left from a man that Scott's red coat had brought to the door, put him on the right line ; and presently Scott saw his guide take the same direction by the fields, followed by a large black and tan hound, whose deep-mouthed baying, as he jumped and frolicked about his master, was echoed back by the surrounding hills. After the man's politeness in directing him, our friend could not do less than court his society ; so he pulled up to a pace at which the man would easily overtake him.

He was a stout young fellow dressed in the conical hat, red and green embroidered flannel jerkin, cord breeches, blue stockings, and laced boots of the hill country.

" You were going the wrong way," said the man, as he overtook Scott.

" Yes," replied Scott ; " how far will it be from here ? "

" Not above half an hour," replied the man, putting his best leg first.

" You're taking your dog to assist the hunt, then ? " said Tom, looking at his black and tan comrade.

" Ay, Muffler, can't do without Muffler ; can they, old man ? " asked he of the hound, clapping him on the back in return for the look up he gave on hearing his name. " The captain has no dog in his pack like Muffler," added the pedestrian.

" And yet he has some good ones, I suppose ? " observed Tom.

" Ay, but he always sells the best," rejoined his companion ; " he's o'er fond of money's the captain."

So Tom and his new friend journeyed on in the usual unreserved freedom of fox-hunters, the captain's character not improving as they went.

*　　　*　　　*　　　*　　　*

" Yon's the bridge," at last exclaimed Scott's companion, as a sudden turn of the road brought them full upon the beautiful

valley stretching away to the foot of the lofty Bevis Mount.
The sun was lighting and sparkling up the broad expanse
of the shallow streams, which narrowed about the centre,
where a low bridge of many arches was thrown. This
bridge carries the cross road over the valley, from the left
hand side of which Mr. Scott's guide intimated the hounds
would come.

Already the rough battlements and the greensward at either
end of the bridge gave indications of the coming sport. Groups
of foot people, mostly in the costune of Scott's companion,
mingled with the horsemen, among whom were already a slight
sprinkling of red coats.

Tom and his companion were presently among them.

After a fairish wait, " *here they come ! here they come !* " at
last burst from a dozen voices, as a hound or two in advance
emerged from the mountain pass, followed by a scarlet-coated
horseman, surrounded by the body of the pack. Nothing could
be more beautifully picturesque than this sudden emergence
from an unknown land, as it were,—nothing more lively than
the gay colours of the group contrasting with the sun-bright
scenery of the mountain pass.

*   *   *   *   *

" But what long ears the horses have ! " exclaimed our
friend Tom as they approached, and a sidelong glance
showed them flopping about. " *Horses !* great heavens, *they're
mules !* "

And so they were—great, dark, glossy-coated, mealy-legged
mules.

' *Well, I think !* " exclaimed our friend. " What will Mr.
Neville say ! The master and servants of the Stout-as-Steel
hounds mounted on mules ! "

The cavalcade advanced at an ambling sort of pace, and the
whole were presently within scanning distance ; at least for
people with the use of their eyes, though half the world

should be put under "Titmarsh"* to learn how to see things.

Captain Cashbox, the master, was a distinguished officer in the horse marines, and he still retains some of the characteristics of that anomalous service.

"*Avast there! avast!*" exclaimed he, as the hounds neared the bridge, and he wanted to turn aside to "heave anchor" on the green.

He was a fierce, square built, chuckle-headed-looking little chap, with a coarse black fringe of beard all round his face, and the gills of a blue striped shirt turned down over a gaping mohair stock, with the dickey strings staring out behind. Scott couldn't help thinking what an admirable study he would have made for the sign of the Saracen's Head on Snow Hill. Though the day was serenely fine, scarce a cloud hanging round even the highest mountain top, he yet sported a shining glazed hat, and had a black oilskin cape tacked on to the brass-bound pommel of his saddle. His coat was the old uniform one of the hunt in Mr. Squander's time—scarlet with dark blue collars and cuffs ; a mixture that looks better than it reads, at least the portrait Scott had of his cousin in it does not look amiss ; but how Stultz or Nugee would have laughed at the grotesque contortions of the captain's cut. Coat, it could hardly be called, it was more like one of those respectable, old gentlemanly articles of dress called a "spencer," with short square laps tacked on. It was plentifully sprinkled with buttons, not even omitting some at the bottom of the laps ; which would afford great satisfaction to the captain's seat when he happened to alight upon them of a sudden. He had a boatswain's whistle attached by a blue ribbon to a button hole, and carried a telescope in a spare stirrup leather across his shoulder. His waistcoat was made of seal skin, and what little breeches were visible above a

---

* The clever author of a "Journey from Cornhill to Grand Cairo," &c., who saw more in a month than most travellers see in a year.

pair of gaping, green-lined, fishermen's boots, fastened up at the side like overalls, appeared to be of canvas or unbleached duck. The boots had a miserably harsh, hackney-coach-head, lack-lustre look, which was unnecessarily heightened by his Britannia metal looking spurs, being newly rigged out with patent leather straps with broad pads. The mules we have already spoken of as fine animals of their sort ; while between Enoch, the old huntsman, and the hounds, there was a striking similarity of appearance. The hounds were of a breed now rarely seen, save in hill or mountainous countries, being bright-coloured, wiry-haired, rough-muzzled animals, combining the power, mettle, and endurance of the fox-hound, with the hard-bitten pertinacity of the terrier. Enoch Tiphill was just such another looking piece of goods. A little, light, wiry, grey-muzzled, keen-visaged old man, looking as though you might trundle him down, mule and all, from the top of Bevis Mount, over rocks, crags, precipices, and points, without hurting. The memory of man runneth not to the contrary when other than Enoch hunted the Stout-as-Steel hounds. In Mr. Squander's time he had a little mountain-bred grey mare, on which he performed such feats of activity and daring as could only be equalised by a chamois, or by the enterprising Mr. Gomersal in the character of Timour the Tartar, Napoleon Bonaparte, or some such vigour-requiring service.

We once heard a gentleman who had wandered into a strange country, give an account of the establishment he there found, and as it contrasts with the opinion our friend Tom passed upon the captain, we will repeat it here. After speaking favourably of the meet, the field, and the style of country, the gentlemen entered upon the more delicate one of the master and establishment. " The hounds," said he, " were really very good-looking animals, and in very good condition, the men were smart, clean, and well mounted ; in short," added he, " there was nothing ridiculous about the establishment *until they threw off!* "

So let it not be said of the Stout-as-Steel! Let not Captain Cashbox's incongruous garments prejudice a hunt that Scott's cousin, Squander, spent the best part of his fortune in supporting. But let us away to the hills, and enjoy the brief sunshine of the hour!

The Captain having eyed Scott with the suspicious curiosity masters—with the fear of pen-and-ink men before their eyes—regard strangers, until they are recognised by some of the field, honoured him with a touch of his glazed hat, as he saw him shaken hands with by two or three of his members; after which he jocosely observed, that he "supposed they might weigh anchor."

Scott then for the first time began to look for the cover. Woods there were none, at least none with any lying; what little apologies of trees there were, scattered on the more rugged parts of the hills, being so open at the bottom as to show all the stones in which they were stuck, and though there might be patches of gorse here and there, they did not seem large enough to hold much temptation to a fox.

"What do we draw?" asked Scott of one of his friends, whose face he knew, but whose name he either never knew or had forgot.

"Oh, just draw the hills," replied the interrogated, nodding his head towards a great plum-puddingey-shaped one, with some fern and brushwood about the middle, towards which Enoch was steering with the hounds. "Foxes lie all about," added he.

So Enoch seemed to think, for he steered all ways as if trying for a hare.

"You don't pay much for cover rent in this country, I imagine," said Scott to his friend.

"Nor for damage either," replied he.

"They've got a scent," continued he, shortly after, as the hounds began feathering towards the fern and brushwood on the before-mentioned hill.

"Ay, yon shepherd by the fire on the opposite hill views

him," added he, just as the outburst of melody from the pack proclaimed they had found the fox.

Down the hill reynard came pouring with his great bushy tail whisking in the air, as much as to say, " I don't care a copper for any of you ; " and hard upon him followed Enoch, full tilt on his mule, with three couple of hounds, Enoch blowing his horn, and screeching like an owl for the rest.

HE CLEARED THE HIGH STONE WALL.

They came pouring over one another like a waterfall !

The fox got such an impetus that he cleared the high stone wall and burn at the bottom of the hill like a greyhound, and commenced the ascent of the opposite hill with a stoutness that looked like wind and condition.

" Hooray ! " cheered a party of miners, at a fire on the crags towards which he was pointing, causing him to alter his line, and run the hill side.

The hounds having once got together, there was no further

call for hooping or hallooing, or blowing the horn. Away they went at a pace that showed how good was the scent, and how hopeless the attempt to follow them. Eclipse himself could have done nothing on the rough, stony, steep mountain sides ; and the hounds streaming away in full cry, with old Enoch toiling along on the mule, furnished an apt illustration of the fable of the hare and the tortoise—the further he went, the further he was left behind.

" *This way! this way!* " screeched little Cashbox, in a state of excitement bondering on phrensy. " *This way!* " repeated he, ramming his mule down a rutty hill-side, and working his arms like a telegraph. So the field rattled and clattered away in his rear, for his mule was in a good humour, and went at a pretty good bat. They soon got into the valley of Dol Velin, along the margin of whose bright stream a broken track-road ran, for there are few places so uncivilised as not to have roads of some sort, if people could but find them out. This most accommodating one led them straight through the mountains, on the left range of which the hounds were running with a breast-high scent, to the astonishment of the goats and sheep, and ponies, herding on the sides.

Though the devious course of old reynard, now ascending, now descending, now going straight ahead, was in their favour, still the pace was too good to allow of much halting to look. The Captain, who led the way with his telescope set, occasionally indicated, as he put it to his eye, which hounds were leading ; and after they had pursued the chase in this peculiar way for some five miles, the Captain having given the foreground a good raking, proclaimed that he saw the fox himself. "He's tried the great earths at Stetley Crags, where the fire is," said he, halting and holding the telescope in the direction of the far-off fire, " and is now stealing down the hill among the sheep and cattle."

Just then a movement among some distant dots indicated the fox's whereabouts, and presently the hounds came pouring down upon the spot followed by a drove of ponies, who seemed to join the chase to show how soon they would be beaten off.

The hounds were well called the Stout-as-Steel, for they ran as hard now after traversing so many miles of rough moorland country as they did at first. Let stag-hunters say what they will, five miles hard running is no joke.

FOLLOWED BY HIS OLD ENEMIES, THE CROWS.

The field had now a perfect panoramic view of the chase, without more trouble than they would be put to at the Diorama, or any London show. A splendid sun lit up the wild mountain scenery, while a slight tinge of frost rarefied the air, bringing distant objects near, and causing the music of the hounds to fall like thunder on the scene—reverberating like Mons. Jullien's band of a hundred and twenty performers at a "Bal Masqué."

Presently they had fox and all in view, and beautiful it was, watching the unerring truth with which the pack followed his every twist and turn and bend. There he was creeping and stealing along, not at the high galloping defying pace at which he started, but coolly and collectedly, as though conscious of the work he had to do.

So he returned about a hundred yards below the line he had taken in going, followed by a large flock of his old enemies, the crows, who kept a noise up overhead second only to that of the hounds behind. Luckless reynard, when so pursued, for you rarely escape destruction !

So it was this day. The striving pack gained on him just as one race-horse gains on another. The fatal view at last ensued ! A dodge, a snap, and a cataract of hounds as usual ended the scene !

CHAPTER IX.

MR. JENKINS JONES.

" Who-hoop ! "

"Who-hoop ! that's a queer way of beginning a chapter, Mr. Author ! "

"So it is, Mr. Reader, but you'll have a good many more of them before you are done."

Our last left the Stout-as-Steel hounds in the act of running into their fox on the far hill-side, the field viewing the feat across the water. Not a soul appeared near them, but ere the " worry " was complete, old Enoch dropped as it were from the clouds, and dived into the middle of the pack. To be sure the latter part of his descent was visible enough in the shape of a red thing sitting as it were on the back of a rabbit, sliding on its hind quarters down the mountain.

Having reached the pack, up went the fox, and baying leaped the hounds, the group forming a lively speck on the wide expanse of mountain scenery.

Few people are willing to admit that a fox has been killed, unless they see him—at all events seeing him seems to add considerably to their satisfaction ; and away Captain Cashbox cut, followed by the field, for ocular demonstration. Through the water splashed the mules, over great boulder stones, enough to throw down an elephant, across the rushy, rugged bottom, and now up the steep hill-side —clatter, clatter, clatter, they went among the loose rumbling stones— blob, blob, blob, they floundered on the unsound ground beyond.

Whohoop!

"*Who-hoop!*" each man exclaimed, on pulling up within "ware-horse" distance of the huge fox, now hanging his head before the pack in all the terrors of grim death. "*Who-hoop!*" yelled little Cashbox, putting his finger in his ear, as though he were afraid of deafening himself. "WHO-HOOP!" screamed he, still louder, throwing himself off his mule and rushing up to Tiphill for the fox. If the Captain had gone on all-fours, and hunted and killed the fox himself, he could not have taken greater credit to himself for the feat. The hounds might kill him, but who brought the hounds? Captain Cashbox—and therefore to Captain Cashbox belonged the honour and glory of the day.

Having got the fox from Enoch, he held him up for some seconds above his head, in the manner of a "Poses Plastique" master, until his little arms tiring, he threw him flop on the ground.

"He's a terrible length from the snout to the stern," observed the nondescript little man, stooping and measuring the fox with his whip.

Without announcing the longitude, he proceeded to divest him of his appendages.

Off went the head.

"There's the head of a traitor!" exclaimed the Captain, holding it up.

Then came the pads, and, lastly, that noblest trophy of them all—the brush!

"Allow me, sir," said he, strutting out in the most grotesque, puss-in-boots style, towards where Tom Scott stood, " to present you, sir, with the brush of one of our mountain breed—sir, a real 'stunner,' sir, as my friend, Joe Banks, would say, sir. Sir, I'm extremely glad, sir, to see you out with *my* hounds, sir; hope, sir, I shall often have the pleasure, sir—shall be most happy, sir, to present you with our button, sir."

Flattered by so much attention, especially from a man that he did not expect any from, Tom incontinently replied, on receiving the brush, that he would be most proud to receive the button, and wear it wherever he went.

Scarcely were the words out of his mouth, than the Captain, having dived into the trunk of his fisherman's boots, produced a packet, from which, having blown the silver paper, he exhibited a complete set of large buttons, to which having added a pinch of small ones from his seal-skin waistcoat pocket, he handed the whole over to Scott, observing, that " he might send him a Post Office order for the four guineas when he got home, and that he would be most happy to have his name down as a subscriber also."

" *He's done you*," whispered a gentleman, with a smile and a wink, as the little varmint waddled back to his mule, and proceeded to what he would call "hoist himself on deck," by the aid of a rusty, most disreputable-looking stirrup.

" I don't know that," replied Tom Scott, with a grunt, thinking the Captain might, perhaps, get the buttons back instead of the Post Office order.

" Well, we've had a very good run—at least, the hounds have," observed the stranger, who had now brought his horse alongside. " Are you staying in this part of the country ? "

" Why, yes—no—yes—not exactly," replied Scott ; " the fact is, I *was* on this side of the country, and, wishing to have a look at these hounds, lay at Sludgington over night."

" I pity you," exclaimed the gentleman ; adding, " I wish you'd come to me. Where are you going to now ? " inquired he.

" Don't know till I get back—perhaps stay there again "

" Come to me," rejoined he ; " we shall be most happy to see you—you've plenty of time," added he, showing our friend his watch, which wanted a quarter to one.

" You are very kind," replied Scott, feeling little disposed to undergo the persecution of Cake and the noise of the Goldtrap Arms again, though the cuckoo clock nuisance was abated

—adding, " I shall be very glad to avail myself of your offer."

" That's right ! " said the stranger, closing the bargain by a shake of the hand : " we dine at six, and there will be a stable ready for you." So saying, he turned up a road the reverse of the one that he pointed out as Scott's, and tickling his horse with the spur was speedily out of sight.

One person in a hurry is very apt to put another person in a hurry, and Scott began to trot too, without knowing why.

* * * * *

" Gently, old girl," at length said he, easing the old mare down into a walk, to enjoy the scenery, the winding mountain-road having brought him before a fresh range of hills. Just then it flashed across his mind that he didn't know who his friend was.

" Well, that's the stupidest thing I ever aid in my life," exclaimed he, dropping the rein, and giving his thigh a hearty slap. " I thought I knew him because he knew me, and I have no more idea who he is than the man in the moon."

Scott then went back to the turn of the road to see if any of the field were behind, but they had all dispersed on their different routes—the horsemen by the roads, the foot people by the mountain tracks.

" Well, never mind," said he, turning short round again, " I can describe him—round-faced, ginger hair, rather stout, hunts, says he lives near Sludgington. Oh, Cake, or the saddler, or the postmaster, or the blacksmith, or any of the wise men of the place will be able to tell me who he is." So saying, he relapsed into enjoyment of the scenery, until the road at length opened upon the vale.

Sludgington formed a not unpleasing feature in the landscape now that Scott regarded it with an unprejudiced eye. Its church tower, its clump of trees, its white dovecote to the right, the now sun-glittering mill-pond on the left, even the very smoke and outline of the houses, made an agreeable break on the tame monotony of the flat vale beyond. The cold, black, whinstone mud made him shudder, though, as he got into the street again ; nor were his feelings soothed by having to ride on the rough M'Adam to make way for a long line of slate carts passing through with the produce of the neighbouring quarries.

" Who is it that lives near here, and hunts with the Stout-as-Steel hounds ? " asked he of the hostler, as he gave him the mare to be fed while he packed up his traps ; " who is it that hunts and rides a clipped horse, and wears black boots, not fishermen's boots like Captain Cashbox's, but Bishop's boots coming up to the knee-pan ? " touching the whereabouts on his own leg.

" Who is it that h-o-u-n-t-s and rides Bishop's boots," drawled out the muzzy idler.

" *No! no!* rides *in* Bishop's boots, black jacks," retorted Scott ; " rides a clipped horse, and lives somewhere about here."

" Why, I should say that would be Mr. Jenkins Jones," replied the man ; " he has a clipped horse."

" But can't you be *sure?* a gentleman with gingery hair. Has Mr. Jenkins Jones gingery hair ? "

" Why y-e-a-s ; I should say he has," replied he; " and rides a clipped horse."

" Where does he live ? " asked Scott.

" At Down House, about six miles from here," replied the man.

" Ay, that's him," said our friend, leaving the stable, and running into the house. " Jenkins Jones, of Down House, *is* the man ; " indeed, I fancied I heard somebody call him Jones out hunting.

*　　*　　*　　*　　*

What with the bother of packing, waiting for the bill, and

THE OLD WOMAN DIDN'T KNOW WHERE IT WAS.

[*To face page* 138.

then for the horse, the limited allowance of a winter's day
began to give indications of declining ere Scott got sufficiently
near the residence of which he was in quest, to gain any decided
information from the few country people and mountaineers he
met as to its precise distance and locality. One man told him
it was three miles, another that it was two ; and an old woman
that he overtook, driving a flock of geese, and who said she had
lived in the country all her life, didn't know where it was at
all—had never heard of Down House before, or of Mr. Jenkins
Jones either—had heard of a Mr. Thomas Jones, but he lived
at Frengford, at the back of the hills, but he had been dead
many years, and " of course," she said, " it couldn't be him."

A woodman, however, that Scott next met, was better
informed, and after running the words " Jenkins Jones, Jones
Jenkins, Jenkins Jones," backwards and forwards on his
tongue, as a lady runs up and down the notes of a piano, he
directed him through a pass at the low end of the mountain
range.

Having trotted through it just as night began to close in, he
came upon a wild, undulating down country—open, spacious,
and far-stretching. Here and there dark patches, occasionally
indicated by the fitful gleam of a passing light, denoted human
habitations, but the extreme distance was completely lost in the
clouds.

To heighten the confusion of the scene, the road, as he had
been warned by the woodman, resolved itself into a mere race-
course sort of track, whose line was marked by little chalk-heap
mounds thrown up on the turf.

The springy down, so tempting under ordinary circumstances
for a canter, was now traversed slowly for fear of losing the
thread of the heaps, and having to pass the night on the wide
dreary waste.

" It must be a primitive place, indeed," thought Scott, riding
close inside the line of chalk heaps, " where a track like this
serves alike for carriage, cart, and bridle road. No fear of

having one's rest disturbed by the rumbling of carts, the yells of drivers, or the music of cats, as it was last night."

A bigger wave of land that the mountain throe had rolled further inwards, obtruded just as the fast-falling shades of night began to make him wish to be at his journey's end ; on reaching the top of which the lights from a house ensconced among trees appeared within a couple of hundred yards, and the quick eye of the mare presently caused her to halt at a light iron gate, dividing the lawn from the downs.

The clatter the gate made in swinging to and fro, caused an outburst of barking and yelling from the kennel, while the raising and hurried dropping of the curtain of a low-windowed room on the ground floor showed that the inmates were aroused, and ere he had dismounted at the sash-windowed door, a shirt-sleeved groom had rushed round from the back of the house to take his horse.

A glass door, while it is pleasant and cheerful in summer, has the advantage in winter of letting a guest see who is coming, and the bright burning oil lamp discovered our friend's host now attired in a comfortable suit of plaid instead of the cloth and leather of the foxhunter.

How we pity people who lived before " tweeds," railways, and writing directions on newspapers, were invented !

The gentleman shaded his eyes with his hand and shut them as some people do who want to have a good look at one ; but a momentary glance produced an " Oh, Mr. Scott, is it you ? I'm glad to see you," confirmed by a cordial shake of the hand.

Scott then proceeded to " hang up his hat."

" You've brought your nightcap, I hope," observed the gentleman as he helped Scott off with his paletot

While this was going on in the passage, Scott overheard the following nursery dialogue in the parlour :—

> " Little Jack Horner
> Sat in the—— ?

" Where did little Jack sit, my pet ? "

" Pie," lisped the child.

" No, my darling, *not in the pie*," responded the questioner.

" Let me introduce my friend Mr. Scott, my dear," interrupted the host, throwing open the door of a cheerful-looking
room, and disclosing a beautiful dark-eyed lady, with a lovely
little child half on her lap, half on the table, studying the interesting career of the gentleman aforesaid.

An attempted rise, with a sweet smile mingling with a half-
suppressed laugh, at Jack Horner's novel position, made Scott
feel quite at home, and he readily accepted his host's offer of an
arm-chair by the brightly burning fire.

As Scott looked at him he thought it was lucky he had been
able to give some other account of him beyond a mere description of his person, for hunting things made such a difference in
men's appearance that it is not always easy to recognise them
in others. The gentleman, however, speedily touched on the
grand ice-breaker of conversation "the run of the morning,"
and his wife having gathered up the child's toys, consisting of
a jumping mouse, a Macassar oil bottle, a tin kettle, a tatter'd
doll, and an illuminated copy of " Jack Horner," departed with
her treasure in her arms.

Scott soon found he was in capital quarters. Indeed he re-
collected to have heard from some of "their hunt" who had
strayed so far out of the world as Mr. Neville's men consider
the hill country, that there were some "capital fellows " in it,
which, in current sporting phraseology, means, men who are
glad to see their friends without any fuss ; or, as in Scott's
case, men who are glad to see fox-hunters at any time.

There certainly is a wonderful freemasonry among fox-
hunters. There is no letter of introduction equal to the few
words, " This man's a sportsman." It is far superior to any
formal application to be allowed to recommend one's particular
friend Mr. Augustus Fitznoodle, eldest son of Sir Augustus
and Lady Fitznoodle, who was a daughter of Hugh fifth Earl

of Bigacres, to their attention in the way of a "ticket for soup," as these unfortunate documents are sometimes termed. But we are getting off the line, and must be running into our subject. They had a capital dinner, some famous mutton broth, with meat in it, thick and strong ; a well-crimped piece of cod with oyster sauce, a leg of dark-gravied four-year-old Welsh mutton, followed by a woodcock and a dish of nice hot mince pies, assisted by sherry and iced champagne at dinner, and a bottle of fine old port and a devilled biscuit after.

The next morning, as they sat at an equally good breakfast, Scott saw a fustian-clad groom arrive on a horse at exercise, and presently a note was brought in, which his host, after perusing, presented to him with a smile, saying, "This refers to you." Thus it ran :—

"DEAR JONES,

"*Have you seen anything of Mr. Scott of Hawbuck Grange? He promised to come to me yesterday, and has never cast up.*

"*Yours truly,*

"JONES JENKINS."

"Good God, ain't I at Mr. Jones Jenkins's now ?" exclaimed our friend.

"Why, no," replied his host, laughing ; "my name is Jenkins Jones, his is Jones Jenkins. I saw you had made the common mistake last night when you came, but was not going to deprive myself of the pleasure of your society by telling you."

"You are extremely kind, I'm sure," replied Scott. "I *did* think, when I saw you, that your hair had got darker, but I attributed it to the shade of the lamp, or to not having seen you with your hat off."

"Oh, I assure you, it's nothing uncommon," replied his host,

" nothing uncommon at all ; we get each other's letters and parcels, and papers, and all sorts of things. A Frenchman brought a bill for a musical clock here the other day, and insisted upon my paying it. It was directed à Monsieur Jones Jenkins.' In vain I protested that my name was Jenkins Jones. ' Vel, sare,' said he, ' it shall be all de same—dey have jost put de Jones before de Jenkins ; *you are de man.*' ' Nonsense !' said I, sporting the old joke, ' there's just as much difference between Mr. Jenkins Jones and Mr. Jones Jenkins as there is between a chestnut horse and a horse chestnut.' "

MR. JENKINS JONES AND THE FRENCHMAN.

CHAPTER X.

TAKING leave of his kind host ard hostess at the Down House, Tom Scott again mounted the old mare, "homeward bound," as Captain Cashbox would say.

He had not got above a couple of miles on the high road before he was overtaken by a man on foot, going at a pace known only to fugitives, servants who have been loitering at public-houses, or people in pursuit of sport. Urgent or exciting must be the cause that spurs a pedestrian past a horse. Nevertheless the individual shot ahead, and that without look or observation.

"He's a good'un to go," said Scott to himself, eyeing the quick short steps with which he got away from the old mare. He was a square-built, bow-legged, stiff little fellow, not at all of the cut that one would imagine a "Hookey Walker." His dress was puzzling, as well as his pace. It consisted of a brown duffle frock coat, black and white plaid trousers, with drab gaiters, and he carried an oil-skin-covered umbrella under his arm ; quite a town turn-out—at all events, not a "week-day" one in the country.

"I wonder what the buffer is," said Scott, watching him as he stepped along. "I'll be bound to say he can't keep that pace up long," continued he. Still he trudged on, and Scott followed, thinking, as he rode, that he had the best of it.

Presently the pedestrian began to look about him, first over one hedge, then over another, as though he wanted his nurse, or an excuse for bolting.

" What now, old boy ? " said Scott, eyeing the proceeding ; "*you* surely have no business in the fields."

He seemed to be of a contrary opinion though, and, coming to a weak place in the hedge on the left, he popped over the rail that protected it, and forthwith commenced a rapid ascent of the hill.

He was quickly out of sight, leaving Tom to pursue his road and ruminations together.

About a mile further on, where a mountain pass runs into the Netherdew turnpike, our traveller was struck with a vast concourse of people coming down, some on foot, some on horse-back, some in gigs, some on mules. " A foot-race," said he to himself, eyeing the numbers ; " the Llandogget Stag against the Bob-Daniel Flyer, or some such fun ; " and he fancied he saw the poles and ropes with which they were going to stake off the turnpike.

" Or'd, hang it, no ! they are a set of dancing-dogs or monkeys," exclaimed he, as the red and gaudy jackets of the animals and the yellow flag of one of the leaders became apparent. " What queer creatures they must be in these parts ! " continued he ; " only fancy a bevy of great men turning out after such animals ! "

Notwithstanding this denunciation, he pulled up to have a look at them himself, and he was so lost in astonish-ment at seeing that the whole party were English, instead of the white-teethed, olive-complexioned Italians, the general attendants of monkeys and dancing dogs, that he was right in the middle of the cavalcade before he saw the animals were greyhounds—greyhounds in all the pomp and paraphernalia of race-horses, coloured hoods, quarter-pieces, and bottle-carry-ing leaders. " Gad," thought he, " what ' a go ' it would be if they were to bring a pack of foxhounds to the cover side in clothing ! "

It's odd if a fox-hunter gets into a crowd of sportsmen, within half a hundred miles of home, without being recog-

nised by some one ; and from the heterogeneous assemblage
of shooting-jacketed, and great-coated, and duffle-coated, and
cloaked, and shawled, and paletoted, and trousered, and Tagli-
onied, and jack-booted, and overalled, and fiddle-case booted,
and gambadoed, and umbrella-handed horsemen, a voice from
a complete mountain of mackintosh exclaimed, " Halloa, Tom
Scott ! is that you ? "

" *It's me !* sure enough," exclaimed our friend ; " but who
the deuce *you* are beats my comprehension ? "

" Don't you remember Charley Travis ? " replied the
questioner, lowering his comforter, and raising a puddingy
plaid off his brow, so as to display a pair of large boiled-goose-
berry-looking eyes staring out of a great red harvest-moon of
a face.

" Charley, my boy ! " exclaimed Scott, starting at the
familiar name and the change that time had effected on its
bearer. " Charley, my boy, how are you ? I'm delighted
to see you," and thereupon they rung a requiem over the
twenty years that had elapsed since they met, and aroused
the spirits of no end of " larks " that had flown with the time.

Upon the evidence of so much cordiality, divers of the
sporting gents lifted their hats and caps to the stranger,
indicating that our traveller's friend Charley was " somebody," and that a portion of his greatness was reflected upon
Tom.

" I shouldn't have known you," said Scott, looking at the
man mountain he now rode beside, and recalling the smart
slim youth he had parted with.

" Nobody does," replied he, " nobody does—my leg's as big
as my whole body used to be," shoving out a great woollen-clad
mackintosh-cased limb, terminating in a black and red list
slipper. " Do you remember when I squeezed through the pot
of Miss Gammon's chimney, and descended amongst all the
bread and butter misses at their tea ? " asked he. " Couldn't
do that now, by jingo ; no, nor ride 8 st. 7 lb. as I used to do.

However, never mind ; I am delighted to see you again, old fellow. Tell me now what's brought you into this part of the world ? "

" Ah ! still as fond of hunting, still as fond of hunting as ever, are you ? " observed he, after listening to a narrative of where Scott had been.

" Just the same," replied Scott, " just the same. If anything, the older I get, the bigger fool I get. I should think hunting couldn't do you any harm," added he, looking at his friend's puffy face.

" Bless you, my dear Scott," shivered he, " *it would kill me*. Consider, my dear fellow, what a mass of complaints, what a lump of corruption I am. Look at the chalk stones in my hands," continued he, pulling off a sable glove. " It takes two men to put me horseback. Hunt ! Suppose I should be spilt ! I should never get up again—I should lie kicking on the broad of my back like a sheep or a bull frog ! "

" But what's made you gouty, old boy ? " asked Scott. " Your parents were healthy, and you had nothing of that sort in your youth."

" *Had I !* " exclaimed he, earnestly, " *you* know I hadn't —never a moment's illness of any sort. As long as I was starving on a hundred a year I was the healthiest and happiest mortal alive ; but the moment the money came, down came a whole bevy of ills, and I became one mass of disorders. Stevens ! " exclaimed he, " is it time to take my pills ? "

While the individual thus appealed to was supplying his wants, it flashed across Scott's mind that the hero he was addressing had been changed into a baronet, and that Charley Travis of former days was now Sir Charles Munchington, having been most unexpectedly metamorphosed one morning while shaving by a fourpenny glass in a barrack-room at Gibraltar.

" I'm afraid you live too well, Sir Charles," said Scott, as the Baronet gulped down the last of the pills.

" *Live!* my dear fellow, I wish you saw me live ; if rice puddings and soda water are living, then I do live.   But, talking of that, come to me to-day after coursing."

" Thank you," said Scott, " but I'm expected at home."

" What, you're married, are you ? " asked he.

" Why, no ! yes ! no ! not exactly ; but the fact is, I'm out of linen—got my last shirt on."

" Oh, I'll find you linen, and be shot if I don't take a glass of wine, too, for ' auld lang syne.'   I'll lend you shirts and shoes, and everything, for I have them of all sizes since I began to magnify, till I think Daniel Lambert and I might now go partners in a wardrobe."

We trust the reader will believe Mr. Scott sincere in saying that he had every intention of going home that day.   Indeed he wished it ; for, independently of being out of linen, he was extremely short of other things, and a man feels the want of trifles that he does not appreciate when at hand.   Besides, he wanted to see how things were going on, whether the red cow had calved, or any of the young horses got lamed.   Still, what could he do ?   Here was an old friend whom he had not seen for twenty years, gouty and unwell, yet willing to take a glass of wine with him.   Prudence said "No," but inclination said " Ay," and accordingly " ay " had it.

" Come and see a course," said Sir Charles, as the cavalcade turned off the road through a gate into some extensive pastures ; " you don't know what fun it is, and we are getting near a tie," added he.

Tom had a pretty good idea though, for he once kept a greyhound himself, and a more daft, mischievous, useless beggar was never seen.   It used to do nothing but run a muck at the poultry, and sheep, and foals, and practise feats of agility through the windows.   Worse still, the insensate brute was continually losing itself, and cost him no end of half-crowns for casting up, until he was fortunate enough to see the animal enticed away by a mugger-man, from whose care there is seldom much escape. The fellow thought he'd got a prize.

Scott followed the motley group, which had now been joined by his pedestrian friend, into the field, and a couple of dogs were stripped of their hoods, and spectacles, and quarter-pieces, and put in the slips. They then made a circuit of the enclosure, following the important Mr. Marksman, the judge, with the rear brought up by a most miscellaneous rabble of foot people, interspersed with brandy-ball and lollypop merchants, the usual concomitants of pedestrian crowds.

They ranged that field and another, and beat a bank-side, and then crossed a nice trout-stream on to some water meadows beyond.

"Let us stand here and see the course," said Sir Charles, sheltering under the lee of a tumble-down building, from one of those heavy, cutting, rattling hail-storms that so disconcert lazy house-maids with bright grates. Patter, patter, patter it came, rattling down upon the harsh dry mackintosh, making the large bullets bound again.

Before it was well over, at least before they had fairly opened their daylights again, a shout proclaimed the course begun, and, looking across the water, Scott saw two great snake-like animals stretching and striding away over the plain after an unfortunate little driblet of a thing, that evidently had a very poor chance with them. It went away stoutly at first, to be sure, and there was little sensible advantage so long as it ran straight ; but the moment it began to swerve, the superiority of the followers was evident.

So it went twisting and turning, the efforts becoming " smaller by degrees and beautifully less."

Sir Charles was in ecstasies ! He jerked, and he jumped, and he worked his arms, and bit his lips, and hung to one side, just as a cockney does in a cab that he thinks is about to capsize. "*Beautiful* course!" exclaimed he; "*beautiful* course!" as the dark dog turned the poor drab thing to the left, and the light dog sent it right ahead again. "Finest course I ever saw in my life!—finest course I ever saw in my life!" ejaculated he, as the hare made straight for a gate.

"By Jove, that's well done!" said he, as the dogs cleared it together. "Now for the tug of war!"

They were now upon a seed field, and gaining painfully upon poor puss. First one strider turned her, then the other, the poor thing's energy contracting with each effort, till the dark dog shot a length in advance, and chucked her right up in the air.

Then up hurried the field, the victor all glee, the loser all glum, while water-bottles and clothing were produced, and another brace of dogs had their spectacles taken off and were put in the slips.

So they went on from field to field, coursing and killing, and losing and missing, amid the betting and cheering of the company.

At last the course came on deciding whether the owner of the dark dog or a red one was to have the honour of keeping a pewtery-looking cup for the year, and of sacking a certain number of sovereigns in the shape of stakes. We dare say there was as much as ten pounds at issue; and if there had been a million, there couldn't have been more noise. "Five shillings on the Dusty Miller!" exclaimed a great, fat, butcherified-looking fellow, in blue woollens or tweeds, mopping the perspiration from his brow, which he had managed to acquire in the "trot" of the last course—a thing that none but a twenty-stoner could accomplish with such an atmosphere.

"I'll lay a shilling on the Miller! I'll lay two! I'll lay three! I'll take three to two!" exclaimed another.

"I'll lay you half-a-crown to two shillings, Jubbins," replied Popkins ; and the quantity and nature of the betting showed that there would be a great demand for silver after the course.

The awkward part of betting on a course seems to be that there is no way of regulating the race. It isn't like a trial of speed between horses, for twisting and turning seems to have quite as much to do with winning as the straightforward fly. So it was here. After much to do they at length got a satisfactory hare ; but, after the usual bowling about, the victory was declared in favour of Bright Star, Dusty Miller, for some unapparent cause, being non-suited, though an inexperienced courser would have said that he followed suit quite as stoutly as his competitor.

Amidst cheers for the victor the scene closed, and many of the field availed themselves of the opportunity afforded by pulling out their purses to pull out their pocket-handkerchiefs too, for it was intensely cold.

On reaching the village of Leighford, Sir Charles abandoned his cob, and a brougham, with post horses, was presently at the Greyhound Inn door, in which he insisted on seating Scott, and carrying him off to his residence.

It requires a strongish intimacy to accompany an invalid with no better prospect than what the baronet had held out ; but friends decrease so, as we get on in life, that it is cheering to put one's hand into the back shelf of time, and pull out an old one, altered, dusted, and damaged though he may be. If a chap is a good fellow at twenty, there's little chance of his being a bad one at forty ; and, barring his ailments, Sir Charles was just the same hearty cock Scott had parted with twenty years before, when he sailed for India. Alas ! the then gay stripling was now the premature old man.

It was just light enough, as they dashed across the ornamental bridge, over the swan and fowl-swarming water, and dived among the undulations of the deer-stocked park, for Scott to see that his friend had "lit on his legs;" and when they stopped, with a jerk, under the wood-paved Gothic porch of the ancient edifice, and two neatly dressed footmen responded to the sound of the bell, it was evident there was what a literary appraiser would estimate at " *ten thousand a year*." Nobody that has " any thing " has less, thanks to the liberal talent of Mr. Warren.

" I don't keep these fellows to *look* at," said Sir Charles, as he sidled from his seat in the brougham on to their crossed arms, and was carried bather-woman fashion into the house, ordering one to get the room next his ready for Scott, and the other to tell the groom to see after our friend's mare, which was coming with his cob.

" Oh, doctor ! " groaned the baronet, as they placed him on a couch, in a perfect snuggery of a room ; " ah, doctor ! " groaned he, to a little white-headed old man, in knee-breeches and buckles, who Scott could have sworn was the doctor if he hadn't been so addressed ; I'm *dreadfully* exhausted—*very ill indeed !* "

" Indeed, Sir Chorles, I'm sorry to hear that, Sir Chorles," replied the little gentleman, advancing solemnly to his patient, at the same time pulling up a great noisy watch by a sort of jack-chain, to which was appended many seals, as if he was going to feel his pulse.

" Oh, no ; it's not physic I want—it's not physic I want ! I've taken *all* your pills and the blue draught into the bargain," exclaimed the invalid. " I want something to *restore* me—to *revive* me, in fact."

" Well, Sir Chorles," mouthed the man of medicine, " suppose you have a little water gruel," looking mysteriously at Scott.

" D—n your water gruel ! " screamed the invalid ; " why, what an inhuman monster you must be to want me to take water gruel on the *very day* I've fallen in with Tom Scott, after an absence of nearly twenty years ! "

" Well, Sir Chorles," responded little blacklegs, taken rather aback, " what would you like to have, Sir Chorles ? "

" I DON'T KEEP THESE FELLOWS TO LOOK AT."

" —Hang it ; I want *you* to recommend, man ! " continued he, precisely in the tone that he used to blow up the waiters and landlords of the inns when they didn't please him. " I want *you* to recommend, man. What's the use of being a doctor if you can't tell what's good for me ? "

The little man was quite abashed.

" Do you think a glass of maraschino would do me any harm ? " at last asked Sir Charles.

" Oh, not the least—none whatever," replied the doctor, glad of the suggestion—" at least, that's to say if you don't take more than a glass, *or two*," added he, seeing the brow begin to lour.

" And a slice of *paté de foie gras*, perhaps ? " continued Sir Charles.

" You might find benefit from it," replied the doctor, " especially if your stomach's empty, and it wants an hour yet to dinner," continued he, looking at the watch, which he still fumbled in his hand.

" Stomach *empty*," growled Sir Charles ; " why, now, is it likely a man would eat if his stomach wasn't empty ? At least *I* know *I* wouldn't."

" And bring two or three dozen oysters, and some pale ale," exclaimed Sir Charles, as the servant was going, after receiving the above orders ; adding to the doctor, " Oysters are wholesome enough, at all events, I hope ? "

" Nothing more so, Sir Chorles," replied the man of medicine.

" A beaker of burgundy would be right after the *paté*, wouldn't it ? " asked he in continuation.

" It would give tone to the stomach, Sir Chorles, especially if you have rather overdone yourself with exercise."

" Well, then, my good fellow," interrupted the patient, " will you have the kindness to go into the cellar for it yourself, and see and wrap it properly up in flannel, so that it mayn't get chilled by the way ? "

With such a " whet " the reader will conjecture what the dinner was like ; nor will it, perhaps, be necessary to point out why Sir Charles is not as healthy as he was with his hundred a year, to prevent rich people parting with their money for fear of getting like him. Should there be any alarmists, however, Mr. Scott says he can take a few sackfuls, which may either be sent to Hawbuck Grange, or left with the publishers of this work. The accommodating reader will now have the kindness to suppose our friend Tom Scott returned to the former place.

CHAPTER XI.

THE DOUBTFUL DAY.

OLD BEN.

DOUBTFUL days— that is to say, days on which one does not know whether to go to hounds or stay at home—are great bores. To be sure, a native has no great business to be bothered by them, seeing that he has no need to " turn out " on other than undoubted days, and can chop over to his other occupation should a day seem unpro-pitious ; but in a sport-stinting season, even natives are very apt to try and get a day that, in a favourable winter, would be rejected. Gentlemen who leave their homes for the purpose of hunting are fairly excusable for going sliding and slipping to a meet. Not but that even *they* had better stay at their lodgings and read the " Annual Register," or whatever work of light reading they have brought with them.

Speaking of the season, 1846–7, our friend Scott, after pre-
facing his observations by declaring that he "doesn't wish to
say any thing unhandsome of the weather, or of anybody,"
denounces it as "the most tricky, capricious, unhandsome
season he ever remembers." "It is not the frost and snow
that I complain of," says he, "though we had enough of them
in all conscience, but it was the dirty, deceitful, delusive sort
of changing that kept raising men's hopes, apparently for no
other purpose than 'dashing them to spinage.'"

Of course he spoke of the weather in Mr. Neville's country,
but we believe it was pretty much the same all over. After an
inordinate quantity of frost and snow, from the end of
November to the beginning of January, there was a slight
cessation, and the wide-awake ones actually got a few days'
hunting in some countries. At the end of the first week, however, just as all the packs were again blooming into advertisement, back came the frost, harder, if possible, than ever,
accompanied by a fresh fall of snow ; and again, about the last
week of the month, they both disappeared, and hunting was
resumed with all the advantages of first-rate scent, to be
again stopped on the 31st, by the return of frost and snow.
Then look at that little snuffling, shabby month of February,
one that in ordinary seasons we reckon as the second best
hunting one of the year. It came in, of course, with a white
coat and an icicled nose, when all of a sudden, on the night of
the 4th, it turned to a thaw, the west wind got up and cleared
the country of snow in an incredible short space of time, when
lo ! as all the snow-broth yet floated on the fields, back came
the frost on the 7th, caking it on the top, to the damage, if not
the destruction of the wheat crops, and then a fall of snow
succeeded to keep all snug. Now that we call very unhandsome—unworthy of the great and enlightened eighteen hundred
and forty-seven ; it's as bad as kicking a man when he's
down.

Not being fond of doubtful days, Tom Scott missed a run or

two during the first interregnum, and paid dearly for it by the persecution of Muff & Co., who happened to be out. Indeed, he could hardly get their township books through at the next meeting of the board of guardians, from first Muff, and then Tinhead, and then Tinhead, and then Muff, bursting into exclamations about it.

"Thomas Felix Badman, relieved in kind—two kicks and a basin of barley water," read the clerk.

"Major! do you recollect that splendid cast the hounds made of themselves at the four cross roads? Just as we came to Briarly Dell, where the fox had met the sheep in the face, and made them 'right about wheel?'" inquired Muff (Tarquinius), who was in the chair, of his docile friend Tinhead, who stood warming himself before the fire.

"Ellen Draggletail told she must behave herself better, or she'll get no more ginger," continued the clerk.

"Ah, but did you see them at Heathhanger Bridge?" asked the major: "I don't think I ever saw hounds behave better."

"January 3.—Mark Scrimagour received into the house at four o'clock without any hat, and a pair of shocking bad breeches—lent him a cap and a pair of union trousers," read the clerk.

"The fox had run the parapet," observed Tinhead, "and when the hounds came up, of course they——"

"January 4.—Mark Scrimagour refused to scour the candle-sticks, because he had not had enough sugar in his milk at breakfast."

"Hang his sugar," snapped Tinhead.

"By the way, Mr. Scott, what got you?" inquired the all-important Tarquinius Muff, throwing open his blue paletot, and displaying an acre of chest, bespangled with studs and encircled with chains. "I thought you were one of the 'never-say-die' sort," continued he—"a regular *sacré matin* man for the *chasse*, as the French say."

The hounds had had good sport, an hour and twenty minutes

one day, and a very sharp twenty minutes the second ; and if
Tom had had an hour and twenty minutes to compose it in,
he'd have said something to Muff as sharp as the last run ; as
it was, he parried his importunities by pretending to be
desperately busy with the accounts, inwardly resolving not to
give him a chance of crowing over him another time.

The foregoing took place on a Wednesday, and an opportunity
was afforded on the Friday. Mr. Neville always advertises his
hounds, in doubtful times, putting " weather permitting " at
the top of the advertisement. This is a good plan, for though
masters may say that it is always understood they hunt the last
advertised meets, or meet at the kennel the first hunting day,
we can assure them there is no such regular understanding in
the world, and people don't like running the double chance of
"weather permitting," and hounds being " somewhere else "
too.   Advertising costs nothing ; the trouble to " masters " is a
mere trifle, while the convenience to the country is very great.
Localities vary so.   The frost sometimes strikes a particular
district, while a neighbouring one is wholly untouched.   We
have seen a difference of three weeks' hunting between adjoining countries—hounds being at a stand-still in the one, while
they were going on, with sport too, in the other.   Sea-side
tracts are often quite huntable, while inland and particularly
upland regions, are perfectly unrideable.   Again, we have seen
the reverse of this.   We have seen a sea-side country bound up
in iron frost, while hounds met, hunted, had sport, ay and
killed their fox, ten miles inland.   At least we were told so, for
we didn't go to see.   It was rather a singular circumstance, for
we got within four miles of the meet before we turned back,
having got our horse from the groom, who had turned too.
The ground certainly was so hard where we changed that we
could scarcely find fault with the man for turning ; but being
so far on the road, and the horse wanting work, we thought we
might as well go on, which we did, till we came to the house of
a friend, who persuaded us it was perfectly ridiculous going ;

the meet being the highest, coldest, bleakest, most frost-
catching place in the world. He wouldn't go for any money.
So we sat an hour or two with him, in the course of which
the horse caught cold, and we returned home with a sore
throat.

These sudden changes and capricious visitations defy all
calculation. The only serviceable observation that can be
made, is the situation of the kennel, and whether it is in a
country liable to be suddenly frost-stricken or not, so as to
prevent hounds leaving it : for though hounds may be
entrapped into a frosty country out of a soft one, yet there is
seldom much chance of their leaving a frosty one in search of
a soft one. " *Too hard*," the huntsman will say the first thing
in the morning, and that settles the business of the day.

It is odd that few days are so bad but that some one will
appear at an advertised meet. Even though they go sliding and
skating at the imminent risk of their limbs, if they mount
their scarlets, they will mount their horses too. They get their
rides at all events, and their horses exercised ; and even should
the hounds come, they know *they* have no occasion to ride a
yard unless they like. It is another matter, however, with
the huntsman and whips. They *must* follow their hounds,
and despite the cavillings and grumblings of fault-pickers and
hole-finders, we maintain that hounds far oftener throw off
when they should not than refuse when they ought.

There is no pleasure in hunting in a frost. None whatever.
Far better stay at home, and read the " Post Office Directory,'
" Annual Register," or any work that is not encumbered with
a plot, than go picking one's ground so as to keep where the
sun has struck, leaving a yard measure behind each hoof on
pulling up. Men who leave their homes for the purpose of
hunting must occupy their time in some way or other, and
those who can't read are perhaps excusable in accompanying
hounds. It is of no use contending with the elements. It is
poor work shivering at a meet. calculating whether hounds will

come or not—magnifying old women's red petticoats into
" pinks," and flocks of sheep into hounds.

There is a sort of desolation attending doubtful days, unlike
the concomitants of regular seasonable hunting ones.   Long
before one gets to the meet—whatever country it may be in—
one sees something indicative of hunting on a real hunting
day.   A lad riding faster than his horse, a countryman with a
stick, pacing along at a very different rate to what he would
be going if he were carrying a message from his master ; the
imprints of light-shod horses on the grassy road sidings, or
careful grooms clustering at the doors of the Red Lion or
Barleymow, taking their early glasses as they loiter to cover ;
but on a doubtful frosty morning, all doors are closed, no one
turns out that can help it ; master rides his own horse on, and
saunters round by the farm, or the factotum's, or some place or
other to kill time and see what effect the sun has as he goes.
If you arrive at the meet at the right time, the chances are
there is nobody there, and you begin to fear you have mistaken
the day.   The children stare with astonishment ; and one urchin
bolder than the rest at length ventures to ask if the " hunds
be a coomin to-day ? "   That's just what *you* want to know.
A quarter of an hour elapses and still no symptoms of hunting.
Your watch perhaps may have stolen a march, or the clocks
may vary.   If it's at a village, however, the clocks presently
undeceive you.   A miller comes past, riding on his sacks ;
you ask him where the hounds come to when they meet there,
and he assures you he knows nothing about them—millers
never do—they are the most uninformed race of men under
the sun.   Some people, however, have the knack of knowing
nothing, and the way they preserve their ignorance is truly
astonishing : they should have a patent for it.   " Ar doan't
know "—" Ar carn't tell "—are the invariable drawls after a
good stare.   Ask a cockney boy where such a street is, and he
tells you in a minute, or slangs you well ; but a yokel can't
declare his ignorance without exposing his stupidity.

But we are reversing the order of things, and converting a real Tom Scott day into an imaginary one, instead of making an imaginary day look as much like a real one as possible. We began by deprecating doubtful days, and showed how Tom had missed two runs during the brief interregnum of January by adhering to the doctrine, and now we propose showing, a very common case if people would but admit it, how Tom was piqued into going by a man—a gentleman we should say—of whose hunting capabilities he has no great opinion. Mr. Neville's Hounds met on this day at the village of Thornfield, on the north side of their country, not a bad rough sort of meet, and one whose woodlands are favourable and accommodating for hounds, especially in frosty weather. Still it is a place Tom very seldom goes to, nor would he have thought of it, but for the crowings of Tarquinius Muff, and the fear of giving him another opportunity. Independently of that, Tom had employed some of his leisure frost in riding over to Snailswell once or twice, and though we are not at liberty to mention (except in strict confidence, of course) what passed between the fair Lydia and him, yet we may say, that it had been so far satisfactory as to induce him to make a fresh appointment at each leaving. " I'll ride over again on Sunday," or " I'll look in upon you again as I'm passing to Edge-Hill on Monday," he would say, for he carried on the courtship more by " innuendo " than by the old point blank, " If you love me as I love you," &c. Indeed, to tell the truth, Tom is rather a cautious cock, and thought if he could but get his own consent, that of the lady would follow as a matter of course. We have already hinted that she would not have any money, but this deficiency Tom had at length induced himself to overlook ; but thinking that a woman who was to be a " fortune in herself," ought to be sound and all right, he had lately stuck at the matter of her teeth, whose beautiful pearly whiteness he thought " too good to stand." Upon this point he determined to take the opinion of his friend Mrs. Sylvanus Bluff, a lady great in the medical art, and it was until her decision was obtained that he now hung "off." All that, however, will hereafter more fully and at large appear, as the lawyers say, though we believe if the frost had lasted steadily, Tom would have dropped quietly into an engagement, an offer at all events, for the visits were getting both more frequent and longer,

OUR OLD FRIEND DOCTOR PODGERS.

when the upbraidings of Muff nettled him into taking advantage of an apparent change in the weather.

So now to the day named at the head of the page. The previous one felt like frost, and the morning of this one was decidedly frosty, but having been called for hunting Tom got up, and having got up he got breakfast, and having got breakfast he got on to his horse, and though his hoofs made that ringing sort of sound peculiar to horses and well-built London carriages on hard roads, he speculated on the influence of the sun and the favourableness of the woodland bottoms, and proceeded on his road as we have described up to the conversation with the miller. Therefore that part of the sketch may stand as "part of the bill."

As the miller slouched out of sight, and Scott rode backwards and forwards on the village bridge, a pair of leather breeches hove in sight—not the genteel cream-coloured things of modern times, but a pair of good old-fashioned yellow ochres, whose owner was further encased in a black dress coat, a black satin stock, and dingy lack-lustre boots.

It was our old friend Doctor Podgers, on his fat black pony, master and nag counterparts of each other.

On ordinary occasions a doctor may be in boots and breeches without signifying a hunt, but a rich grandfather-looking silver-mounted hunting whip, and a ribbon to his shaved black hat, committed him beyond all extrication.

" Good morning, Doctor," said Scott ; " do you think the hounds will come ? "

Doctor (raising his hat to the extremity of the ribbon). " Upon my word, sir, I don't know. What do *you* think ? "

" Why, I think so of course, or I shouldn't be here."

" It's very cold. Do you think the frost is going to hold ? " at length Scott asked, rather ashamed of his tartness.

Doctor. " Upon my word, sir, I don't know. What do *you* think ? "

Though a man may "trot" himself into a belief that there will be hunting, the sad reality of " standing " generally produces a candid opinion.

Scott could not but admit that the ground about was very hard, that the atmosphere was very frosty, and the only chance there was of hounds coming seemed to be the possibility that it might not be quite so hard or so frosty in the neighbourhood of the kennel.

The only alleviating circumstance there is in a case of non-hunting is the coming of the hounds, which shows that a man is not so wide of the mark as he would otherwise appear.

Indeed, it almost amounts to a case of " big foolism " being
there without them, and Scott strained his eyes and cocked his
ears up the Gunnerton Road, in hopes of seeing them or of hearing one of those knowing notes that fall so musically on the ear,
so symptomatic of hunting, so unmistakable for anything else.

It was all in vain.

There was a crack of a whip, but it was a cartman's—there
was a holloa, but it was from a boy frightening crows. There
is no more similarity between these and the genu*ine* thing than
there is between the jovial mirth of the village school broke
loose upon the green and the determined tallyho of the man
who has been thrown into convulsions by viewing the fox.

Scott began to be rather ashamed of having come, especially
as he could not but feel (though of course he would not admit
it to anybody) that he had been rather " talked into it " by
Tarquinius Muff.

Just as he thought of Muff, his other greatest abhorrence of
life, Dolores Brown of Bleakhope, cast up.

There are some people in the world whose looks or whose
manners are so melancholily lugubrious as to make one
unhappy to see them, and Dolores combines both these unfortunate qualities. He is the most unhappy-looking wretch
that ever was seen. He is a sort of ill-omened bird, for
people say they never have sport when he is out. Some
people's jolly good-natured phizzes set one agog and cheer one
up, but Dolores never does anything but depress the spirits.
It isn't his nasty looks alone, but he is an ill-conditioned
creature into the bargain. Nobody ever heard him say a good
word of any one without his adding as much spite as counter-
acted the praise. He may be called a praising detractor, only
he does much more in the detracting than in the praising line.
He is a grumbling, dissatisfied, cantankerous animal, never
happy but when he's miserable. He has always some fault to
find, some hole to pick, or some misfortune to forebode. The
master of the hounds is generally his stock victim. He, poor

man ! never does anything right. After the master, the huntsman comes in for his maledictions, and then the whip. It is
gratifying to know that Mrs. Brown takes her " change " out of
him at home. There, he daren't say his " soul's his own," and
we have often heard it suggested that he comes out hunting to
escape her. Whatever his motive may be, it is a frequent
observation that Dolores Brown never brings luck. A doubtful day seems just the sort of one for him to cast upon.

If we had a Daguerreotype machine we would sketch him
as he sits under the stunted, crooked, decaying ash tree, and
impale him on our page ; but that not being practicable and
our friend " Phiz " not being at hand, we will just do what we
can with the pen.

Dolores is a farmer—a large farmer—he keeps four or five
draughts, and has two or three thousand sheep herding on the
downs about his appropriately-named residence of " Bleakhope "—one of the highest, coldest, most exposed places in the
country. Still, as if by a frolic of nature, there is some good
land upon it, and, cold as he looks, Dolores is supposed to be
warm. To look at his nasty, lank, straggling, sandy-coloured
hair, impoverished whiskers, and clay-coloured cheeks, you
would fancy he was the follower of some noisome trade instead
of a wholesome out-of-door-living farmer. He may be any age
from thirty to fifty ; indeed, one often sees far fresher-looking
men at sixty or even seventy. His features are harsh and
sharp, and there is a cunning watchfulness about his little
watery grey eyes.

His clothes are as unwholesome looking as his person. His
napless, low-crowned hat is all glue-stained round the band, the
marks widening out in front into a thing like a chimney-
sweeper's badge. The frost makes the hat's browning hue
more apparent. A good hat is about the only thing that looks
well on a frosty day, and if anything will bring a thaw it surely
is the temptation a new one offers to Jupiter Pluvius.
Dolores' coarse draggling gills are guileless of starch, and his

washed-out, blue-striped neckcloth, dirty, twisted, and knotted into what the French call a " Tyburn tye," exposes, rather than covers, his long scraggy neck. The greasy collar of a browning black cut-away coat, and the frayed top of a shabby striped waistcoat, appear above a seedy, well-worn brown tweed, slightly slit up behind for the saddle, and covering the greater part of the hard, crackey-looking patent cords, and almost black top-boots in which his spindle shanks are shrouded.

His horse was a bay, until it was clipped and singed into a dun-duckety sort of mud colour. The cold makes the uneven jagging of the scissors and the blotches of the singer more apparent, for badly clipped greys are the only horses that will stand the searching investigation of a frosty day. This horse is a sour - headed, sunk - eyed, cock-throppled, ewe-necked, ragged-maned beggar, though with some apparent breeding about him. Light feeding seems the order of the day both with horse and master, and despite the laziness of the season, Dolores has contrived, by the substitution of bran mashes and boiled turnips for corn, to keep his horse's girth in much the same moderate compass as his own. Between its ragged, rubbed-out tail and Dolores' shabby, straggling locks there is a striking resemblance, and altogether, what with the bother of the little doctor, the nastiness of Dolores, and the unpromising appearance of the day, we hope the considerate reader will excuse Tom Scott slipping up to the sign of the " Haymaker " to get a glass of brandy and water.

*   *   *   *   *

Hark ! here come horses ! Three red coats heave in sight on the sheep-walk road, visible as they pass the gaps and bits of walls built into the ragged hedge, where the village and pedestrian depredations have extinguished all hopes of the quicks being permitted to grow.

The sight of red coats is cheering. " No knowing but the hounds may come yet," said Scott to himself, as he returned, feeling like a giant refreshed, " throw off, have a glorious run, old Dolores be trundled into a black bog, and the hounds run into their fox on the hill above Hawbuck Grange."

" The horses' hoofs sound louder than I like," continued he, cocking his ear to the east wind, " forbiddingly keen ; " but no sportsman ever forgets that the celebrated Billesden Coplow run took place under similar unfavourable circumstances.

The tramp of horses approaches.

What a noise the riders make ! Their jabber sounds on the clear frosty air as if they were close by, though they are still a quarter of a mile off. " Hah ! hah ! hah ! " what a laugh. There it is again ! " Haw ! haw ! haw ! " deeper and deeper still. " He ! he ! he ! " a third volley. The hounds must be coming, and they know it. There goes the baccy ! Smoking and all. How clear that puff by the gate curled up in the pure air : Lord, how they laugh ! That must be a capital joke, for they are all " haw ! haw ! hawing ! " together. Who can they be ?

" As I live," exclaimed our friend Scott, " the Muffs, and old Tom Tinhead ! "

Fortunately Scott made the discovery just in time to enable him to slip back to the sign of the " Haymaker," from the cow-shed at the end of which he surveyed the scene and overheard the conversation.

Up came great " Muff Tarquinius," as Trumper calls him, full fig, in a spick and span hat, new bright scarlet coat, with the corner of a white cambric handkerchief peeping out of the breast pocket, a sky-blue satin cravat, embroidered with roses and lilies, a roll collar waistcoat, most unexceptionable leathers, and shining jack boots, set off with bright heavy spurs, running most desperately to neck. Tarquinius Muff is an immense man ; we dare say he rides eighteen stone, and sits full souse on his horse, for all the world like a five thousand a year man, as he is. Could he have been certain that the hounds would not come he would not have had a care, in the world, for

he was " got up " for the drawing-room and not for the cover
side. Just the man for a frosty day.

Bad as old Muff is we really think he is better than his
brother, Blatheremskite. Blatheremskite affects the coachman ; but his favourite " Rover " and " Telegraph " being off
the road, he mourns their glories in the dress of a coachman,
which he cleverly adapts to all the pursuits of life. His
shining silk hat is " as round as a cheese, and as flat as a
flounder." His hair is close-cropped, and his white shawl
cravat is secured by a massive gold coach-and-four pin, forcing
its way above the step collar of his long, coachman-cut, rough,
drab velvety - looking waistcoat, with a double row of flap
pockets. His stout, india-rubber cloth, strait-cut, cuffless
scarlet, is a compound of stitching, back strapping, and flaps.
The narrow collar has a strong double hem, the seams behind
are back strapped, and there is a curious device of strength
just above the waist buttons, looking as though he expected a
trial of strength with the garment generally, or a game of
"pull devil, pull baker," with the laps. The outside pockets
are guarded with ample double-stitched flaps, out of the mouth
of one of which what he would call a " bird's eye fogle '
appears, while the other has got a decided drag downwards
from the frequent occupation of his hand. The front buttons
are firmly set in on a separate strip of cloth, and about the
centre of the breast is a small sort of watch-pocket, as if he
had to time himself constantly. The broad greenish-coloured
patent cord breeches, buttoning in front with mother-of-pearl
buttons, come a long way down the leg, where they at last meet
a pair of receding tops, the length of the breeches and the
shortness of the boots producing the observation from Tom
Bowles, the first whip and wag of the hunt, that " he supposed
Mr. Blatheremskite paid double price for one and half price for
the other." The long tops are of the roseate tint, and the
thick double soles are of a texture to resist any quantity of wet ;
all very well for a coachman paddling about a coach in sloppy

weather, but perfectly unnecessary for even the most inveterate "leader over" of a fox-hunter. His action, as well as his dress, is that of the coachman. He holds his reins, and works his arms, as if he were on the box ; and, altogether, he is about as great a snob as the great historian of "Snobs" himself could wish to draw.

"Hallo, doctor!" exclaimed Muff to our friend of the yellow ochres, as the trio turned into the road, "halloo, doctor! *at it again;* keen dog, keen dog, very."

Doctor Podgers acknowledged the compliment by raising his hat to the limit of the hunting string.

"Where are the hounds?" asked Muff.

"Not come," replied the doctor.

"Not come!" retorted Muff ; "why what's happened?"

"I think it will be the frost," observed an earthstopping game-keeper, touching his hat, and cracking an ice-star with his staff.

"Frost?" exclaimed Muff ; "there's no frost to hurt."

"None whatever!" assented Blatheremskite, breaking an upshot column of smoke against his hat brim.

"Oh, they're *sure* to come," rejoined Muff, after a pause, hoping they wouldn't, adding, "there's no frost in the ground, none whatever."

"It's hard here," observed the gamekeeper, tapping his hob-nailed shoes against the ground.

"Oh, but that will give by twelve o'clock ; see what a sun there is overhead," continued Muff, looking up at the heavens.

"They can't plough," observed the keeper, thinking to clench the argument.

"Ah, that's because they won't," replied Muff, turning to Brown with a "what do you think of the matter, Mr. Brown?"

Of course Brown, like all men at a meet, thought hounds were "sure to come;" but mere opinion not having the effect of drawing them, after about ten minutes consumed in smoking and flopping their arms, the conversation began to take a downhill turn, derogatory to the hounds and their management.

"Well, this is the slowest thing I ever saw in my life," exclaimed Muff, as his fears were quieted on recognising Tom Muffinmouth's face under a hunting cap, instead of that of one of the servants coming as he feared with the dread intelligence that the hounds would be there at twelve.

"Well, this is the slowest thing I ever saw in my life," repeated he, tendering Tom the unusual compliment of a hand ; for Muff tries to combine the courtesy of the candidate with the open frankness of the fox-hunter.

"What ?" inquired Tom, blushing, thinking Muff meant that his new sugar-loaf-shaped cap was the slowest thing he ever saw in his life ; nor would it have been far from the mark if he had said so.

"The hounds not coming," replied Muff, with ill-feigned disgust ; Tom Muffinmouth assented, notwithstanding his blue nose and red-rimmed ears gave striking evidence of the severity of the frost.

"Neville's getting too old," observed Muff, with a toss of the head and flourish of the hand. "One doesn't like to say anything in disparagement of an old man who has been a good one in his time," continued he, "but, between you and I, it's about time he was laid on the shelf."

"Old Ben's all bedavered, too," observed Dolores Brown with a sneer ; "he never rides over a fence if he can get any one to pull it down. He set all my South Downs wrong the other day merely because he wouldn't ride over a hurdle."

With this and similar conversation the next quarter of an hour was beguiled, the perfect incompetence of the whole establishment becoming more clearly developed as the discussion proceeded, until, like Gil Blas's mule, it seemed all faults. A successor, who lived more in the centre of the country (like Muff), was faintly hinted at, and having allowed the discussion to run up to appropriating point, Muff adjourned the meeting, and, attended by his staff, Blatheremskite and Tinhead proceeded to Honeybower Hall to lunch and flirt with the Miss

Oglebys—for, shocking to relate, such is the lamentable desti-
tution of country society, that these fine girls are forced to
tolerate the Muffs, while Tinhead is pawned off on the old lady.

As they disappeared in the distance, Scott came sneaking out
of his hiding-place, intending to be off too, when a joyous
" Yonder they come ! yonder they come ! " diffused pleasure
over the faces of the hitherto disappointed-looking countrymen
who had been losing a day in hopes of a hunt. We always pity
a countryman under such circumstances. Strong must be the
passion for hunting that induces a man to sacrifice his total
income for that day for the pleasure of the chase. " Little
think the great men," as Mr. Canning's friend of humanity
said to the needy knife-grinder, when interrogating him about
his misfortunes, " little think the great men," say we, " mounted
on their spicy steeds, with cigars in their mouths, and good
dinners in view at the end of the day, how much better they
are off than the poor pedestrian, who returns leg-weary and
worn to his home, without even the usual humble fare his
labour would have procured him."

The cynic may say he had no business out hunting ; but
sportsmen will take a kinder view of the case, and feel for the
man whose ardour has carried him into a pleasure that he cannot afford. Let sportsmen do more ! Let them put their
hands in their pockets and give them a shilling.

Money thus bestowed is not always wasted, as we will prove
by an incident that happened to our friend Scott last season.
He was riding over a half-finished bridge on the " Grand Gammon and Spinach Junction Railway," when the taskmaster,
timekeeper, overlooker, or whatever they call the man in
authority, exclaimed, as the hounds caused the navvies to pause
and look up from their work, " Come ! *drop it at once,* or stick
to it ! " causing a struggle between duty and inclination, end-
ing, however, in the general triumph of duty, and return to the
digging. Two men only out of above forty threw down their
spades, and, mounting their flannels, set off after the hounds.

" You are fond of a hunt then ? " said Scott, as they came running past them.

" 'Deed am I, your honour ! " replied the first, whose good-natured open countenance proclaimed him an Emeralder, even before he spoke.

" Well, then, I'll give you a shilling," said Scott, handing them each one.

" Long life to your honour ! " exclaimed one.

" Sure you're a worshipful jontleman," observed the other.

After crossing the railway they came upon the rich vale of Grassmere, rich in agricultural possessions, lavish in black bogs, and renowned for the width and bottomlessness of its drains. What persuaded old Ben, who was merely going from cover to cover, to cross it, we don't know, but the field were presently at a cut that set the " funkers' nerves a-shaking," as the song says. It wasn't a large place, but it was a deep one, and the three or four first horses breaking the somewhat under-mined banks, it began to look wider and wider, till Tarquinius Muff's famous water-jumper, Harlequin, coming up full tilt, made a regular " stand and deliver," shooting his luckless rider overhead in the muddy water.

Splash, splash, blob, blob, up and down, backwards and forwards, Muff went, now calling out for help, now emptying his hat, now fishing for his whip, now feeling for his gloves, in the dripping, forlorn, drowned-rat, pitiable-looking state of an extinguished exquisite, setting those who had got across laugh-ing, and those who were on the wrong side wishing " they were well over."

There wasn't a man there but whose horse would have taken the cut (according to their own accounts), if Tarquinius's had not set them the example of refusing, and diverting it was to see the half resolute, half timid way some of them rode at it, pretending to " shove," but in reality holding for a crane.

" None but the bold deserve to clear the brook," and unless horse and rider are well agreed upon the point and go at it resolutely, it is far better to tie the whipthong to the snaffle rein, and lead over, or to blob in and out, anything rather than a "stand and deliver," or a mutual recumbency in the bottom. We don't know a more humiliating sight than a man " rocking-horsing it " in a brook—now the head up, now the tail, now the tail, and now the head—till they either struggle out (perhaps on the wrong side), or part company, the horse perhaps setting off on an expedition of its own to discover the source or defluxion of the stream.

Scott was riding the "young-un," the chestnut, a sweet horse, well worth a hundred to any of our readers, but with the common complaint of well-bred young-uns—*rayther* given to bucking at water. In getting away from Coldbrook Gorse one day after just two rounds that showed there was a rare scent, and the crash and music of the bitches had raised any little remnant of pluck to its highest pitch, when, careering down the grass-field on the north side of the cover, Scott came upon Tarquinius Muff's former bed of roses before he knew where he was. He was up in his stirrups though, and seeing master Reynard travelling away at a very business-like pace over a famous large pasture, he dropped the " Vincents " into the young-un, giving him a shake of the head, as much as to say, " Look what you're after."

Down they came upon the brook.

Tom thought nothing in the world could prevent their being over, when, lo! up bucked the young-un, Tom doesn't know how high, and dropped right into the middle of it. If he had only stretched himself to the extent that he rose, he would have cleared two such places.

But we will draw the curtain over the remainder of that scene, and proceed to " Brook No. 2."

With a lively recollection of the misfortunes of No. 1, Tom contemplated the scene at No. 2 with anything but pleasurable emotions.

The " young-un " had not seen water since his immersion,

HE SENT HIM FLYING BEYOND THE FOREMOST HOOF-MARK.

[*To face page* 174.

though he set up his back and snorted as he came up as if he had a perfect recollection of it. Cold-blooded water leaping, especially on a cold day, is always to be deprecated, and Tom was just going to practise what we preach, by knotting the point of his whip to the rein, and leading over, with "lots of line," when his Irish friend nudged his elbow.

"Sure, your honour, I'll ride him over for you," said Paddy.

"Will you?" said Scott; "but are you sure you can ride?"

"Arrah, by Jasus, and is it myself you ax that question on? Sure I was groom to the great Squire O something, of O something Castle, who kept a stud of forty horses, besides milch cows, and a dacent sprinkling of pigs."

With this his friend began poking his high-low into the stirrup, and having got the reins clubbed in his hand, in the true "hang-on-by-the-head" style, he was presently in the saddle, and turned away to get a run at the brook, so as to take it flying. And very flying-like he looked, his wild hair stragling away from beneath a muffin cap, his loose flannel jacket filling with wind, and his red and green garter ends flowing about the saddle flaps as he went.

Having taken a liberal distance, he forthwith began kicking and talking to the horse, increasing his speed and raising his voice as he went till he got him full gallop, when, with a flourish of his arm and a wild *hier-r-r-o-s-h* sort of shout, he sent him flying many feet beyond the foremost hoof-mark across the cut.

"Ride mine over, Paddy! and I'll give you a shilling!"

"Ride mine over, Paddy, and I'll give you half-a-crown!" shouted several.

"Sure but I'll be losing the hunt if I do," replied Pat, dismounting and running away.

There's a long story by way of parenthesis, supposed to be told on a frosty morning while waiting for hounds. We had just got to the outburst of joy that proceeded from the group

of pedestrians as old Ben and the hounds appeared, rounding
Wenburg Hill in the distance, after giving the field a somewhat
long wait, that looked very like not coming. The bustling
pace at which they approached, while it looked very like business, would have cut our story through in the middle, if we had
been allowed no longer time for the telling it than intervened
between the view and the arrival.

"Gently, Rantipole ! *hie back !* " rated Tom Bowles, as
Rantipole dashed in advance to seek for her master in the
crowd.

"Here again, hounds, here again ! " exclaimed old Ben, with
a whistle and wave of his hand, pulling up short at a gate to
take the hounds into a grass field.

"Good morning, Ben," said Scott, thinking that looked like
throwing off—"What are you going to do ? "

"Oh, I suppose we shall hunt, Sir," said Ben quite gaily,
with a touch of his cap as he spoke.

"Is Mr. Neville coming ? " asked Scott.

"No, Sir, but he said we had to hunt, if we could. It'll do
the hounds no harm."

"Foxes nouther," observed Tom Bowles.

"Tom Scott nouther," added our hero, cheered by the
intelligence.

"We hav'n't been here since cub-hunting," observed Ben,
"and the foxes want routing out sadly. There were three
litters hereabouts, and the farmers are beginning to complain
of the poultry. In such a season as this we must just take
every day we can get."

"It's a bad season," observed Scott.

"*Shocking !* " rejoined Ben, with a solemn look and shake of
the head.

"I see the sessions are coming on," observed Tom Bowles,
"and they are advertising for people to send instructions for
indicting prisoners. I wish some one would send instructions
for indicting the weather. Talk about ether," added he, "for

cutting folk's heads off when they're asleep, without hurtin' of
them, I wish they'd etherise me, and let me sleep during a
frost."

It is odd how people "turn up" at a meet of hounds, let
the hour be what it will. The select party had not consumed
above five minutes in this sort of conversation before half-a-
dozen horsemen of one sort and another appeared.

Tom Griston and Giles Clapgate, both farmers, turned out of
the Falcon, while Mr. Sheepskin of Bossall and Mr. Randall
of Reay came riding together, and then there was Tom Muffinmouth, and Podgers, and the earth-stopping gamekeeper, who
had now got upon his pony. Best of all, Dolores Brown had
taken his departure in the wake of the Muffs, the whole swear-
ing that hounds not coming was the "slowest thing" they
ever saw in their lives.

"Well I suppose we may as well be going," observed Ben,
eyeing the workpeople going home to their dinners, adding,
"it's twelve o'clock by these clocks, it seems, though I should
say it was half past twelve by the day."

So saying, he whistled his hounds together, and trotted out
of the field to the cover.

This was a chain of woodlands, beginning at the village of
Thornfield, and stretching into a wider range about two miles
further on, where a wild and broken sort of country intervenes
between the vales. Rossington Wood comes in here, a sort of
amphitheatre, formed of wooded hills round an area of warm,
well-cultivated land, just the sort of place for a doubtful day.
In went the hounds.

They had not been in cover ten minutes before Tom Scott
saw by the increased motion of Ben's shoulders and heels, that
there was a scent afloat, though no hound as yet having spoke,
Ben did not care to break the silence.

At last, a low short whimper, more of a catch than a note,
brought out a "*have at him*, Brilliant, old boy!" and presently
Brilliant threw his tongue in a downright "I'll stake-my-

reputation-there's-a-fox " sort of way, that convinced Ben there was one, though none of the others taking it up, Mr. Sheepskin, the solicitor, hinted that it was in consequence of Ben's cheer, and muttered something about its "not being right to lead hounds in that way."

Brilliant presently dropped another note still deeper, that old Ben cheered to the echo ; and first one and then another joined in the proclamation, upon which Sheepskin observed, " if there wasn't a fox they ought all to be *sus. per col.*"

" *Hoic ! hoic ! forrard ! forrard !* " screamed old Ben, and with one twang of the horn he went scrambling and tearing through the wood regardless of branches, briars, breeches, and boots.

What a crash they made ! There were five-and-twenty couple of hounds, and every hound throwing his tongue, making the woods echo and re-echo to their music.

They soon got to where the full width of the woods made it advisable to keep inside, when the softness and splashiness of the rides satisfied Tom Scott that old Ben had done right in throwing off. The horses sunk in the ground as they went, and threw the clay and mud about in a manner that was quite delightful considering the frost. Scott got stained in a way that would have done credit to November, and Sheepskin's great splay-footed black horse put his foot in a trod that sent the yellow water squirting up into his master's face, and nearly blinded him.

" You've got six-and-eight pence worth there, I think, Sir," said Tom Bowles, cantering past, as Sheepskin sat mopping his face, dyeing a cheap white silk handkerchief yellow.

How much finer, wilder, and more natural is the cry of hounds in a large, resounding wood, than the close, suppressed muffle from a small, confined gorse. Artificial covers are doubtless useful, but they detract sadly from the fine, riotous spirit of hunting. Our friends had a rare chivey to-day. We don't know how many foxes they viewed, but if the hounds changed they must have done it very quickly, for they were never off their noses. It takes a good deal of persuasion to induce a fox to leave a wood of several hundred acres, especially a wood where the travelling is more favourable to him than to the hounds, and possibly nothing but the fact of his having been hunted before, and being about as good a judge of pace as a Newmarket " tout," could have induced him to be satisfied with the two rings that he made of the amphitheatrish ground before he proceeded up the Dean to the west of it.

There he was viewed by the foot people, " an enormous big-un ! " and " dead beat," of course ; and as he was getting into more circumventable covers, and the scent was first-rate, Mr. Sheepskin expressed his opinion that he was as good as " realised."

It is seldom that anybody says a good word for a fox, but this certainly was a most accommodating one ; for instead of taking the high ground, and sending the field skating and sliding about at the risk of their limbs, he ran the bottoms, and those he selected with considerable judgment. He took them up Apedale Dean, through the Buckland Bog, and past the Decoy at Casterton, scarcely crossing a dozen inclosures the whole way. His line was then Swinbrook Plantations, where he hung a bit, having been headed by some shooters, and probably driven from his point, for he took down the little valley of the Dingle, and was presently into Hardingham Plantation.

One loses one's latitude and longitude so desperately out hunting, especially in cover, that Scott had no idea which side of the plantations they came out at, or where they were going, further than that some well-hung green gates, and better cultivated land, betokened prosperity.

They clattered through the gates, making the hard ground resound with their horses' hoofs, while the frosty air was filled with the cry of the pack, now running frantic for blood.

The nimble and accommodatingly disposed reader will now

perhaps have the kindness to transport him or herself
to Honeybower Hall, and imagine the Muffs palavering
the young ladies, while old Tom Tinhead is billeted on
"Mamma."

We need not trouble them with their balderdash ; how they
abused "old Neville," and ridiculed the idea of hounds not
coming, and how Tarquinius talked of "taking the country
himself if they didn't make him represent it," and so on, as
being matter quite as easily imagined as described. For that
piece of leniency, however, we must request the reader—
non-luncheon eater though he* may be—to accompany the
party to the parlour, where the usual savoury hashes are
commingled with jellies, roast potatoes, and cold fowls—
Hie-sos-sos-sos-sos !

" *Hark !* " exclaimed Muff in the middle of a merry
thought : " I thought I heard the horn," continued he,
rising and going to the bay window which opens to the
ground.

Muff was right. It was old Ben sounding a *requiem* over
his fox in the park on the east side of the hall, a view that
never having taken of it before caused Scott not to recognise
it, till Muff stepped out of the window on to the lawn.

" Why, there's Mr. Muff ! " exclaimed our friend as he
recognised Muff's great white stomach between his black jacks
and red coat.

" So it is ! " replied Ben. " This will be Honey-bower
Hall, I dare say," observed he, looking at the house, with the
right of entry air of a Fox-hunter.

Ben had now got the brush and head in hand, and the pads
being distributed, up went the fox and down it came rolling
right into the jaws of the whole fifty hounds.

" *Who-hoop ! tear him and eat him ! Who-hoop !* "

---

* Ladies are always luncheon eaters, so we need not put "she"
here.

Muff refuses the Brush

" I'll tell you what, Tom," said Scott to the whip as soon as the latter had satisfied himself with hooping and screeching while the hounds worried the fox, " I'll tell you what, I'll give you a guinea if you'll go and present Mr. Tarquinius Muff with the brush," pointing to Muff as he stood at the window, surrounded by the ladies, like a cock of the midden.

" I'll soon do that for nothing," replied Tom, taking the brush from the huntsman, and shuffling away in the crab-like fashion of a whipper-in, up to the house.

       *   *   *   *   *

" Please, sir," said he, touching his cap, as he saw a frown o'erspreading Muff's ample face instead of the smile that usually irradiates a man about to be honoured. " Please, sir, Ben has made free to send you the brush, and is sorry you've missed the run."

"*Is he ?*" sneered Muff. " I feel much flattered by his condescension," at the same time sticking his hands under his coat-tails to remove all idea of his accepting the offer.

" Pray where is Mr. Neville ? " asked he, after a pause.

" He's not out, sir," replied Tom, with another touch of the cap.

" *Not out !* " exclaimed Muff. " You don't mean to say you've thrown off without him ? "

" Master said we were to hunt if we could, and there was anybody there."

" Well, and who have you had ? " asked Muff.

" Oh, there's Mr. Scott, and Mr. Sheepskin, and Mr Brown, and Mr. Randall of Reay, and several others," replied Tom.

" They are not owners of covers, I think," snapped Muff.

" Hazelhanger belongs to Mr. Scott," observed Bowles.

" Well, you know your orders best," observed Muff

pompously, "but if you were my servants, I should say you
had done extremely wrong in throwing off on such a day,
especially to such a field, disturbing such an extent of
country;" whereupon he gave a loud *hem*, and returned with
the ladies to the luncheon, repeating as he went, "*extremely
wrong, indeed!*"

" Vain his attempt who strives to please them all!"

CHAPTER XII.

THE BAD MEET.

" OH ! yau—au—Neville's at the chase. Monday," puffed great Captain Rasher through a mouthful of mustachios in his barrack-room at Scrapetin, as he read the county paper. " *Sha'n't go*—never get a run—confounded woodland place— up to one's horse's hocks all the day in mud and clay—bad for curbs "—with which observation the man of war settled the matter ; and being the hunting authority of the regiment, of course all the subs followed suit. Lieutenant Scrimagour denounced it as the most uncivilised place that ever was seen ; and little Cornet Muttonjaw, who is just weaned and entered to hunting, swore " *he* wouldn't go if anybody would lend him a horse and give him five pounds into the bargain."

So they settled the matter in barracks.

" I sha'n't hunt to-morrow, William," said Tarquinius Muff, strutting into his stable at the four o'clock feeding time, with his friend old Major Tinhead, to show off his stud. It's the most confounded nasty place to get away from that ever was seen, and a very likely one for an accident. Strip that horse Tom," said Muff to helper No. 1, who had just replaced the clothing, " and let the major see him."

" *There !* " exclaimed Muff, as the lad swept the highly-finished richly-lettered clothing over the horse's quarters again. " *There,*" repeated he, extending his right arm, " I call that shape. You may go up to him," continued he, seeing the major stand in the vacant way people do when called upon to admire a horse in a stable, " you may go up to

him—he's quite quiet ; " whereupon Tinhead availed himself
of Muff's liberality, and squeezed up the stall till he got beside
the servant, when he underwent the usual penalty of spanning
the horse's knee, grasping his pastern, admiring his loins, and
criticising his colour.

Muff then rewarded him by making him do "ditto" by
another, and so on through the five ; four hunters and a hack
being Muff's complement, though one would do all his work.
We need scarcely say that Tinhead is Muff's toadey. He
looks like a toadey—a little shrivelled, parchment-faced,
precise, old-maidish sort of animal, that nine men out of ten
would take a dislike to at first sight without knowing why.

"You may exercise the horse to-morrow, as well as the
mare," said Tom Talkington to his half groom, half flunkey,
"I sha'n't go to that beastly Chase—was nearly smothered in
a bog the last time I was there."

"What horse will you ride to-morrow, sir ? " asked Joe
Beans of his master, Mr. Muffinmouth, as the latter came in
from coursing. "To-morrow ! " exclaimed Muffinmouth, "to-
morrow—what's to-morrow ? "

"The Chase," replied Beans.

"The Chase be hanged," replied Muffinmouth, turning on
his heel as though it were not worth a thought.

Every country has its proscribed meet—its place that
" Nobody thinks of going to," which redeems itself every now
and then by some tremendous run, drawing all the chatterers
back, to be choked off by degrees, and Abbeycroft Chase is the
" beastly place " of Mr. Neville's hunt ; not that it is a bad
place, looking at it as far as the interests of hounds are
concerned, for it is sporting-like and spacious, and lying on
the verge of two countries, is always full of foxes belonging to
each. In short, it is one of those sort of places that require
routing out every fortnight or so, in order to be sure of
finding foxes in the smaller ones. Its great imperfection
undoubtedly is the absence of fences and leaps, which are

hardly compensated for by sundry terrific bogs that dye a red coat black in no time. Still that is not the sort of excitement Capt. Rasher, Cornets Muttonjaw and Shaver, or such like cocks, delight in ; they want a cutting whip, and a line of flags through four miles of stiff country, with a break-back brook in the middle.

Long life and two necks to each of them, say we !

Neither is the out-of-the-way locality of the Chase, nor the wild sylvan beauty of its scenery, attractive to men like the Muffs, who prefer basking in the sunshine of sloping lawns, or the gentle undulations of the deer-stocked parks of turreted towers.

If a large extent of rideable woodland, with wildness and boldness at every step, has any charms for fox-hunters, Abbey-croft Chase ought to rank high ; and though too many foxes undoubtedly lead to changing, still if hounds have the luck to get settled to a good one at starting, and there is anything of a scent, he must either fly or be twisted up in cover.

If it were a favourite place its situation would be convenient for the commingling of the apricot-coloured coats of the Dazzlegoose Hunt with the British scarlet of Mr. Neville's ; but save just after some redeeming run, which is most likely magnified to stag-hunters' measure who, we are sorry to say, often *lie* (under a mistake, of course, as Lord Byron said), they seldom muster more than ten or a dozen, independently of farmers.

But we will take Monday's meet as a sample.

It was almost the first *real* hunting day our friends Tom Scott and Co. had had after the most disreputable season of 1846-7, turned the Tattenham Corner of 1847 and as Tom got on to his hack, he felt the sort of spring glow that almost persuades one into growing. The colt's coat had a kindly glossy hue, which underwent no change on opening the stable door, though he stood immediately opposite. A horse's coat furnishes a pretty good criterion of the state of the atmosphere, far better than one of those curious old instruments in bottles which profess to show everything, though, if they are all like ours, they only show the purchaser's stupidity in buying them.

"The Chase" is an unmeasured fourteen miles from Hawbuck Grange, to do which Tom allows himself two hours and a half. When he got to where the Galton cross-road joins the Hardingham turnpike, he saw by the great splay footmarks on the lifting mud, that the hounds were "on," and he presently got a glimpse of a red coat passing a gap in a plantation beyond. Hounds' feet certainly do not show to advantage in sticky soil, and nobody would have thought that Mr. Neville's round ball-footed dog pack would have left such great slovenly-looking imprints behind them.

The meet was at a beggarly farmhouse just on the confines of the Chase ; a farm that has brought more people on the parish than all the rest of the township put together.

When our friend arrived, he found even Mr. Trumper's attention was drawn from the powerful pack, now stretching and rolling about on the soundest part of the much plunged green, to the picture of misery and desolation before him.

"Did you ever see such a place, Mr. Scott ? " asked Trumper, pointing to the dilapidated house, with the windows pasted over with paper, or stuffed full of straw and old hats. "Just look at those stacks," added he, pointing to three or four crooked half-covered corn stacks, slipping out of their ropes, on which the pigeons, poultry, and sparrows were regaling.

"Good morning, Mr. Trumper," exclaimed Mr. Neville, bustling up on his hack, and shaking hands with our hero ; adding, "I'm very glad to see you out with *my* hounds."

"Thank you, sir," replied Mr. Trumper, making his obeisance.

"And how are *your* hounds going on ? " asked Mr. Neville, for he is one of the few masters of foxhounds who are not jealous of harriers.

"Oh, middling well, sir, thank you," replied Trumper ; "we began our season early, and had some good running up to the end of November, but we've done nothing almost since."

"Nor we," replied Mr. Neville, "nor we ; nothing, at least, to speak of. Runs that we should have thought nothing of last year are magnified into splendid ones this."

"Ay, that'll be your fine pen-and-ink gentlemen, I presume," said Trumper ; adding, "I've been suffering a little in that way myself. I'll goose and dumplin them," continued he, with a shake of the head.

"You've got the old horse still, I see," said Mr. Neville, eyeing our friend Golumpus.

"Ay, the Yorkshire horse," replied Trumper, lifting his long green lap up so as to show the horse's great round barrel, adding, "good horse, *varry.*"

"What a size he is ! " observed Mr. Neville.

"I don't like to be stinted," replied Trumper, quite incontinently.

"I know you don't," rejoined Mr. Neville, with a smile.

"What age is that horse, now ? " inquired Mr. Neville, after a pause.

"He'll be seventeen this grass," replied Trumper. "This is his tenth season, and he's as fresh as a four-year-old."

"You didn't begin riding him till he was seven, I think," observed Mr. Neville.

"He wasn't broke till he was six," replied Trumper, "but then he comes of a good sort—a M'Orville—all the M'Orvilles are natural hunters, and you save a season or two that way. Mr. Muff Tarquinius wanted to buy him," added Trumper ; " indeed he sent his groom for him with a blank cheque for me to fill up, and very much astonished the man was at not getting him away. 'Do you think he is strong enough to carry your master ? ' asked I.

" ' Indeed I *think* he is,' replied the man, cautiously.

" ' Then I think he's strong enough to carry me,' added I ;

' so I won't part with him.' Tarquinius has never been quite friendly with me since," added Trumper.

"Whose horses are those?" asked Mr. Neville of a diminutive tiger who now rode round the corner of the stack-yard with a couple of splendid animals, just as Mr. Neville had exchanged his hack for his hunter.

" My Lord Lazytongs'," replied the lad with a touch of his hat.

" And whose are those?" asked Mr. Neville, as two more hove in sight.

" My Lord Lazytongs', too," replied the speaker.

" What's his lordship going to ride *four?* " asked Mr. Neville, with a smile.

" No, sir, those are for Captain Windeyhash," replied the lad.

" And where are they coming from?" asked Mr. Neville.

" From Dawdle Court, sir," replied the lad. "We are from Newbolt this morning."

"Dawdle Court!" exclaimed Mr. Neville—"why, that's thirty miles off."

" Five-and-twenty, sir," replied the groom, who had now come up, having given the benefit of his superior weight to the Windeyhash detachment.

" *They'll never come,*" whispered Scott, remembering the Ecclesford Green day.

"We must wait a few minutes," observed Mr. Neville, "for gentlemen who are coming so far."

" Is his lordship riding?" asked Mr. Neville of the groom after a pause.

" He comes in the carriage as far as Danebury Hill, sir," replied the man, "where there are hacks waiting to bring him on to Newbolt, and there are fresh ones again at Newbolt."

" Humph," considered Mr. Neville, meditating how long he ought to wait for gentlemen who had made so much preparation.

LORD LIONEL LAZYTONGS.

[*To face page* 188.

" Do you think they'll come ? " asked he, after a pause and a lapse of some minutes.

" Why, I should *think* so, sir," replied the groom. " Our orders were very particular—half-past ten to a minute ; it's a quarter to eleven now," added he, pulling out his watch.

" Is there any one at Dawdle Court ? " asked Mr. Neville.

" Oh, yes, sir ; the house is full of company. Indeed, I know his lordship wants to be back at half-past two, to shoot a match."

" *The deuce he does !* " exclaimed Mr. Neville ; " then I think I'd better throw off, and have a fox on foot for him against he comes." So saying, he gave the usual jerk of his head to old Ben, and the glad pack at length bounded away to Ben's whistle.

" Shoot ! " said Mr. Trumper to Scott, as the latter came alongside, adding—" That's the queerest style of hunting I ever heard of. I should have thought fox-hunting was amusement enough for any man for one day."

Before they reached the first straggling brushwood on the rising ground of the " Chase " that the hounds condescend to draw, a brimstone-coloured coat was seen sailing through the fields below at a very first-rate pace.

" *Crash* " the wearer went through a rotten wattled hurdle ; " *swich* " he divided a live thorn fence ; " down " he sent a row of rails, and so the wearer went careering triumphantly on till he was most ignominiously brought up by a sheep net.

" That'll be my lord," said Mr. Trumper, eyeing his lordship's long legs working away at the nag to make it face the nets. " He'd better leave that game alone," added he, with a shake of the head, as the animal turned tail to the stakes.

Tootle, tootle, tootle ! blew Mr. Neville on his horn, to let his lordship see where the hounds were ; for there was a direct

way up from the enclosures into the chase, through a most
conspicuous new white gate, but Mr. Neville's intimation had
just a contrary effect to what was intended, and converted the
affair of the nets into a sort of " eyes-of-England-are-upon-
you " point of honour. Seeing he was observed, his lordship
was more determined to take the nets, and making a considerable semicircle, he again charged them most stoutly.

No ; deuce a bit ! the horse wouldn't have them, and round
went the tail as before.

A third charge ended in a similar result.

Just as his lordship's hack turned tail for the fourth time,
the biggest fox without any exception, that Tom Scott ever set
eyes on, crossed the glade towards which they were riding in
the most haughty, disdainful, arrogant manner imaginable.
He had his head in the air, and his brush in the air, and went
careering along just like a colt turned into a strange field.
He sniffed the air, and threw his head about, as much as to say,
" What the deuce do you mean, you disorderly dogs, by
disturbing a gentleman in this way ? " As yet nothing but the
horn had been heard.

" *Tallyho !* " screamed Mr. Neville, enlightening him on
the subject, when down went the brush, and away shot the
owner across the open, amid the tallyhos, and screams, and
screeches of the field, till a friendly copse screened him from
view.

How the dog pack made the welkin ring, as they scored to
cry, and every hound owned the scent ! Echo answered echo,
till one might have thought there were a hundred couple of
hounds at work.

" *Moy O-oies !* " exclaimed old Trumper, sucking in the
melody, " but that's *f-o-o-ine*."

Screech ! screech ! went the horn, " crack, crack," went the
whips, but there wasn't the slightest occasion for either, only
servants are afraid if they don't make a noise, people may
think the hounds kill the fox and not they.

They now dived into the thick of the Chase, where lofty forest trees supplied the place of stunted oaks, and crags and rocks appeared hurled promiscuously around.

The riding, though not bad, at least not bad for woodland riding, required a sharp eye both above and below to keep the riders' heads on their shoulders for the trees, and their horses on their legs for the bogs.

The Chase bogs are a very peculiar kind of bog ;* not that nervous, protracted blob, blob, blob, "deeper and deeper still," of moors and heaths, but deep, black, over-head-and-ears-at-once sort of places that a horse should clear in his stride. Some of them are awfully deep, though not very holding, a late occupant looking more like a man out of an inkstand than out of a mud cart. To be sure the places are tolerably marked by the unhealthy green, and yellow, and grey moss on the stunted birch trees, as also by the hassocky ground and coarse reedy grass about, but strangers are seldom satisfied of the real importance of a Chase bog until they have fathomed one After that they ride to a "leader," as they all did to-day. That leader was old Ben, who has a sort of map of the bogs in his head. How he sailed away to be sure, hopping over them just like water furrows, trusting as much to his voice as his reins for making his old mare leap. Horses are much like sheep in the leaping line, when one begins, the rest generally follow ; much in the same strain, too, as will often have been observed by men whose horses have made tremendous leaps over "nothings," merely because the one before them leapt wide. Ben had the best of it, barring the risk, for before they had gone very far, the black daubs, and spots, and stains on the white breeches and ties showed who rode behind and who didn't. It was no time for stopping, however ; indeed we question that any horse worthy the name of a hunter would have submitted to be pulled up with such ravishing music

* "New Foresters."

before him. If he did, we are sure the man on his back
wouldn't deserve to be called a sportsman. *Forrard!* they
went, making every bunny on the ground and tom-tit in the
trees quiver with fear.

We often wonder whether there is such a thing in the
world as a man whose heart wouldn't leap into his mouth at
the sound of a pack of hounds in full cry. We should think
not ; at least, if there is, we should be very sorry to back a
bill for him. To-day would have been a grand one to try him.

None of the field who were out seemed deficient in sporting
spirit, for they went at a pace that might be called truly awful
—awful considering the squire traps, trees, and other contingencies.

There was no time for politeness—no time for saying, "Take
care, sir, or you'll be getting your eyes scratched out," or,
" Mind what you're after, sir, or you'll be getting your head in
your hand ; " it was every man for himself and the mud take
the hindmost. If the hounds ran musically, the field rode
mute. And here let us pause to pay a tribute of respect to dog
packs generally. There is something fine and noble in the
appearance of the great strong animals, and theirs is a far
honester, more substantial, John Bullish style of hunting, than
the quick sharp whimper and cut away of the bitches. The
dogs seem to say to the horses, " Come along, my hearties, and
let us enjoy ourselves together," while the bitches seem as if
they were always wanting to steal a march upon the nags, and
to have all the sport to themselves. The dogs look grand and
noble ; something to " fill the eye," as Trumper says.

Away, away, away the field went, now alongside of the
hounds, now behind, now perhaps a *leetle* before. Reynard
picked his ground with judgment.

A check at last ensued.

*   *   *   *   *

" He's into the enclosure ! " said old Ben, eyeing Brilliant jumping at the high palings—"*yooi over!* they go," hallooed he as a whole bevy of hounds charged the palings in line.

"*He's down!*" cried Ben, holding his hand in the air for silence whilst he listened for the sound of their tongues in the dean.

"They're on him again!" (added he, as a slight whimper burst into full cry).

"*Get together hounds! get together!*" hallooed Tom Bowles, cracking his whip, though there wasn't a straggler to be seen.

"We must be inside," observed Mr. Neville, hustling along with a great patch of black mud on the side of his hat that looked for all the world like a cockade.

"There's a bridle-gate just below," observed Ben, who knows every point and pass in the country.

They were presently at it;—a nasty place it was, too, as most wood bridle-gates are—boggy and plungy, with a pair of most resolute posts for a hot horse to dash his rider's legs against.

"One at a time, and it'll last the longer!" exclaimed Mr. Neville, cocking up his knees to avoid a collision.

"*I'll lead*," observed Mr. Trumper, throwing himself from the now lathered Golumpus.

"Why, what a mess you're in, Beaney!" observed Trumper, eyeing Beanstack's desperately bespattered front.

"Am I?" replied the now purple-faced Beanstack; "I can't be much worse than yourself; look at your breeches!"

The time for estimating dilapidations, however, was not yet come, and having all blobbed through the gateway in some fashion or other, and Mr. Trumper having climbed on to Golumpus again, they now found themselves in a better managed part of the Chase. In lieu of the natural straggling glades and rotten inundations of land, they were among regular grassy rides, diverging in all directions through thriving plantations, whose open bottom afforded every facility to the chase.

The hounds pushed their fox through as straight as an arrow.

" If there's half such a scent in the open as there is in cover," observed Mr. Neville, " we shall have him in hand in ten minutes."

" Hark ! *he's down,*" exclaimed he, as a sudden burst of melody to the left proclaimed the fox had turned at last.

" He *must* break," said Mr. Neville, turning too, " or be killed in cover. Hark ! I believe they have him," added he, as a sudden lull ensued.

*   *   *   *   *

" No, he'll be away," said old Ben, spurring his horse into a canter, and making for the spot ; adding, " I'll be bund he's just slipped back at the woodman's cottage below."

A loud, long, shrill tallyho ! almost instantly confirmed Ben's surmise, and on scuttling away to the gate they found the second whip with his cap in the air, in the high state of excitement lads are generally in who have " viewed the fox."

" *Hoop ! hoop ! hoop !* " screamed he, turning his horse, and sweeping his cap towards the ground on the line the fox had gone.

Out poured the hounds ; crash came Ben, horn in hand, through the wattled fence ; and the scene-shifter having changed the slides, the second act of the drama commenced in the open.

What an open it was, too ! And how the top of the rising ground, up which the fox had gone, favoured the view ! After hugging and holding up the hill, they looked upon the rich vale of Brightwell, the vaunted " crack " of the Dazzlegoose country. Large grazing grounds stretched away in fertile greenness, while what arable land there was showed sound and brown on the surface. There is something fine in running slap into an adjoining country. It is a sort of sporting *foray,* which enables us to compliment our friends on the sport they unwillingly afford us. The old spirit, in fact, that instigated the Pytchley man of old to exclaim to his horse, as the fox went away into Leicestershire—

—————— " Now, Contract," said Dick,
" But we'll show these d—d Quornites the trick."

Loving and sociable as fox hunters undoubtedly are in the aggregate, still there is always a strong feeling of jealousy between neighbouring packs. On this occasion the Dazzle-goose men began to hustle their horses and show in front as the hounds pointed for their vale, as though they thought it incumbent on them to do the honours of the country. "Recumbent"—one of them—Dick Jellyhead—very soon was, for his trouble. The fox having taken the old Swinbrook road, for a couple of hundred yards, which runs parallel with the hills from whence they had all just descended, the hounds, after running that distance nearly mute, suddenly burst into chorus on the grassy side of the road next the vale, and in another instant they flew over the fence, formed of a bank with a hedge on the top, into the adjoining pasture.

The fox had run the inside of the fence, and there was a gate from the road into the field a little before, but Jellyhead, disdaining such chicken-hearted work, pulled his hairy-heeled steed across, and shoved him at the bank.

Perhaps there is not a more promising way of getting a fall than pulling a horse up short, and shoving him away from his companions. Independently of this, Jelly's horse didn't look like a flyer. We don't want to buy him, therefore we have no interest in disparaging him ; but we shall convey an idea of the style of the animal when we say that he was a sort of horse that a dealer would declare "looked solitary without the gig at his tail "—a good machiner ; thirty pounds' worth, perhaps.

One sometimes sees an affinity between rider* and horse ;

---

* Sir Robert Peel, for instance, stamps about on a bay, the counterpart of himself.

indeed we have seen them alike in the face, and between **Jelly**-head and his there was a decided similarity of cut. They were both stout, square, clumsy-made looking creatures, and the broad cut of Jellyhead's laps corresponded with the square dock of the horse's tail. This resemblance was painfully apparent when, having mounted the fence, the laps flew up in response to the tail, the master " spread-eagling " as the horse went down on his head on the far side—a melancholy example of disappointed " show off." Fortunately the ground was soft, or there is no saying but such a head as " Jelly's " even might have suffered.

When the rest of the sportsmen got into the field by the gate, they found him busy pulling his head out of his hat, with the unconcerned air men assume when the crown lies at their feet. The insensate author of the misfortune was grazing quietly at the hedge-row, just as if nothing had happened. This, too, in spite of the hounds pouring up the side of the field, pointing straight into the vale in defiance of all conjectures that the fox was back to the " Chase."

Leaving the open for the vale is like leaving the camp for the thick of the fight ; but no one seemed at all concerned at the change. Even Mr. Trumper, who declines leaping altogether, pounded along on Golumpus, as though he had perfect confidence in getting through. Indeed the field soon resolved themselves into a sort of mutual assistance society, and keeping with the hounds was all they looked to. The rest of the apricot coats took warning by their fellow, and discontinued the pioneering trade.

Good farming is certainly a great promoter of hunting. Instead of high, rough, ragged, briar-choked, water-soughed fences, through which a horse can scarcely bore, and which occupy no end of ground, our friends now got among nice, level, well-laid, well-pleached fences, that a horse could both see his way " on and off." The total absence of hedge-row timber, too, aided the sight, which would otherwise have been rather impeded by the extreme flatness of the land.   What a change of opinion we have seen in the matter of hedge-row timber !   We remember when the wise ones used to counsel a man to stick trees in his fences at every yard, and used to calculate to a fraction what they would be worth at the end of the world ; whereas now " Mechi * and Co." teach us to shave our fences as close as our faces.   All fox hunters are Mechiites in that matter.

The burst of the early part of the chase had now settled down into a good hunting run—not a scent-diminishing run, but a good holding steady pace, that looked like mischief. Every hound threw his tongue, and first one and then another took the lead—a most sporting, mud-stained, varmint-looking, working-like pack they were, as they bustled and carried the scent amongst them—not one would go a yard without it.

When they got upon grass, they ran hard, but master Reynard seemed to have preferred the light land of the fallows, indeed rather to have gone out of his way for them.

This caused a division of opinion as to his point, Mr. Neville fixing Linton Woods, while Ben and Mr. Trumper stood up for the main earths at Castlebar.

These main earths are a drawback upon running a fox into a neighbouring country ; for if he reaches them, there's an end of the matter so far as his brush is concerned ; and a fellow sitting, straddling, and " whohooping," cap in hand, as though he were full of delight, over a main earth, is a poor substitute for the joyous, upstanding, baying of the " fox in hand " of a kill.

Mr. Neville was right, and Trumper gladly acknowledged the superiority of his judgment.   If the fox had any doubt on the point himself, it would appear to have been settled in his

---

* Mr. Mechi, the celebrated cutler of Leadenhall Street, and of Tiptree Hall, in Essex, is one of the great authorities of the day on farming. His " experience in drainage " is excellent.

mind in the course of his progress up a long slip of rubbishing wood, between a turnip field and a fallow ; for on getting to the end of it, he put his head straight for the woods, despite the rising ground over which he had to travel.

" Yonder he goes ! " exclaimed Mr. Neville, viewing him somewhere, though " where " nobody could tell but himself.

Some people have a wonderful knack at viewing foxes, and think those desperately " dunch " who don't see them.

" Where ? " exclaims one.

" Why there—*there to be sure !* " replies the viewer, as if the fox's line, was set out like a railway.

Our friend hadn't much " where "-ing to-day, everybody being satisfied that Mr. Neville knew a fox from a cur, and the hunting of the hounds held out every expectation that they would shortly have a closer inspection of the one they were after. Moreover, a few of the nags had begun to sob, and Mr. Trumper thought it well to take the castle off the elephant, and lead up the hill.

On reaching the rising ground, after easing their horses, grinning and holding on by the manes up the hill, they all saw the fox sailing away down the other side towards the river. Nor did his pace and action give much prospect of speedy relief to the now panting and perspiring steeds. On the contrary, he went high, and though he had lowered his standard, he kept on at an even pace that looked very like lasting.

The hounds hunted him as true as beagles over the wretched starvation land that he had now chosen for his course, stuff that one would be sorry to take at two-and-sixpence an acre. Little advantage was perceptible on either side, so long as they kept on the high land, but when the fox descended, and ran the river margin, the hounds evidently gained upon him, until Dangerous and Hannibal caught view, when, as if by magic, the whole pack flew from their noses to the worry, and rolled one over another with their victim into the river.

" God bless us, what a f-o-i-n-e run ! " exclaimed Mr.

Trumper, pulling up, his horse and himself all running down with sweat. The lathered Golumpus gave himself a hearty shake, as much as to say to his master, " Why don't you get off, you great slush-bucket ? "

Mr. Trumpet then plunged down, and the scraping of his whip-stick under the horse's belly was followed by a regular flow of water.

How different the poor dripping rat-like fox looked as he was brought out of the river to the dashing, staring, brush-whisking, high-going flyer they had started with an hour or so before—an hour, a glorious hour ! What a deal had been compressed into that time ! The field had done a week's work in it.

How variously we estimate time ! We knew a man who went to a dentist's to get his dinner set overhauled, and after having been some twenty minutes in the chair he went away declaring he had been three hours. And he was a man of veracity too, but doubtless calculated the time by the pain. So with a run. The ground we go over, the incidents of each moment, the change of scene, the varieties of pace, all tend to magnify the time—especially if there happen to be two or three checks, when every minute is like a half hour, except when one's nag is rather blown, or there is a big leap that we don't yet see how to avoid.

" One hour and ten minutes, *exactly*," observed Mr. Neville, shutting his gold hunter against his cheek.

" *So*," replied Mr. Trumper, " I thought it had been more."

" Well hunted he was," said Mr. Neville, alighting from his horse.

" *Oh well !* " rejoined Trumper in ecstasies.

" What an old villain he is ! " exclaimed Ben, opening the fox's mouth as he lay distended on the ground. "He's hardly a tooth in his head. He's had many a turkey poult, I'll be bound."

Ben then proceeded to the usual ceremony of decapitation, de-paditation, and brush-i-tation.

" Give me *that !* " said Mr. Neville, as Ben was proceeding to pocket the yet dripping brush.

" Now, Mr. Trumper," said he, wringing it out, " you often send me a very fine hunted hare—let me present you with the brush of the animal I hunt."

" Thank you, sir," said Mr. Trumper, receiving it with a low bow. " I'll put this in a glass case, and write the *partick- lars* below it."

" Ay, you may say it was a ' *tickler,*' " observed Mr. Neville.

" So it was ! " replied Trumper, " a *reglar* one."

The pads were then distributed to Jellyhead and the Dazzle- goose gentlemen, who in the harmony of the kill buried the jealousies of country.

It was carried unanimously that he was a good fox, had shown them a good run, over a good country, and Ben very truly observed, that he was just as likely to be one of Mr. Neville's foxes as one belonging to the Dazzlegoose country.

So the mixed field parted in the greatest harmony.

*   *   *   *   *

Let us now take a glance at the absentees.

" Aw—yaw—aw—they say Neville's had a run," said Captain Rasher, throwing his cap into the corner, as he rolled into the mess-room in the tight-laced ease of a full-figged heavy.

" I don't believe it ! " exclaimed Lieutenant Scrimagour.

" Aw—yaw—aw—why I don't much," said Rasher, twirling his resolute mustachios, a process that he generally has recourse to when short of ideas.

" People tell such lies about hunting," observed Major Tinhead, who had done somebody out of a dinner, it being band day.

" They do," exclaimed little Cornet Muttonjaw.

"LET ME PRESENT YOU WITH THE BRUSH."

[To face page 202.

Captain Rasher demonstrating

" There isn't one man in fifty knows what a run ought to be," said Tinhead.

" Aw—yaw—aw—I defy them to have a run from such a place as that Chase," observed Rasher ; adding, " It suits old Neville and old Ben, and a few old potterers of that sort ; but who the deuce could take any pleasure in such riding ? "

Captain Rasher then resolved the mess table into a model of the country, making the plateau-stand in the centre do duty for the Chase, and the lamps and wine-coolers to represent the Linton Woods, Castlebar earths, and covers generally, from which premises he made the most satisfactory deduction that it was *utterly impossible* for hounds to have a run—a position that he established to the satisfaction of all, just as the tawdry mess-waiter came in with the soup.

Next day Tarquinius Muff having come into town to see his aunt, get his hair cut, or something of that sort, met Rasher in the High Street, sabre-tache swinging, heel-spur ringing, bonnet staring under, as usual, and confirmed the opinion.

The verdicts of the others, our readers will perhaps excuse our entering on the " record."

They were generally delivered in the laconics, " Oh my ! " " No go ! " " Not possible ! " " Won't believe it ! " " Hookey Walker ! " " Tell it to the marines ! " and so on.

We may, however, add, that our friend Tom was so delighted with it, that he wrote a long account of it to his lady-love, instead of one of the three-cornered laconics with which he generally favoured her.

CHAPTER XIII.

THE BLANK DAY.

AT HOME!

IT'S four years since last February, though our friend Tom says he remembers it as if it were but yesterday, so rare are the calamities of blank days in the catalogue of his misfortunes.

The Duke of Tergiversation, having the Prince of Spankerhausen, Mynheer Von Cled, and several other great Dutch swells, whom he wanted "galvanizing," had written to Lord Harry Harkaway to bring his unrivalled hounds to Fast-and-Loose Castle, on that most forlorn of all forlorn speculations, the " chance " of finding a fox.

Dukes are people that generally have their own way, let them be ever so unreasonable ; and even if Lord Harry had been inclined to object to trashing his hounds and horses such a distance, the offer of hospitality to himself and establishment would have caused him to think that he might as well avail himself of the opportunity for paying the duke and duchess a visit.

Accordingly the hounds were advertised to meet at Fast-and-Loose Castle on "their" day of the week, with a non-hunting one on each side of it, though what that day was, we don't pretend to say, dates and distances being things we seldom trouble our head about.

It was the first season of Lord Harry's hunting the country, the hounds having just come out of Yarnshire with the usual high-flown renown of new packs.

Fast - and - Loose Castle, indeed the whole Tergiversation territory, had long been looked upon as extra-parochial in the hunting-line, neither Sir Charles Wildblood nor his predecessor Lord Heavysop ever having thought it worth while to play at drawing his grace's covers a second time. Not but that his grace is a patron of fox-hunting, a patron in his own peculiar way,—just as he is a patron of racing, to uphold which, he keeps two or three wooden-limbed brutes that go the rounds of the district. Fox-hunting he looks upon in much the same light as racing ; a sort of amusement of the hour, that requires no care or consideration during the rest of the year. He therefore gives hounds leave to draw his covers, on certain set days of the season — the 15th of December, the 15th of February, and again on the 15th of April, provided none of those days fall on a Sunday, in which case, the hunt stands adjourned to the Monday.

But the system will develop itself with the narrative.

The talk people make about anything new, especially anything new in the hands of a nobleman, made Tom Scott take a fancy for seeing Lord Harkaway's hounds, and though the distance from Hawbuck Grange is great, five and thirty miles to the kennel, yet the town of Barkeston being within easy distance of the castle, by lying out a couple of nights, he could easily accomplish his object, especially as, like Lord Harry, he

could kill two birds with one stone—get a hunt, and pay a
visit to his old friend the Rev. Peter Blackcoat, the worthy
rector of Barkeston.

Accordingly Tom arranged it so.

It was not until he got to Barkeston that he heard the exact
state of the fox question. His grace having lately made one of
his periodical changes of politics, Tom thought he had very
likely turned over a new leaf in the hunting book too, and that
things were going to be different.

" I am afraid you've come on a forlorn hope," observed Peter
Blackcoat, wringing Tom's hand, as he met him at his neat
parsonage gate.

" How so ? " asked Tom, fearing the whole thing was put
off. " The duke hasn't changed his mind, has he ? "

" Oh, no," replied his friend ; " the thing is to take place ;
that's to say, there's to be a grand spread of a breakfast, cherry
brandy—cheese, and so on—but as to finding a fox, there isn't
such a thing in the parish."

" The deuce there isn't ! " exclaimed Tom ; " then what are
the hounds there for ? "

" Oh, just for the duke to show them to his friends. He's
got a lot of great barge-built Dutchmen there, who can't speak
a word of English, and he'll persuade them that the hounds are
his, and that Lord Harry is a sort of retainer of the castle, and
so they'll go back to the place from whence they come, and tell
all the great boundless burgomasters and fellows what a
tremendous great man the Duke of Tergiversation is."

" The *deuce !* " exclaimed Tom, wishing himself home again.

" Nay, don't look glum," replied the parson, patting the
mare's neck. " I dare say the gamekeeper will manage something in the shape of a fox. All the world will be there, and it
won't do to disappoint a whole country side."

" *Manage something in the shape of a fox, my dear Peter !* "
exclaimed our friend, in disgust. " You don't think a fox is
like a coat, that you can have to order and turn out when you

want it ? Believe me, my dear fellow, a fox is very like what the young ladies, bless them ! say of love; there is but one real love, though there may be a hundred different copies of it ; so there is but one right sort of fox, though there may a hundred imitation ones."

This very philosophical observation brought Tom to his friend's stable door, a comfortable three-stalled edifice, with a gig and harness room adjoining.

We never get into a parsonage house without thinking if it wasn't for writing the weary sermons, we'd like to be a parson ourself. They are always so snug, and have such capital port wine !

But we will pass over the feeding and friendship, and proceed at once to the festival.

Tom's friend said the thing that was true. As he rode away in the morning through the usually quiet little town of Barkeston, all heads were at the windows, those who were to be left behind looking wistfully after those who were going, and one-horse chaises and two-horse chaises were loading and driving away with mirthful parties, to say nothing of an omnibus full inside and out. There were Mrs. and the two Miss Sugarlips in their yellow phaeton, driven by young Mr. Whateley, the rising apothecary ; and there were Mr. Luxford, the bookseller, and "his lady," as the genteel ones call their wives ; Mr. Kidd, the hosier, rode with Mr. Holmes the saddler, while their respective ladies, with some seven or eight children between them, followed in the public "private" landau of the Duke's Arms. The duchess—that is to say, the landlady—had just been confined, and couldn't show. Nevertheless every horse they had, both from the hotel and the farm, was in requisition, and great was the demand for saddles bridles, and tackle generally.

The plot thickened as Tom proceeded until the road swarmed again. More gigs, more horsemen, more horsemen, more gigs, and pedestrians without end.

The most astonishing thing, however, was the appearance of a troop of yeomanry that came jingling and clattering down the Heckfield-lane on to the turnpike, in all the pomp and terror of cart-horse cavalry.

" *Who's dead, and what's to pay ?* " exclaimed Tom Scott, as a most insignificant little officer, almost extinguished by his horse-tailed helmet, was borne against him by a great pulling powerful black mare, who seemed fully intent upon running away with him.

" Co-o-o-m-e and s-s-e-e, old b-o-y," ejaculated the victim pretending to be quite at his ease.

" Why, Billy Bobbinson ! is that you ? you little unfortunate devil ; what have you been about now, that they have dressed you up in that way ? " exclaimed Tom. " Who looks after the shop when you are out soldiering ? " But Billy was deaf to the inquiry, and the troop rattled on as if they were going to quell a rebellion or extinguish a fire at the least. Little thought Tom that they were the Duke of Tergiversation's cavalry going to form a hunting guard of honour on Mynheer Von Cled and Co. !

Our friend Tom had never seen Tergiversation Castle except from the Cockington Fort road, where it is visible in the usual style of castle visibility, towers above trees, and a flag above towers. Its ground dimensions he had no idea of, neither did he care much, seeing he was not likely to be wanted inside.

The castle certainly had a very imposing appearance, when he got the whole concern mustered in one grand view—body, wings, giblets and all. There was great liveliness and animation apparent, both inside and out, quite relieving the austere frownings of the cloisters, and the heavy Gothic architecture of the building.

Powdered footmen, in gorgeous plum - coloured liveries, bedizened with silver lace, with massive covered dishes, pushed their way among "gentlemen's gentlemen" and heavy-looking moustached Dutchmen, who seemed as if they had nothing

THE POMP AND TERROR OF CART-HORSE CAVALRY.

To face page 208.

whatever to do but smoke ; while occasional glimpses of the
" real quality " might be caught through the plate-glass
windows of the receiving rooms, and good steady studies made
of ladies' maids staring out of the windows or disporting themselves on the leads and turrets above.

The spacious court-yard behind presented a curious medley
of war and pastime, soldiers and fox-hunters. The yeomanry
had dismounted, and were busy rectifying the little derange-
ments of dress and appointments incident to the march.
Those whose saddles had threatened to come over their horses'
ears for want of the crupper were now slamming them back in
their places ; others were scraping the frothy sweat off the
stinking, hairy-heeled brutes, while some were combing out the
manes and tails of theirs, by way of trying to make them look a
little decent.　There was a strange contrast between the
cumbrous, misfitting uniforms of the ploughman soldiers, and
the trim neatness of the hunting and stable servants.　Nevertheless, the former seemed very well pleased with themselves,
and clamped and strutted about the yard in their heavy jack-
boots, dragging their noisy swords after them, looking about for
admiration from the maids.

The hounds were advertised for eleven, but that hour had
long passed without any indications of a move.　To be sure, a
little after eleven, sundry footmen emerged from the castle,
bearing trays, covered with cakes and biscuits, with bottles of
sherry and glass jugs full of water for the schedule B people
outside, while bread and cheese and ale, with something in a
most profane looking black bottle, circulated freely among the
troopers and trampers at the back.　The servants of the hunt,
being billeted in the castle, surveyed the scene in easy indolent
attitudes from the stone steps leading from the offices into the
court-yard, and criticised each comer just as the first-class
company criticised the outsiders from the windows in front.

Little Billy Bobbinson, with his face all flushed with liquor
and tight girthing, conveyed the first symptoms of active

animation by floundering along the stone passage in his iron-heeled jacks, with his spurs draggling and his sword banging and nearly tripping him up as he went, to give the word of command for the men to "prepare to mount." Billy is the most unfortunate-looking little object that ever was manufactured into a heavy dragoon, being split up far too high—all legs, and no body. Still Billy was in great force. He would not have exchanged figures with Hercules, nor his rusty, mis-fitting, dragging, lace-tarnished scarlet with green facings, or his parchment looking leathers and lack-lustre jacks, for the outfit of the youngest and smartest officer in the Life Guards.

"*Prepare to mount!*" hallooed little Billy from the top of the steps, standing on one leg and putting his right hand to his mouth, so as to convey the sound right among the soldiers. "Prepare to mount!" repeated he in a still louder tone.

"Hurrah for the cornet!" exclaimed Tom Curlin, the half drunken farrier, tossing off a third potation from the black bottle, and "Hurrah! hurrah! hurrah!" was shouted and repeated from all parts of the yard.

Billy the hatter and Billy the soldier are very different people, and he does in his red coat what he would never think of doing in his black. Seeing Scott standing in the desolate way a man does outside a great house waiting for hounds, he came with a patronising air of one with the *entrée,* and asked if our friend wouldn't "walk in" adding his conviction, "that the duke would be extremely happy to see him."

Tom didn't think the duke would ; and not knowing what practical jokes some of Billy's half-drunken heavies might play on the old mare if he went to try the experiment, he contended himself by saying, that "he had breakfasted," and was anxious to know whether it was to be "a fox-hunt or a review ?"

"Oh, it's a fox-hunt," replied Billy, quite gravely, adding, confidentially, " the fact is, *we* are here as a guard of honour on the prince."

" PREPARE TO MOUNT ! "

"To prevent the fox eating him, I suppose," said Scott, as puss-in-boots waddled away to get his men mounted.

All this gathering, and quartering, and liquoring, and soldiering, so unlike the " real thing," was anything but encouraging ; nor did the prospect appear brighter when sundry postillions in bullion-laced, plum-coloured jackets, spic and span leathers, with tasseled caps, and glass-blown wigs, emerged from the servants' hall, whips in hand, and wended their ways to the coach-house department in the adjoining court to where the soldiers were.

Presently the tramp of horse announced something coming, and a light blue landau, drawn by six blood bays with their manes full of ribbons, followed by a barouche and four, drew up in the inner court, for the "army," as the Irish call a handful of recruits, to arrange themselves around, so as to proceed in proper form to the front.

This was no easy matter ; for few of the honest Dobbinses being accustomed to such lord mayor's shows, they flew in all directions as the postillion wormed his leaders among them ; and more than one heavy dragoon measured his length on the ground. A wicked wag, too, whom Billy Bobbinson had rather "done" in the matter of a hat, had figged the old black, who began lifting her hind quarters as he mounted in a sort of cross between a kick and the action of a dancing horse at Astley's. Drink ! all glorious drink, however, had strung Billy's nerves, and he rebuked her, and jagged her in a way that plainly said, "he wasn't the Billy he was when he came."

At last they all got mounted and under way, and a brandy-nosed trumpeter having made the castle courts echo with his battered instrument, Billy Bobbinson gave the order "to draw swords," and having got his own great cheese toaster hoisted over his shoulder, the cavalcade proceeded to join the greatly-increased crowd in front.

It was now twelve o'clock — "our great-grandfathers' dinner hour," as Nimrod said in "The Quarterly"—and they had not yet started to find the fox. The day, we should observe, though bright, was clear and cold, with certain indications of frost in the air, just sufficient to make people thump their hands against their thighs, and urge their horses into little backwards and forwards trots before the castle, by way of giving the inmates a hint that they ought to be coming.

*　　*　　*　　*　　*

After numerous false alarms, at last one of those un-mistakeable moves was perceptible in the castle, and ere the lumbering heavies had got themselves into "attention," a rush of servants threw back the great doors, and the Prince of Spankerhausen appeared, with the Duchess of Tergiversation, in feathers and sky-blue satin, on his arm. The prince was a full-sized, stout, heavy-shouldered, enormously big-chested man, with a great meaningless yellow face, little ferrety blue eyes, straight sandy-coloured hair, and bushy mustachios. He was dressed in a half uniform, half-hunting sort of costume, a cocked hat and feather, a double-breasted red hunting coat, buttoned up to the neck, with leather breeches and jack-boots, and wore a small *couteau de chasse* at his side. The Duke of Tergiversation was dressed in the costume he used to pretend to hunt in when a young man, a loose bed-gowny frock coat, yellow-ochre leathers, coming low down the calf, and very short mahogany-coloured top-boots.

Having stood on the stone step inside the portico for a few seconds to show themselves becomingly to the crowd, the prince handed the duchess into the landau, in which she was followed by Mynheer Von Cled, who, as our readers are aware, is encumbered with a cork leg. Two other swells having filled the back seats, the landau moved on, to allow the barouche to take up the ladies, Chop and Change, and a party of juveniles. The prince, having seen them all in, mounted his Flemish prancer, sheep-skinned, netted, tasseled, and capa-risoned according to the custom of his country, and the duke taking his place on the right, and Lord Harry Harkaway on the left, the army placed itself so as to keep a space open for the great guns to ride at their ease. The brandy-nosed trumpeter announced their departure on his instrument ; the emblazoned flag on the tower was lowered, so that all the country round might know that the Duke of Tergiversation and Co. had gone forth to give battle to the foxes. Minute guns began to boom from the battlements. Amid all this sporting magnificence, the party proceeded in state up to Tower Hill, which commands an extensive view of the park and neighbouring country.

Lord Harry Harkaway quitted the curious cavalcade as it reached the foot of the hill, to join his poor neglected hounds, now wending their way with the servants in the bottom, his lordship wearing the dejected air of a man under orders to make a fool of himself.

" Well, this is the rummest go I ever saw," observed his lordship to Tom Tiptop, his huntsman, as he reached the latter.

" Oh, it's all my eye, my lord," replied Tom, taking off his cap ; " there hasn't been a fox here these five years ; " adding, " they are going to turn down a brace of things on the other side of the hill that have been in a sack these three days, poor things."

" The best thing would be to make a drag of one of them," observed his lordship.

" I believe it would," replied the huntsman, " and so be done with it at once, and then we might draw homewards, for it'll be night before we get away, if we don't."

The humbug then commenced by drawing several belts of plantations, and clumps of trees and tufts of brushwood, scattered and dotted about the park, from whence issued hares, pheasants, rabbits, deer, wood pigeons, partridges, tomtits, every thing except a fox. Meanwhile, his grace availed himself of the opportunity for pointing out to the prince and Mynheer Von Cled the vast extent of his park and territory, and the most remarkable of the distant views.

Here, there, and everywhere, Lord Harkaway tried with a patience and perseverance deserving of a better fate. At length he neared Gullington Wood, where fox No. 1 had to be turned down. Turned down he had been ; but the supine keepers having omitted to spring the rabbit traps, they found poor reynard in one of them, when a hound very quietly finished him.

Clumps and belts intervening between Gullington Wood and Poppington Dean, and his lordship anticipating no better luck with the second fox, he desired his pad-groom to drag the carcass of the one they had killed at the back of the hill, while the company were staring and gaping in front. " Just drag him alongside your horse," said his lordship, " keeping on the far side of all the plantations and places, so that they mayn't see you, and after making a good round of the park, finish in old Absolom Brown, the keeper's garden, by the South Lodge, where we can bury him, if the hounds won't eat him, and come out with the brush and pads, and all things proper."

This was a very good instruction ; for though " No. 2 " did raise a cry in cover, the melody was very soon terminated by a kill, which his lordship seeing, he out with his horn and blew for hard life, while Tiptop and the three whippers-in set up such screeches and yells, and made such cracks with their whips, that the whole cavalcade seemed to be suddenly electrified, and soldiers, and fox-hunters, and gigs, and carriages, and omnibus, and grooms, and prince, and duke and duchess, and Mynheer Von Cled, were all mixed up in a minute in one glorious state of indescribable confusion.

" Yonder he goes," roared Jemmy Fitznoodle.

" Hold hard ! " screamed Tom Crawley.

" Halt ! " roared Billy Bobbinson.

" Go it, ye shavers ! " exclaimed Jack Hobler, pushing through the crowd, as all eyes were strained after his lordship, in hopes of viewing the fox.

The hounds poured out of cover, down went their sterns, and out came the music, as they crossed the line of the drag, and settled like a swarm of bees on the scent.

Away! away! away! went the field, the bold dragoons mixing up with the rest, leaving the prince to look after himself, while gigs, and cars, and phaetons, and landau, and all strained over the green sward as best they could. It was a splendid burst!

The prince's Flemish punch even seemed to catch a little of the infection, and gave two or three squeals and hoists up behind, indicative of what he might do if his highness did not loose his head a little. This the nag accomplished just as the Duke of Tergiversation, who had been nearly capsized by a dog-cart, came alongside, and suggested that they ought to be getting forward if they meant to see the sport.

On then they bumped together in about equal enjoyment of the run, which was dexterously prolonged by sundry doubles, that would have led the knowing ones to think it was a hare if Jemmy Fitznoodle had not had ocular demonstration of the brush.

At last the conical roof of old Absolom's thatched cottage was seen peering from among the laurels and evergreens in which it is stuck ; and when the great guns arrived, it was announced to the duke, who put it into French for the prince, that the fox was at bay in the garden.

Great were the rejoicings thereat, great the exultations of each party on coming up "piping hot" to the finish. "Glorious run! splendid sport! finest sight that ever was seen."

" Who shall say there are no foxes at Fast-and-Loose Castle !" exclaimed his grace, wiping the perspiration from his brow.

" *Who*, indeed !" echoed Jemmy Fitznoodle, adding, "This is the biggest one I ever set eyes on !"

"WHO-HOOP !" screeched Lord Harry Harkaway at last,

poking his way under the ivy-twined arch of the little garden-gate, with the brush and pads high in hand.

" *Who-hoop!* " echoed half a hundred outside.

"Give the brush to the prince, my lord!" exclaimed the duke, as the outburst of joy subsided—"give the brush to the prince, my lord : he rode like a hero and deserves it!"

His grace then interpreted the compliment, while the great phlegmatic Dutchman sat on his horse looking as unconcerned as a cow. Mynheer Von Cled got a pad, (rather an equivocal compliment, considering his deficiency in that line,) and the compliments and congratulations being at length exhausted, the duke capped the performance by exclaiming, "My Lord Harry! you'd better come to the castle and have a little refreshment after your fatigue."

Lord Harry thought otherwise, and having paid the last tribute of respect to poor reynard's remains in the garden, he groped his way through the now squeezing and jostling crowd to his horse, which having mounted, the brass music of the horn and bugle drew off their respective cohorts, the hunters passing outside the park, while the soldiers *again* formed into something like line to conduct the heroes back to the castle.

In ten minutes the lately distracted park had resumed its usual placid grandeur. The grey-headed green-coated gate-keeper rolled the heavy iron gates back as the last donkey cart took its departure, closing the fox-hunting scene, let us hope, "for ever and for aye."

"Well, but where's your blank?" we fancy we hear the reader say. "You've killed a brace of foxes! how's that? that's no blank!"

Gentle reader, we admit it ; it wouldn't be a blank to some, but it was to Lord Harkaway and many of the gentlemen who "harkaway" with him. Will you, however, take it seriously amiss if we tell you that all this is merely preliminary to the

" blank day ? "   We hope not, for unless you close the book, you have all your medicine to take yet.

Perhaps, however, unlike Lord Harry Harkaway, the reader may require a little refreshment after such a run, so we will reserve the real blank for another chapter.

CHAPTER XIV.

ANTHONY TUGTAIL.

THE Duke of Tergiversation's park - wall encroaches so on the township road outside, that the field was lengthened into something like military line until they cleared its precincts. Indeed it was not until they got upon the liberal width and grass-sidings of the Cockington Fort road, that Tom Scott had an opportunity of diving into the *mêlée*, and seeing "who was who." Others had been in the same predicament, for Tom had not advanced far into the crowd of horsemen, ere he was hailed by some of the "best fellows under the sun," exclaiming, in the wild outburst of surprise, "Damme, here's Tom Scott!" "What the deuce has brought you here, old boy?" "Well, Tom, did you ever?" "No, I never!" and so on, alluding to the recent Fox and Goose exhibition in the park.

Despite the retirement of the prince, and the carriages, and the cavalry, and the costermongers, there was still an immense field : from a hundred and fifty to two hundred horsemen at least. The country papers of the next week, who devoted three columns and a half each to the details of the pageant, " Grand Sporting Pageant at Fast-and-Loose Castle, in honour of his Serene Highness the Prince of Spankerhausen and the great Dutch merchant Mynheer Von Cled," declared there were a thousand —a thousand, exclusive of the handful of yeomanry, whom they magnified into " two hundred of the flower of the country."

And here we may observe, how much better it is for a respectable paper to have a regular cut-along correspondent, who sticks to the truth, and tells what he sees, calling things by their proper names—fools, fools—humbugs, humbugs—and so on, instead of one of your word-sprawling gentry, who are perfectly bewildered when they come to handle a hunt, and who only make absurdity more ridiculous.

Who doesn't remember the mess they made when her Majesty went out at Belvoir, and again when glorious Tom Smith* revisited the green haunts of Leicestershire !

But to the adjourned hunt.

" Why didn't you come in to breakfast at the castle, Mr. Scott ? " asked Sir George Stiffenecke, who had got straggled all the way down to the "duke's," and was still prosecuting the chase, notwithstanding his grace's return, in hopes of gaining an appetite for dinner. " Why didn't you come in to breakfast at the castle ? " repeated he, adding, " The duke would have been happy to see you."

" I dare say would he," replied our uncourteous Tom ; "just as happy as I am when I find a straw. Dukes are only for

---

* Thomas Assheton Smith, Esq., one of the best sportsmen the world ever saw. This scene, we are happy to hear, is in course of redemption by the unrivalled pencil of Mr. Grant, and we hope the public will be favoured with an engraving of it.

such great men as yourself, Sir George," added he, thinking to
smooth over the roughness of the former part of the speech.

"Well, but his grace is extremely affable and condesending,
I'm sure," rejoined Sir George.

"Oh! devilish affable—especially about election times,"
replied Tom. "Then one may expect a visit from his agent,
Mr. Saucyjaw, with his forty-horse power of impudence,
reminding one of the breakfast, and his grace's condescension,
and saying that his grace having just discovered 'black's
white,' hopes Mr. Scott won't object to voting in the affirmative ;
and if one refuses, the duke storms and fumes as if he had
been robbed of his birthright. I don't buy my groceries quite
so dear, Sir George," added Tom : "if great men wish to
retain their influence over little ones, they must be
consistent."

Sir George was rather posed, for he's a short-noticed Jem
Crow-er himself.

The Stiffenecke conversation was here interrupted by a most
dislocating thump on the shoulder from Tom's very sincere, but
very heavy-fisted friend, Foxey Wollop, of Tod House, a ginger-
haired gentleman, with a coarse cane-coloured beard, and a
strong cross of the fox in his face.

"Why, what the deuce has brought you to this scene of
absurdity ? " inquired Wollop, after he had followed up the
blow by nearly crushing Tom's fingers in his vice of a
hand.

"You *may* ask that," replied Tom, wringing his tingling
hand against his horse's side : " I came to hunt, but we don't
always get what we come for."

" Indeed we don't," replied Foxey Wollop. " However, if
you'll come home with me, I'll tell you what you'll get, and r o
mistake—you'll get a cut off a beautiful round of beef, three
weeks in the salt, with the gravy springing out of the centre,
like a fountain, and a pie or a pudding, or something of that
sort."

"That's a very good offer," said Tom, "but at present I'm for the fox, *et preterea nihil.*"

"Oh, fox! we shall find no fox," replied Wollop, with a smile, "unless it is such another as we had in the park."

"That's a pity," said our friend, "for I've come a long way to see these hounds, and should like to have a round with them of some sort."

"Ah! then you must come another day; or, I'll tell you what do—stay over to-morrow with me, and hunt Saturday at Crashington brake; a sure find, and a capital country."

"Can't," replied Tom with a shake of the head; "got to be at home; but tell me," added he, "what are they going to draw now?" as a whip opened a gate on the left of the road, for the hounds to pass into a field.

"Oh! it will be Thorneyhalf Dean, one of the duke's," replied Wollop; "one of the duke's—might as well draw the turnpike—Lord Harry, I suppose, thinks he may as well make a day of it, and go through the form."

Nevertheless, "a lively-faithed" field ranged themselves orthodoxly for reynard to break: the whips scuttled to their respective points, and the swell huntsman yoicked his hounds into cover, and stood erect in his stirrups eying the Dean, as though he really expected to find.

"*Have at him there, good dogs!*" holloaed he; "yoicks, wind him! yoicks, push him up!" and then he gave his own patent note, something between a screech and a demi view-holloa; a cheer, however, that we are sorry to say is not reducible to paper.

Most huntsmen have a pet noise of their own, and that was Mr. Tiptop's.

While this make-believe work was going on, Gurney Sadlad came up grinning from ear to ear, with a "I say, Scott, old boy, they've been hoaxing the 'cretur' that you are the Duke of Devonshire, and we want you to carry on the joke."

" They've been what ! " exclaimed Tom in astonishment.

" Hoaxing the ' cretur : ' you know the ' cretur,' don't you ? " inquired Sadlad. " Everybody knows the ' cretur,' Toe Tugtail. Well, they've been hoaxing the ' cretur ' that you are the Duke of Devonshire, and we want you to let us introduce him to you in form."

"Nonsense," replied Tom ; adding, "*I* can't do Duke at short notice—*I* can't personate the Duke of Devonshire, a man I never saw in my life."

" Oh ! that's nothing," rejoined Sadlad ; " the ' cretur ' never saw him either ; therefore you'll be matched in that respect."

The gentleman thus indicated, although then a perfect stranger to Tom, was so well known by the field as to make them suppose he must at all events have heard of him ; and so, lest we should fall into a similar error with the reader, we will here give a slight sketch of him from the knowledge Tom afterwards obtained.

Toe Tugtail, whose real name is Anthony, Anthony Tugtail, Esq., derives his appellation, either from the natural abbreviation of his name, or from a propensity the unkind ones say he has of making people's acquaintance through the medium of their toes. He is a watering-place bird, and has mustered an extensive acquaintance by a dexterous application of his foot. If he sees a ring formed round a quadrille, or a staring circle environing a set of peticoat-whirling waltzers, Toe elbows his way in till he gets beside the party he wants to know, when dropping his hat, or his glove, or his handkerchief, he contrives to touch the person, which is immediately followed up by ten thousand apologies, and a sort of imperceptible glide into conversation respecting the performances, the lights, the music, the any thing that happens to be handy. The foundation of the acquaintance is thus laid. If it is a "don," off goes the hat the first time Toe meets him alone ; but if Toe is in company, he tries the familiar half nod of a bow, and says, " That's my friend, Sir John, or Sir Tom, or Lord Harry."

Before Tom Scott had time to arrange his thoughts or ideas, he saw a move among the horsemen about twenty yards lower down the hedge, and presently a little wizened, ugly old man, in a rusty old scarlet coat and moleskin breeches, backed a mealy-legged, mealy-muzzled, fiddle-case headed, bay horse out of the rank, in answer to Sadlad's summons, who had gone half way back to give it.

Scott had a good view of him as he came primming himself up, and certainly he did not seem undeserving of the name of the " cretur." It was visible at a glance that he dyed his hair ; indeed it does not require a conjurer to see that, for a practised eye may almost tell what o'clock it is by the various shades a dyed head assumes during the day. The pheasant-coloured tint of the " cretur's " showed that it was long past noon.

Scott had observed Mr. Tugtail in the park ; indeed he saw him come out of the castle close on the Prince of Spankerhausen's heels, but from seeing him running a muck, first at one great man, and then at another, Scott had concluded he was either a great man himself, or an *attaché* to one at all events. That " birds of a feather flock together " holds as good with peers as with pigeons.

Sadlad, we should observe, is one of those harum-scarum creatures whom it is no use being angry with. He *will* have his joke, let what will be the consequence ; and even if our friend Tom had had presence of mind to ride away, we dare say Sadlad would have followed with Tugtail at his back. It was, therefore, perhaps best to surrender at discretion. Sadlad's was the fault, Tom's the misfortune.

" My lord duke, will you allow me to present my particular friend, Mr. Tugtail," said Sadlad in a sonorous voice, and the most respectful manner, extending his right arm a little behind to where his particular friend came creeping along.

"MY LORD DUKE, MY PARTICULAR FRIEND, MR. TUGTAIL."

[To face page 226.

The " cretur's " hat made an aërial sweep, finishing at the spur.

"Great pleasure in making Mr. Tugtail's acquaintance," replied Tom, raising his hat, string high.

"Your grace is very fortunate in the day," observed the "cretur," after a grin.

"*Very,*" replied Tom, not knowing whether he meant in the sport or the weather.

"It was a splendid run, indeed," said Tugtail.

"*Oh, splendid,*" rejoined Tom, looking at the creases in Tugtail's coat and the moth-holes at his breeches' knee, and wondering how long it was since they had been aired.

Twang—twang—twang! went Lord Harry's horn ; *screech —screech—screech!* went Mr. Tiptop's too, who was not to be done out of his blow.

"*To him, hounds—to him!—get away!* " hallooed the men, cracking their heavy thonged whips.

"No go, here, I'm afraid, my lord duke," observed the "cretur," with pretended concern.

"I'm afraid not," replied Tom, gathering his reins, thinking to escape from the listening, laughing, gaping, giggling, crowd.

Vain hope! Whenever Tom turned, the "cretur" was at his heels ; worse still, the crowd followed to hear the fun. How he did be-duke, and be-grace and be-lord him !

From Thorneyhalf Dean they went to Cressingham Copse, another cover of Tom's noble brother Tergiversation's. As they proceeded, the wicked author of his misfortune rode up alongside, and whispered into his ear, " *Pitch into him.*"

"*Daren't,*" replied Tom ; "he'd have me up for an assault."

"I don't mean that," said Sadlad, " but *cram him well.*"

"Your grace hasn't much hunting in Derbyshire, I think," interposed the "cretur," crushing up on the other side of Tom's horse.

"Not much," replied Tom, thinking the cretur might know more of Derbyshire than he did.

"Noble place, Chatsworth!" observed Tugtail, confirming Tom's worst suspicions that he had been there.

"Why, yes it is; and yet I don't know," replied Tom, doubtfully, as if there were things he didn't like about it, or his modesty prevented his praising what was his own.

"Oh, *splendid* place!" rejoined Tugtail encouragingly; "*splendid* place, indeed!"

"You've been there, have you?" asked Tom.

"Oh, yes," replied Tugtail; "as a sight-seer I mean—merely to see the place, you know, your grace."

"I hope I shall have the pleasure of seeing you there as a *guest* next time," observed Tom, with true ducal condescension.

The "cretur" nearly kissed his ugly horse's ears.

Having "done the polite," Tom made him a sort of half bow, as if going to talk to some one else, and got his mare jogged into a trot, which, by dint of spurring, he worked far into the yet remaining crowd, ere he again ventured to look over his shoulder.

"By gar, there was *Monsieur Tonson* again!" Tonson, followed by a longer tail than before, all laughing, *he-he-he-ing, haw-haw-haw-ing,* "you *don't* say so"-ing, as if they would split their sides.

"Your grace was building your pointer kennels the last time I was at Chatsworth," said the "cretur," bringing his horse alongside again, to the displacement of Gurney Sadlad, Foxey Wollop, and some other wicked wags who had crowded round Tom Scott to prompt him. "Let me see, when would it be! I was staying at Matlock. Ah, well, it's immaterial; but I ventured to suggest that the floors should be made of asphalte, which was then just coming into vogue."

"And they *are* made of asphalte," replied Tom, "and very much obliged I was to the gentleman who made the suggestion, and most happy I am to have an opportunity of thanking him personally," continued Tom, tendering him his hand, to try if he couldn't shake him off that way.

No go ; the "cretur" stuck to him like a leech, and shoved poor Sir George Stiffenecke aside, as if he were the veriest plebeian under the sun. Ungrateful man! There are times when even the knight is ardently worshipped.

"Your grace has splendid shooting at Chatsworth," observed the "cretur."

"Pretty well," replied our newly-jumped up duke ; "pretty well ; nothing compared to what I shall have ;" adding confidentially, "I have an idea in my head that, if carried out, will make the sporting at Chatsworth one of the finest things under the sun."

"Indeed, your grace," observed Tugtail with well assumed interest.

"I'm going to substitute peacocks, ostriches, cassiowaries, and other eastern birds, for our common-place pheasants and partridges. What think you of a peacock *battue* or an ostrich hunt ?" asked Tom.

"Splendid! magnificent!" exclaimed Toe, as though he could hardly contain himself.

"I will tell you what my idea is," continued Tom, lowering his voice, "but this, of course, is between ourselves, and in strict confidence ; but my idea with regard to Chatsworth is this—it's a fine place, no doubt, and the present mansion has its advantages, but I think I could Orientalise the whole thing, and combine every English comfort with Eastern magnificence."

"Indeed, your grace," said Tugtail, all attention.

"My idea is this—but of course it goes no further—to buy the Pavilion at Brighton, and place it on the site of the present house, or to take the Pavilion for a model, and try to improve upon it."

"It would have a very fine effect, indeed, your grace," interrrpted the "cretur."

"You know the Pavilion, then ? " asked Tom.

"Oh yes, your grace," replied he ; "I frequently go to Brighton ; was there last summer—stay at the York, on the Esplanade, close by the Pavilion, you know."

The "cretur" had the advantage of Poor Tom again, for he has never been there, and his only acquaintance with the Pavilion is through a picture on his old housekeeper's workbox, where it certainly looks like a most gingerbread affair.

"Well," said Tom, determined to brazen it out, "I'm in treaty for the thing, and I think I shall get it too. The Queen evidently doesn't like it ; but it doesn't do for a purchaser to appear too keen. We all like good bargains, and royalty is not exempt from the feeling."

"I should think her Majesty would be too happy to give it to your grace," observed the "cretur," "especially to ornament so fine a site as Chatsworth."

"I don't know that," replied Tom. "You see if she was to give me the Pavilion, some one else might take a fancy to Buckingham Palace, or St. James's ; not that I think any one is likely to trouble either of those ; but still the principle is the same, and she might be left houseless, which would be unbecoming the Queen of a great nation of foxhunters like this."

"It would so," assented the "cretur."

"However," said Tom, "if the worst comes to the worst, and she tries to ' Jew me,' I can always build a similar thing, and perhaps improve upon it too."

The hounds had now got to Cressingham Copse. It is an oval dean, with a strongish stream, fringed with sedgy banks, the water running into the large reservoir of the Dusty Binn Mills, a little below. After the usual "make believe" drawing, Lord Harry crossed the mill race at the sluice, and, scrambling up a rough brush-woody bank, horn in hand, surveyed the scene below.

It requires a steady horse to insure your safe transit over a mill dam, and some of the field did not seem to fancy giving

theirs a chance of tumbling them in ; among the number the
"cretur," who, sliding down the bank below the dam, began
exploring a south-east passage.

"DUKE !" exclaimed he at the top of his voice, as he saw
a footpath winding up the bank from the road he was now
taking, "DUKE !" repeated he, though Tom answered at the
first shot, "Here's a better way ! here's a better way ! "

"Oh, your grace, I'm not going to draw any more ! "
halloaed Lord Harry Harkaway, fit to drop out of his saddle
with laughing. So saying he took off his hat with great defer-
ence, and having acknowledged his courtesy, Tom cut away as
hard as ever he could lay legs to the ground.

* * * * *
* * * * *

Well, it's four years ago, as we said before, and Tom had
forgotten all about the "cretur," and the "duke," and the
"pavillion," and all the nonsense he had talked, until they
were most unpleasantly forced on his recollection last
season.

Mr. Neville's hounds met at Scruffington Clump, one of the
wildest and most out-of-the-way places they have ; but proscribed meets being rather in vogue since the "Chase" day,
there was a fairish sprinkling of sportsmen, including our unfortunate friend, the "duke for a day." Why he went we
don't know, save that oats were very dear, and he had had very
little hunting for his money ; for Scruffington Clump, independently of being a most uninviting place, is only an uncertain
draw, especially in the spring. It lies handier for the Dazzlegoose hounds ; but Mr. Neville, who is one of the old hard-
bitten uncompromising order of masters, and would as soon
part with an inch off his nose as an acre off his country, keeps
it as a sort of Botany Bay to send his hounds to in bad
weather, or on days that he doesn't mean to go out himself.
When asked to give it up, "as it is of no use to him," he

always says, "*I don't know how soon I may want it,*" and muttering something about railways he closes the discourse. It's a nasty place—a landmark clump of Scotch firs, that haven't grown an inch these twenty years, placed on the summit of the swelling Whitcliffe Hills. The land around is of the poorest, most impoverished order ; the wretched water weeds, the yellow moss, the unhealthy rushes, and the scattered broom and brushwood scarcely covering the thin water-gruelly-looking soil. It seems to grow everything but what it should. Some enterprising individuals enclosed a considerable portion of it some years ago, and the weak hedges are in that delightful state of mossy rottenness as to make gates superfluous articles. The cattle just walk through the hedges where they like. The country indeed is fast returning to its pristine, goose an acre, state. Its fox-hunting feature is not amiss, and if it were a sure find it would not be a bad place ; but there is no regular holding cover in the draw, and Mr. Neville's hounds are generally indebted to the Dazzlegoose people for a run when they get one. Such was the place which our friend Tom Scott cast up at, and, not having been there for five years, he got such a fright that we don't think he will venture there again.

Unpromising as the place was, they had a field—Trumper was there, also the Hobbletrots, and one or two other Goose and Dumpling men.

Of red coats they had Muffinmouth, Colonel Buckskin, Mr. Palmer of Walford, Mr. Moulden of Bradfield, Mr. Harford and his son, Mr. Murray of Hadham, a few Dazzlegoose men in apricot colour, and some of the great unshaved from the barracks.

Judge of our poor friend's horror on leaving the clump to draw some loose-bottomed belts of plantations below, at seeing Tarquinius Muff's great white stomach coming along with a diminutive-looking companion, who, at a glance, Scott saw was the " cretur."

He had hardly time to shove his great Grahamlike* gills into his cravat, push his coat collar up, and stick his hat on sideways (*à la* Jerry, the race-list seller), make himself as unlike himself as possible, ere they were within descrying distance of each other.

Scott pretended not to see Tugtail, but with a sidelong sort of glance watched the first view strike his frame, and saw that if revolving years had deepened the wrinkles in his old cheeks, the day had not yet taken the lustre out of the hair-dye, his precise locks being as black and as trim as a raven's wing.

Moreover, Scott saw Tugtail point him out to Muff, and could almost tell by their manner what each said.

" There's the Duke of Devonshire ! " exclaimed Tugtail.

"Not a bit of it," replied Muff.

" Who is it then ? " inquired Tugtail.

" Which do you mean ? " asked Muff.

" The man on the chestnut."

" Oh ! that's—haw—Mr. Scott—haw—a sort of a—haw— gentleman—haw—farmer—haw—lives at a place called Haw— Buck Grange—haw."

Muff was the great man of the day, and the poor " cretur " who doats upon titles, was absolutely high and dry for want of one. In this sad dilemma he actually sought the acquaintance of our friend Tom at the hands of Tarquinius Muff, all because Tom looked like the Duke of Devonshire, or a man he had been told was the duke, for he is no more like him than we are.

Tom had dodged them for nearly an hour, till they pinned him in the corner of a field from whence there was no escape but over a high stone wall.

" Scott, let me introduce my friend Mr. Tugtail," said Muff, bringing Tuggey up.

* Sir James Graham is very liberal in the matter of shirt collars, as used to be ably depicted by *Punch* during the *virtuous* administration that did so much for the farmers.

"Happy to make the acquaintance of Mr. Scott," said the "cretur" with a most patronising bow, just such a bow as Tom made to him on the former occasion.

Tom sky-scraped in return.

After a common-place or two, the " cretur " thus began :—

" Do you know, Mr. Scott, I was very nearly making a most ridiculous mistake just now ? " observed he.

" What was that, Sir ? " asked Tom, with a pretty good idea of what was coming.

" Why, do you know when I first saw you, I abso*lutely* took you for my friend the Duke of Devonshire."

" That *would* have been a mistake, indeed," observed Tom.

" Well, I assure you it was so," replied he. " Our friend Muff will tell you the same. ' That's the Duke of Devonshire ! ' said I, as you rode up. ' Nonsense ! ' said Muff ; ' it's Mr. Scott.' By the way, may I ask if you are any way related to the great Sir Walter ? "

" Not that I know of," replied Tom.

" Most likely, I should think," observed the " cretur," anxious to make the best of our friend. " Most likely, I should think," repeated he. " Pray do you spell your name with two t's ? "

" Yes," replied Scott.

" You don't know my friend the Duke of Devonshire, then," observed Tugtail, after a minute scrutiny of Tom's features.

" No," replied Tom ; " I never saw him."

" Ah ! well, you'd know him if you were to see him, for there's certainly a resemblance between you," observed he ; " and your voice is something similar. It *must* be so, indeed, or I couldn't have mistaken you for a man I know so well "

" Does his grace hunt ? " asked Tom, thinking to " trot Tuggey out " a little.

" Oh, yes," replied he ; " rides well, too ; I should say, but his mind inclines more to shooting."

" He'll have good shooting, I suppose," observed Scott.

" *Capital,*" replied his—*not* friend, but persecutor. " He's great with his gun," added he. " Indeed it is in the shooting way that I see most of him. I've a room at Chatsworth whenever I like to go," added Tugtail.

" Which you will occupy pretty often, I imagine," observed Tom ; adding, " at least *I* would, I know."

" I've many other friends," replied Tugtail " desirous of my company."

" Ay, but I'd always go to the biggest," observed Tom.

" Well, there's something in that," replied Tugtail, with a sagacious nod of his now puce-coloured head.

Here Tom managed to shove in between old Trumper and Tom Hobbletrot, and escaped the " cretur " for half an hour or so.

After the usual promiscuous rambling about of a " wild draw," going first to one nameless place and then to another, just as they turned up, and seemed likely for a fox, the field arrived at Willowby Brake, the first really plausible-looking place they had been at.

Here the " cretur " pinned poor Tom again.

" You don't know Chatsworth, I think you say, Mr. Scott ? " observed Tugtail.

" No I don't," grunted Tom.

" Beautiful place," observed Tugtail ; " at least will be, when the duke makes his grand alterations."

Tugtail then entered into a long and confidential communication with Tom respecting the Pavilion, which, singular enough, was then lately stated in the papers to have been sold, or for sale, detailing how, " by his advice," the duke, having held off for some years, had now got it at his own price, and how his grace was going to establish an ostrich hunt, and have *battues* of peacocks ; a " *rechauffé,*" in short, of the information Tom had given him four years ago, with a few variations tending to Tuggey's own glorification and exemplification of his intimacy with the Duke.

So the "cretur" persecuted poor Tom from cover to cover, throughout a long blank day, who declares that if everybody suffers as much for telling a lie as he did, he's sure they won't tell any more.

Now, if that isn't a blank day, we don't know what a blank day is.

THE END OF A BLANK DAY.

CHAPTER XV.

" WHAT queer books you write ! " observed our excellent but rather matter-of-fact, friend, Sylvanus Bluff, the other day, who seeing us doubling up a sheet of paper in a rather unceremonious way, concluded we were at what he calls our " old tricks." "I buy all your books," added he with a solemn shake of the head, as though we were beggaring him—" I bought your 'Jorrocks' Jaunts, and Jollities ' I bought ' Handley Cross, or the Spa Hunt,' I bought ' Hillingdon Hall, or the Cockney Squire ; ' but I dont *understand* them. I don't see the *wit* of them. *I* don't see the *use* of them. *I* wonder you don't write something useful. I should think now," added he seriously, " you could do somethimg better. I should say now you would be quite equal to writing a dictionary, or a book upon draining, and those would be really useful works, and your friends would get something for their money."

Gentle reader ! we plead guilty to the charge of writing most egregious nonsense. Nay, we are sometimes surprised how such stuff can ever enter our head, astonished that we should be weak enough to commit it to paper, amazed that there should be publishers rash enough to print it, and lost in utter bewilderment that there should be good, honest, sane, nay sensible folks not only idle enough to read it, but, oh wonder ! of all wonders ! extravagant enough to part with their good current coin to buy it !

And talking of friends buying our books out of politeness, we may here avail ourself of the opportunity to say that there is

nothing we dislike more ; nay, so great is our objection, that if
we knew any honest, mistaken man about to commit such
an absurdity, we would absolutely forestall our own market by
offering him a copy.   At least we *think* we would.

We don't know why any one should do so, we are sure, for
neither by name, dedication, or date, do we ever provoke so
suicidal an act.   We may say, with our excellent friend Peter
Morris, that " if putting our Christian name and surname at the
beginning of a book were necessary conditions to the dignity of
authorship we should never be one while we live."   Like Peter
" we want nerves for this."   We rejoice in the privilege of
writing and printing *incognito,* and think with him that it is the
"finest discovery " that ever was made.   Peter, to be sure, got
bolder with age, but then he felt that he was " somebody."

Writing, we imagine, is something like snuffing or smoking
—men get into the way of it, and can't well leave it off.   Like
smoking, it serves to beguile an idle hour.   Individually speaking, writing makes us tolerably independent, both of the world
and the weather.   We are never regularly high and dry for
want of a companion so long as we can get pen, ink, and paper;
and though we should not like to back ourself against such a
winter as the last (1846-7), yet writing enables us to contend
with a tolerable amount of bad weather.   An author has
pretty much the same pleasure in seeing his ugly cramped
hand turned into neat print that a traveller has in receiving
five and twenty francs for a sovereign on landing in France.
Revising is something like returning to the realities of English
money again.   But we are getting into the mysteries of
authorship.

Next to buying our books out of politeness, our greatest
objection is to having them exposed to view.   If the great
Lord Mayor was to " look us up," and invite us to one of those
gorgeous feasts that annihilate so many turtles, and if on the
table in his reception room we were to see one of our books—
Hawbuck Grange, for instance—(and what author does not

recognise his own works at a glance!) our appetite would immediately fail us, and his lordship would save both "his meat and his mense," * as they say in the country.

Some men "stand fire" better than others. We remember once dining at a great Russian Jew's, whose drawing-room table was garnished with nothing but New Monthly Magazines —New Monthly Magazines in every stage of life, from the well-thumbed "yearling," down to the newly-issued number of yesterday.

Presently the door opened, and Sir Edward Lytton Bulwer, the avowed editor, was announced.

*   *   *   *   *

"Shir Edward Shir," said our host, taking up a number as soon as the baronet's back had subsided into still life, "Shir Edward Shir, I do not like dis article of yours, on de state of parties, it is far too——" something, we forget what, and so he went on lecturing and commenting on the numbers in succession, till "dinner" put an end to the scene.

Our former admiration of Sir Edward's talents was now divided at the heroic way in which he stood fire.

This digression will have told the reader two things, first, that we don't want any body to buy this book on the Bluff principle; secondly, that we shall consider it a greater compliment of those friends who do buy it, if they will keep it out of sight, than if they were to parade it before us.

We now come to the more immediate purport of this chapter. Our friend Bluff's reproof has made us anxious to give this volume a flavour of usefulness, were it only to save us from the labour of writing a dictionary, but the difficulty is, how to give a work relating so entirely to a pleasurable pursuit a flavour of usefulness.

---

* This we believe is a localism : at all events, it does not seem to be a Londonism ; for the printer had it, " his meat and his mouse."

In the course of our cogitations, it has occurred to us that the only possible way of doing it is to give a sort of meteorological register of the season in which our friend Tom Scott's adventures are laid. Tom's adventures will do as well for one season as another, because, generally speaking, they refer to the sport and not to the weather; but an actual matter-of-fact register may be useful hereafter, and perhaps save some from supposing that future seasons are the worst that ever were known. To do the full measure of usefulness we will begin with a glance at the season which preceded it.

The season of 1844-5 was perhaps the best hunting one of modern times. The harvest was late, and some packs got little or no cub hunting, but from November up to the last week in March, there was a continuous run of fine hunting weather, and generally speaking first-rate sport. A snow storm then intruded, but like all spring storms it was of short duration, and April again presented a fine moist favourable month to those who live in countries where hunting can be pursued so late. The summer of 1846 was unusually hot, and the harvest remarkably early. Cub hunting began correspondingly early as we have shown in Chapter I. of this work, yet, with such a favourable commencement, what an apology of a season it was! What a hope-raising, spirit-crushing affair all through! If we look back upon it from the commencement, have we any pleasing recollection of it, any " run of the season," any joyous reminiscence, any realised pleasure, any greenest or reddest spot on memory's hunting waste, any thing handsome to say of it ? Is there anybody to speak to its character ? as the judge asks prior to trouncing a prisoner. No one. Let us review it.

We will begin with November. What was November like ? More like a bad March than the glorious, sloppy, poachy, wet-me-through month we have long known by that name. We contend that a free-born fox-hunter has a perfect indefeasible right to have his feet well wet every day he goes out hunting in the month of November. Yet we know we didn't get ours

wet once, and as to a general good soaking, a sort of return
when one first sends a shower from the hat by running the
finger round the rim, down to the squeeze out of the purply
coat tails, and the sucking, cork-drawing blob of the boots,
our garments are none the worse for any thing they did last
year.

In fact, we don't feel as if we had any hunting. True we
saw a stud of boots standing ranged like Major Ponto's library,
and a "pink" folded lining outwards, lying atop of the
drawers, but they were so seldom used, that the whole thing
appears more like those occasional visits that one makes to
fairs or country races throughout the year than the compact
three or four months into which we compress as much hunting
and pleasure as lasts us the twelvemonth. We have had no
such winter these ten years. The season of 1836-7 was
unfavourable in some countries, and was well cut through
in the middle, particularly in the south, by a tremendous snow
storm, but it did not arrive till Christmas Day, a period when
nobody has any right to object. The papers of that day said,
that "On the twenty-fourth and twenty-fifth of December the
country generally was visited by a fall of snow, heavier and
more serious in its consequence than has been experienced for
many years, which not only put a stop to hunting, but
interrupted the internal communication of the country." The
great storm, however, was only of short duration, and hunting
was resumed in the course of January, and continued in a
catching sort of way, now on, now off, according to the arrival
of the floods, the frosts, the falls of snow, and the gales with
which it was interspersed. Indeed the seasons of 1836-7 and
1846-7 have been somewhat alike, with the qualification, that
the latter being the freshest in our recollection, of course
appears the worst of the two. There was snow in the middle
of April, 1837, but we have had snow at Epsom races since
then, which of course throws the April performance into the
shade. There was a long stop to hunting in 1838, but we had

better say nothing about it, lest we should rouse young 1848 to retaliate. We will therefore just stick to our text, the season 1846-7. November we have seen through. We now come to December. What shall we say of December? Oh lauk! up to the hocks in snow all the month. But we will take the rough outline as booked in our pocket-book. Thus it stands. We should, however, premise that November went out with snow. The twenty-ninth and thirtieth have that ominous word opposite their dates. December entered with a hard frost atop of the snow, which continued throughout the first week. On the seventh there was a thaw, which lasted till the ninth. The tenth brought a hard frost with more snow; the eleventh ditto with more ditto; the thirteenth, fourteenth, fifteenth, sixteenth, and seventeenth, ditto in the way of frost; on the eighteenth came another thaw, which on the nineteenth was very rapid, and continued on to the twenty-third, when, with Thursday the twenty-fourth, came a hard frost, backed on the twenty-fifth by more snow, and so the month continued to the end, with the trifling variation of a make-believe thaw on the twenty-eighth and twenty-ninth. Not a day's hunting throughout a month!

The new year opened doubtfully. We had alternate snow and thaw for the first week. The seventh of January we have booked as wet. But what ominous words follow!—Ninth, frosty; tenth, frost; eleventh, hard frost; twelfth, very hard —and so on from the twelfth to the twentieth without variation, save that the words "and snow" are added to the last day. Twenty-first was frost and snow, twenty-second ditto and sleet, twenty-third ditto, twenty-fourth very cold rain and high wind, twenty-fifth thaw, twenty-sixth thaw continued, with the usual ominous predictions resulting from the snow still lying on the hill tops, the twenty-seventh was very fine, and hounds began to stir again, but the month closed with a white frost and snow on the evening of the thirty-first. So much for January.

February the first has the word "snow" booked opposite to

it ; the second has " more snow and frost " affixed to it ; the third and fourth have " frost ; " the fifth, " thaw ; " the sixth, " thaw, changing to frost at night ; " the seventh the ominous words " hard frost ; " the eighth is distinguished by the words " bitter frost ; " the ninth ditto ; the tenth has " snow " to it ; the eleventh, " more snow ; " the twelfth, " frost ; " which appears to have continued to the fourteenth, when there came a thaw, followed on the fifteenth by a frost, succeeded again on the sixteenth by a thaw, which lasted till about the end of the month—the twenty-seventh—the day on which our pocket-book says " hare-hunting ends," though Mr. Trumper says " it does nothing of the sort," for he reckons a March hare as good as most foxes. March we do not expect much from, and therefore have not much right to find fault with it. It is generally a worse month than either January or April, supposing all countries admitted of hunting in April. This year we had snow in the second week, making the fourth winter of the season, and there was frost enough to stop hounds in many parts about the middle of the month. In the third week the fallows were flying, and the ground was too dry for anything but farming towards the end. April, however, rectified that, for the smiling month, entered with another fall of snow, the fifth winter of the season, which continued to fall at night and clear off during the day for the first three or four days. So we think we may say the season was a *very bad one*.

And now having said our utilitarian say, we will conclude this chapter, and finish our volume with a description of Tom Scott's visit to the man who provoked it.

CHAPTER XVI.

THE MORNING MEET.

OUR friend Tom had put his red coat to bed, that is to say, in the topmost drawer of the wardrobe, and had commenced stripping his horses, when he got the following note from his friend Sylvanus Bluff :—

"CAVIL HOUSE,

"DEAR SCOTT,

"*I'm worried alive with Mr. Neville's foxes, and heartily wish you'd come over and kill me some of them, for I really think they won't leave me a lamb, or a goose, or a head of game about the place. I have written to Mr. Neville and Old Ben till I'm tired, and it's perfectly ridiculous expecting me to preserve foxes, which I do most sedulously, when they never come near to hunt them. I have therefore got the Scratchley dogs coming over on Thursday, and we are going to turn out by daybreak to see what we can do with a drag. I wish you would come over and assist, as you know more about these things than 1 do. Dinner at six.*

"Yours sincerely,

"S. BLUFF."

Bluff—like a great many of us—is a capital fellow in his way—that is to say, if he has his own way—but he doesn't like to be thwarted ; least of all to have any of his live stock injured or destroyed. Still he preserves foxes ; indeed he calls himself a sportsman—a sportsman who is content with two hunts a year, one in the spring, the other in the autumn. When among non-hunting men, he talks big about hunting, and his doings with the hounds ; but when among members of the hunt, he always parades his patriotism in preserving what are a " downright nuisance to him." Like a good many other men, he never makes allowances for the seasons, and if he has not the hounds at his house when he wants them he considers himself slighted. Mr. Neville not having got to him, had caused him to worry and fidget himself into a belief that he was in danger of being eaten up by foxes ; and, partly as an act of self-preservation, and partly, perhaps, by way of what he calls " keeping Mr. Neville in order," he had invited Sam Jubberknowl of Badstock to bring over the Scratchley dogs. Jubberknowl is a loose fish of a brewing, inn-keeping saddler at Badstock, who, what they call, " heads the Scratchley dogs ;" that is to say, is answerable to the tax-gatherer for the ten couple which they return as seven. It is generally observed that half the Scratchley dogs disappear about taxing time.

When we see a pack of hounds advertised to meet at half-past eight or nine o'clock in the morning, or hear them spoken of in the country as " dogs," one has a pretty good idea what to expect ; and, even if Scott had not known Jubberknowl and his establishment, he would have had little difficulty in picturing the concern. As it was, our friend Tom had often been puzzled to make out whether Jubberknowl is a sportsman, or merely one who busies himself about the " dogs " for the purpose of furthering his other callings of saddler, publican, and sinner. The few times Tom had seen him out with Mr. Neville, he observed that he always came very late, and went away very early, and never passed a public-house without stopping to refresh himself. The latter, however, might be on the reciprocity principle.

It so happened that Scott was going over on the afternoon of the day on which he got Mr. Bluff's letter to have a field day on the flags with the entry, and he took an early opportunity of telling Mr. Neville about it, expecting nothing but that ne would give Bluff, and Jubberknowl, and the Scratchley dogs, a good blessing for their intended unceremonious intrusion.

"I'm very glad you've mentioned it," observed Mr. Neville, "for it reminds me that I've had two letters from Mr. Bluff about the damage the foxes are doing him, which I have quite forgotten to answer, and Ben has had no end of complaints from Steeltrap his keeper. What can I do ? You know," added he, with a shrug of the shoulders, "I can't make the season. I should only have been too glad to have gone over and hunted his foxes for him ; but *we* couldn't go in the snow—*we* couldn't go in the frost—*we* couldn't go in the wind—and it was no use going when the country got as dry and as hard as these flags," continued he, stamping upon them as he spoke.

"But what do you say about the Scratchley dogs ? " asked Tom, expecting to get Mr. Neville's bristles up at the very idea of anyone invading his country.

"Why, as to *that*," replied our master, shaking his head and looking very solemn, "I suppose Mr. Bluff must just do as he thinks right. It's true he always preserves foxes for us, and he has some good covers in the centre of our country, so that it wouldn't be prudent to quarrel with him. One can't tell a non-hunting man like him that he shall not do what he likes with his own, and if he does not kill a vixen, he mayn't do us any great harm."

"Perhaps," added he, after a pause, "the best thing you could do would be to go over and see what they do do, and if you *should* have such a misfortune as to kill a vixen, which is almost the only chance Bluff has of getting blood this dry weather, you could secure the cubs at all events. We are short on the Cannonbridge side of the country, notwithstanding we have killed so few there this season."

So unexpected a permission completely staggered our friend Tom, and it was not until he was on his way home that it

occurred to him that a visit to Cavil House would again enable him to kill two birds with one stone—see the fun, and consult Mrs. Bluff about the teeth. Accordingly he so arranged it, and on the Wednesday rode over, "bags and all," trusting to chance for getting his horse taken care of.

It was a fine afternoon, the weather everything that a farmer could wish, and a fox hunter object to—warm sun, cold east wind, cracking clays, flying fallows, and parched roads.

When Tom got to Cavil House, he found Mr. Bluff with the now common accompaniment of a country gentleman, a draining-pipe, in his hand, which he flourished about like a fiddle-stick, or a field-marshal's baton. He was in the usual stew of people who have got hold of something they don't quite understand. We don't mean his draining-pipe, for with these he is quite at home, but he found that boarding and lodging the Scratchley dogs was not quite so convenient as having Mr. Neville's well appointed pack trotted on to his lawn at twenty minutes past ten.

"Most ravenous devils! most ravenous devils!" exclaimed he, grasping Tom's hand, and flourishing the draining-pipe like the leader of a band, with his face as red as a turkey cock's thropple, and his green cut-away thrown back, displaying not only his striped calamanco waistcoat, but his cotton braces at the arm-holes. "Have lapped up all the skim milk! have lapped up all the skim milk! and now they want porridge! and *now* they want porridge! Glad to see you, however! glad to see you!" and thereupon he again shook Scott heartily by the hand.

Tom was just going to say, "What they've come, have they?" when a most appalling chorus from the back yard saved the question, and caused Bluff to point his draining-pipe towards it.

"By gad, what a row they make!" said he; "by gad, what a row they make! I really think they'll drive Mrs. Bluff mad, for she hates dogs any-how, and our youngest boy's just out of the whooping-cough, and she'll swear that this will throw him back ! and she'll *swear* that this will throw him back."

Another chorus more riotous than its predecessor filled the air, and echo prolonged the sound. "If we are to stand this all night," observed Bluff, with a solemn shake of the head, grounding his draining-pipe as he spoke, "we might as well have a menagerie at our door."

"Let's have them out," said Scott, getting off his horse, "and see if we can't quiet them by walking them about a bit."

"*Out!*" screamed Bluff. "*Out!*" repeated he ; "but how do you expect to get them in again ? We have had to carry them in one by one as it is, and they've bitten two of my men *desperately*. Mrs. Bluff declares they are all mad, and has locked herself into her room, and won't come out at any price."

"Well, but where's Jubberknowl ? " asked Scott, seeing poor Bluff's perturbation—"he can quiet them, at all events."

"Jubberknowl be hanged," responded Bluff, "Jubberknowl be *hanged*" repeated he with greater emphasis—"he's behaved very ill ! he's behaved very ill ! See what he's sent ! see what he's sent ! " added he, producing a dirty slip of paper with the following :—

"DEAR SIR,

"*I send the dogs, and hop they will answer your purpose. Am sorry he can't come myself, having got for to go to Croppydock Fair, but Joshua knows all their names, and is very bidly. They had better be coupled before they leave the kennel.*

"*Your dutiful Servant,*

"SAMUEL JUBBERKNOWL."

The "bidly" gentleman now appeared, carrying two pig pails in a stable hoop.

"By Jove, there goes all my pigs' meat ! " ejaculated poor Bluff, inwardly wishing he had let the whole alone. "Might

as well have a regiment of soldiers billeted on one—might as
well have a regiment of soldiers billeted on one ; " adding,
" It's to be hoped he'll get them pacified at last—it's to be
hoped he'll get them pacified at last."

Joshua was a stout-set, square-built, drayman-like fellow, of
a uniform breadth from the shoulders to the heels ; he was
dressed in a sort of third-hand suit of hunting things, the cap
being a rusty brown, the scanty coat deep purple, the abundant
breeches very dirty, and the almost black boots so short and
scant as to keep the majority of his swelling calves above the
tops. His square, coarse-featured, freckled face was indicative
of little except drink.

We will now take a glance at the internal arrangements of
Cavil House.

Mrs. Bluff is any thing but what the name indicates. Indeed she seems to have made a serious mistake in changing her
maiden one of Green—Rosamond Green—for that of Bluff.
The roses and lilies of youth having fled, she is left the
most nervous, pallid, washed-out looking creature that ever was
seen. The slightest thing throws her into convulsions. She is
one of those ailing sort of bodies with whom nothing is really
ever the matter. Still she always lives in dread ; and whatever ailment happens to be uppermost, she immediately invests
herself and family with it. When the cholera was astir, she
had it many times ; typhus fever is a standing dish with her,
and meazles, whooping - cough, influenza, are all frequent
visitors. She buys all the quack books that are published, and
all the quack medicines that are sold, and experimentalises upon
the poor people in the neighbourhood.

No sooner did the news of the men having been bit reach her
than she conjured up all sorts of horrors respecting hydrophobia,
and resolutely barricadoed herself and children into her room.
Even poor Bluff was only permitted to hold communion sweet
through the keyhole. Of course the party at Cavil House had
not her company at dinner ; and almost equally of course, Bluff,

Tom Scott, and the few neighbours Bluff had assembled, drank
more wine than they ought. We don't mean to say they got
drunk ; but having no break, caused either by the retirement
of the ladies or by their summoning them to tea, they settled
more determinedly to the bottle, added to which, they drank
the first three bottles as two, without finding out the mistake.
Indeed it was not until he got three-quarters of a bottle aboard,
that Bluff could fairly be said to be himself again, when, having
got his waistcoat loose all but the two bottom buttons, they
gradually got his conversation coaxed through the medium of
his favourite subject, draining, on to that of fox-hunting itself.
It was plain, however, that his inclination was for the destruction, and not the pursuit, of the animal. He was uncommonly
blood-thirsty. The blood of his lambs and his leverets seemed
to call for vengeance, and the number of victims increased as
the evening advanced, until he got the lambs up from ten to
near thirty. The shepherd told Tom in confidence that they
had lost three, but one he believed had been worried by a
greyhound. The neighbours gradually dropt off until Bluff
and Tom were at last left alone, when, having fixed . the
time for turning out, said every thing they could think of,
and some things twice over, they both seemed to think
they might as well save the fatigue of further conversational
effort by going to bed ; and pulling out their watches
simultaneously, they found it was on the point of striking
twelve.

Accordingly off they bundled.

Tom had scarcely got into bed when the violent bang of the
door in the next room, which was only separated from his by a
thin lath and plaster wall, followed by a heavy footstep, and an
ejaculation that sounded very like " D—d fool," announced
that his host was hard by. Bluff stumped and banged about,
hitting this, knocking that, occasionally letting fall an oath or
an observation, such as, " Curse the table " — " Absurd
nonsense "—" Women such fools "—" D—n the boot-jack ! "—

until at length a creak and a heavy souse proclaimed that he had turned into bed.

The poor man was condemned to sleep in his dressing-room, for fear he might be mad. Tom Scott might be included in the list of unfortunates, for he was victimised by the arrangement. His room, though an extremely good one, was not that terrible bugbear, the best one, with a lofty bed as big as a field, but a cozey, comfortable, easily-got-ready one, looking to the north, or back of the house. It so happened that the Scratchley dogs were lodged in the brewhouse just below ; and these unruly spirits, unused to the restraint of civilized packs, kept howling and yelling throughout the night. It was not the cheery chorus of hounds in kennel filling the air with their merry voices, but a sort of melancholy drawl resembling what is called the death howl. This they set up about every half hour, bursting out in full chorus at first, with the sound of scratching and gnawing at the door and wood-work, until the howl gradually died out in a moan. Nor was this the worst ; for Tom's host could hear them also, though not so distinctly as Tom did ; and what with the drink, the noise of the hounds, and the strange bed he was in, Bluff evidently could not get to sleep. This was plainly indicated by his tossings and talkings. First he began calculating the number of draining tiles to an acre, at various distances. a calculation that was interrupted every now and then by abusing the hounds, wishing they were all in a warmer place than the brewhouse ; then he banged over against the wall, and snorted, as if trying to get to sleep with a snore. The next thing Tom heard was, " Curse the thing," and apparently stripping off the counterpane. Then there was another lull, and the dogs had their turn ; after which Tom heard his friend at the novel recreation of saying his multiplication table—twice two's four, twice three's six, twice four's eight, and so on. This Bluff carried on very perseveringly till he got into the fifth column, when, after boggling at five times six, he was regularly brought up at five times eight, and the mul-

tiplication table seemed to die away in a mutter.   Tom really
thought they would both accomplish a sleep about this time, and
he was as near dropping off as could be, when the vagabonds in
the "lock-up" fell a fighting, and if there had been fifty couple
they could not have made a greater noise.   They yelled, and
they tore, and they bit, and they worried, and they howled, and
they growled, and they rattled and knocked the butts, and tubs
and casks about, as if they would destroy every thing in the
place.

Fortunately their din had the effect of waking Joshua, and
presently he began clattering with a bromstick at the door, and
rating and calling to them by name.   "Miscreant!" shouted
he ; "*Miscreant!*" he repeated in a still louder tone.   "MIS-
CREANT!" roared he, with a tremendous *rat, tat, tat, tat, tan*,
of the broomstick against the door, adding, "Ord, dom ye, ha
don! Ord, dom ye, be quiet! Oh! PROWLER, it's *you*, is it!
PROWLER! ar say, ha don! PROWLER, *for shame* of yoursel!
PLUNDERER! what are you after there?" inquired he, as the
scene of action shifted to another quarter.   "Whistler!
WHISTLER! ar say, Flasher! *for shame!* TOWLER, be quiet!
GUIDER, ha don! ord dom ye! ar'll hang ye all, and put the rest
i' the small debts *coourt*!"added he, with a kick at the door that
made it shake again ; and after rating, and *rat, tat, tanning,*
and kicking and clattering for some quarter of an hour,
peace was at length restored.

Still Bluff couldn't get to sleep.   He, however, abandoned
the multiplication table, and tried another tack : he took to
saying over the kings and queens of England—William the
Conqueror, William Rufus, William Rufus, William the
Conqueror, and so on down to Stephen, where he stuck.   He
then skipped on to Edward the Fourth, from whom he brought
them on with a very fair hunting scent down to Queen Victoria.
Still that wouldn't do.   He then began spouting—"My name
is Norval! on the Grampian hills," &c., but that did not seem
to answer any better, and he presently struck off with—

"The curfew tolls the knell of parting day,
The lowing herds wind slowly o'er the lea;
The ploughman homeward plods his weary way,
And leaves the world to —— "

" *D—n those hounds!* " roared he, as the brutes again fell a fighting. Tom then heard him groping for his bell, which having found, he gave such a pull as left the rope in his hand. This presently went smash through the window.

Bluff then lay quiet for some time, and Tom was in hopes he had fallen asleep ; but he had most likely only been listening if his footman was coming, for in less than ten minutes he was back at his multiplication table, trying to put his memory over the leap it had stuck at before. It wouldn't do, however, so he at last turned away from it again, and began spouting ; and two o'clock found him most appropriately rehearsing Henry the Fourth's soliloquy to sleep :—

" How many thousands of my poorest subjects
Are at this hour asleep ! O, gentle sleep,
Nature's soft nurse, how have I frighted thee,
That thou no more wilt weigh my eyelids down," &c.

which really seemed to operate beneficially, for a few incoherent noises were followed by a deep snore ; and having got rid of his nearest persecutor, our friend dropped asleep too, though when the servant called him at five, he was ready to swear that he hadn't had " a wink of sleep."

Poor Sylvanus looked ten years older when he came down the next morning than he did when he went to bed. Instead of the healthy, ruddy complexion he generally has, and the full bright eye, he was a sort of a bad green, much of the colour of the cushions in the library of the Conservative Club, with eyes like boiled gooseberries. His chin was all jagged and hacked with the scrapings of a blunt razor, or the shakings of an unsteady hand. Nevertheless he had got himself into the old swallow-tailed scarlet and yellow ochres that Tom Scott remembers ever since he (Tom) was a boy. A red coat is a red coat with some people, and year after year we see them putting themselves into the most old-fashioned, extraordinary articles with the most self-satisfied air. Sylvanus's had been made when mother-of-pearl buttons were the fashion, and he had great black animals engraved upon them that might pass either for wolves or foxes. The collar stood right up, in a sort of Gothic arch, half way up his head, and the closely set on waist-buttons were about half way between his shoulder blades and where the small of his back would be, if it had any small—Bluff's outline is pretty straight.

"Well, Scott, old boy, how are you?" exclaimed he, with ill-assumed gaiety, extending a feverish hand as they met in the passage leading into the breakfast room; "hope you slept well."

"Pretty well, thank you," replied Tom, adding, "the hounds rather disturbed me at one time."

He sunk "My name is Norval," the "kings and queens," "multiplication table," and all that sort of thing.

"Curse the hounds!" muttered Bluff, adding, "they disturbed me too. One would have thought all that pigs' meat would have kept them quiet; however, let's to breakfast, and go and take our change out of them."

Very little breakfast did for Bluff. A devil'd kidney and two cups of coffee were all he could master, though, as Tom slipped up the back stairs for his gloves, he detected him in the butler's pantry, getting a bottle of soda water on the sly.

It was fortunate Mrs. Bluff's room did not command a view of the back yard; for if she had seen the great bloody, dirty, sooty, unruly devils rush out full cry, and scour the yards and courts, and outhouses, tearing here, there, and everywhere, regardless of Joshua's yells and threats, and screams and tootles, and the cracks of his great flail-like whip, she might well have thought they were mad.

" Give us a leg up ! " exclaimed Joshua, as, after shooting the bolt of the brewhouse door, he stood beside a wretched, iron marked, bay Rosinante, whose galled back was protected from the puddingy saddle by a piece of old green and yellow Scotch carpeting.

" Which way's the cover ? " inquired he, as he thrust his great feet into the rusty stirrup irons.

" Up the hill," replied the gardener, telegraphing with his arm ; and forthwith Joshua tickled the old nag with his solitary spur, and hobbled off the stones at a most woe-begone shuffle, blowing, and hooping, and hallooing as he went. It was hard to say which leg the old nag was lamest on.

" They certainly are very unsteady, those hounds, I should say," observed Mr. Bluff, whose black cob seemed to have caught the infection, and began kicking and capering, regardless of Bluff's remonstrances and the diggings of his spurless heels.—" *Quick* " was the word, and having mounted, our friends hurried after the noise made by Jos as he led the charge.

*   *   *   *   *

" —— the fellow ! he's not going to put them into Reislip plantation, surely ! " exclaimed poor Bluff, as, on clearing the well-wooded avenue, they saw Joshua careering over the turf in that direction with some six or seven couple of hounds apparently hunting his horse, for they were going full cry.— " Oh my God ! " exclaimed Bluff, looking the very picture of misery : " they'll kill every hare in the place. Oh dear ! oh dear ! whatever shall I do ! Scott, my good fellow ! Scott, my good fellow ! your horse can gallop ! *do* get forward and turn them, or they'll utterly ruin me."

Tom shot off at best pace, and just got within ear-shot of Joshua, as the resolute devils tore past his horse, and rushed full cry into cover. Stopping them was quite out of the question ; half a dozen Jos's couldn't have done it ; no, not even a Jos to each hound, mounted at least as this Jos was.

In they went as if they would eat it.

"A! they gan in bonny!" exclaimed Jos, pulling up his cripple, apparently pleased at the feat. "If he's there, they'll soon root him out. Forrard in! forrard in, Tapster, old boy!" continued he, as a great black and white devil came lobbing along, towling and howling as he went.

"They'll all be here enow," added Jos, looking down upon the surrounding country, where one hound was baying the cows, another chasing a jackass, a third running a muck at the geese, and a couple of beagles that had been beat by the pace of their great four and twenty inch cousins were establishing a little rabbit-hunt of their own.

Poor Bluff's prophecy was speedily fulfilled; for the hounds had not been in cover a minute ere the most lamentable screams and cries began to issue from all parts, as first one poor hare and then another was chopped by the savage invaders. Pheasants rose in clouds with noisy whir, and hares streamed wildly out in all directions, some rushing into the very jaws of the arriving stragglers; and when Bluff's cob got him to the scene, every dog had his hare, either dead or alive.

Steeltrap, the keeper, was frantic. He abused Joshua like a pickpocket, asking him in the most open way if Joshua "thought he was such a fool as to allow a fox to set foot in the preserves?" It was, however, no time for talking. The screams of the hares still continued; and the keeper and the foot people having armed themselves with sticks and rails, and whatever they could lay hands on, rushed to the rescue, and presently there was a rare battering, and scrambling, and howling, and fighting in the plantation, as the savage hounds disputed the possession of the mangled pussy remains with the assailants.

At length, by dint of blows from the cudgels and blows from

the horn, some six or seven couple of hounds were got out of cover ; and the only plan with scratch packs being to keep moving, when you get a majority, Joshua again set off over the downs in the direction of Hailweston Woods, which were pointed to him in the distance as the place where he ought to have gone to throw off.

When they got to Hailweston Woods they found the field

"FORRARD IN ! FORRARD IN, TAPSTER, OLD BOY !"

consisting of a few neighbouring farmers, a keeper, and a blacksmith or two, who had been waiting some time for the hounds, each man, according to his own account, having winded a fox as he came. Some of them were ardent admirers of the Scratchley dogs, and anticipated their throwing Mr. Neville's completely into the shade. " Mr. Neville's dogs are very good when there is a scent," observed Willie Wander-head, " but they can't work a fox in dry weather like these," said he, eyeing the great bloody-faced savages as they passed.

"That's Rollocker!" exclaimed Toby Butcher, as a great mastiff-headed creature, half foxhound half bloodhound, came throwing his tongue as he travelled. "Ah, what a fine note he has!" and so they were severally criticised in detail as they passed into cover. Joshua was already in, "yoicking" and cheering such as were inclined to listen to his voice.

Several of the stanch dogs giving tongue as they drew, and all being desperately addicted to hare, they had kept up a pretty continuous noise in different parts of the cover before a decided stream of melody indicated anything better than riot, when a loud, oft repeated, most masterly "TALLYHO!" to the south, announced that reynard had been seen. Away they all cut to the place, where they found a young plough-man, purple with shouting, in the act of loosing a horse from the harrows to join in the chase, leaving t'other ar'd nag to follow with the harrows, if it liked. The ground was very dry, but there was a good scent in cover, and not a bad one out; indeed, if truth must be told, wet is not indispensable to scent, and one of the best scenting days we ever saw was when the ground was as dry as in summer. But to the hunt.

The great business of a huntsman to a scratch pack is to lay his dogs on the scent—"casting," and "lifting," and "throwing in at head;" all scientific manœuvres, in short, are only for your fifteen hundred, or two thousand a year packs. What can you expect for eight pound ten? The scratch gentleman puts his hounds on the scent, and it is their business to tell which way the owner of the scent goes, and not his. So it was with Joshua. His poor, half-starved, broken-down steed was quite done by the time it got to the halloa, and, instead of setting to, and riding in the naughty way Mr. Holyoake did in the "Quarterly," with a couple of hounds or so on the scent,

'Ware Sheep!' 'Ware Sheep!'

Joshua very deliberately got off, and sitting astride the fence rails, began puffing and blowing his horn to get all the redoubtable dogs out of cover that he could. That feat being accomplished, at least as far as he could judge by the absence of noise, he shifted his saddle back off the poor galled jade's withers, re-adjusted the piece of carpeting, and proceeded at a gentle trot along the higher ground of the line they had gone ; his next business being to catch and couple the dogs at the end, for which purpose he carried two most formidable bunches of couples at his saddle. So he hobbled and jingled away at his leisure.

The majority of our readers, we dare say, will have had experience enough of the elongated, straggling style in which scratch packs do their "splendid work ;" the difficulty there is in telling which field has the head, and which the tail. Perhaps some of them may have unpleasant reminiscences connected therewith, so, as our paper is short, and our dinner we sincerely hope nearly ready, we will wind up this part of our sketch by describing the scene that burst on Joshua's astonished vision as, on rounding Fourburrow Hill, he came all at once upon Woolridge Valley.

What "strange confusion there was in the vale below !" as the poet sings.

First and foremost were **Mr. Sylvanus Bluff's** swallow tails flying out, as, horsewhip in hand, he hurried from one upturned ewe to another rescuing herself or her lamb from the fury of the savage pack. Others were similarly engaged, while their horses fled or grazed at their leisure. Dead ewes and lambs were scattered around, while some of the more depraved of the pack actually did battle with the rescuers for the bodies of their victims. Others sneaked stealthily around, diving up to the very eyes in blood as opportunity offered, and those that had gorged themselves with tender lamb, curved their distended sides, and sought repose among the bushes on the hill.

So the last state of Mr. Sylvanus Bluff was a deal worse than the first.

MORAL.

All you kindly disposed, generous-minded, country gentlemen who encourage fox-hunting without partaking of it yourselves, make allowances for masters, and beware, oh ! beware, of the Scratchley dogs.

CHAPTER XVII.

AND LAST.

THE END OF HUNTING.

ND now we really think, what with the chapter on the weather and this moral on the "muttons," we have done something to rescue our work from the charge of utter uselessness. It is somewhat singular that we should extract a moral from the misfortunes of the man who made the complaint; but truth is stronger than fiction, and performs far more unaccountable feats. The obligations we were under to Mr. Bluff for buying all our works, without wanting them, made us desirous of showing him some little civility in return ; accordingly, we despatched our friend Phiz to make the sketch illustrative of the scene we have described, and which we hope the worthy man will like. We have kept a proof before letters on India paper, which we purpose framing and presenting to Mrs. Bluff, for her *boudoir* or physic-room rather. Phiz, when down on this errand, made a sketch of Hawbuck Grange on speculation, **which,** as things have turned out, **was** fortunate.

Our friend Scott doffed his red coat on his return to Hawbuck Grange with very different feelings to what sportsmen generally experience on parting with their " pinks," and as he replaced the breeches with tweed trowsers and the dusty tops with good honest double-soled shoes, he felt rather glad than otherwise that there was at last an end to the humbug of hunting.

"I wouldn't give twopence to have any day over again," said he, running the winter quickly through his mind as he sat changing his stockings, when his thoughts were suddenly directed into another channel by the protrudance of a big toe through a great hole.

"*Confound the thing!* " exclaimed he, pulling the stocking off again and throwing it from him, "that's the care one's housekeeper takes of one ;" whereupon his thoughts immediately flew to Snailswell and matrimony, and if he had not wanted most particularly to see how his drainers were getting on, and whether Jack Hoggers had harrowed out the oat field or not, we have little doubt he would have trotted over to Snailswell, and finished the day with a little tea and courtship.

"I'll go to-morrow, any-how," said he : "I'll not bother mother Bluff about her teeth : at all events I'll go over and see her," continued he, relapsing into cautiousness, and thinking he could make the old excuse of trying the brother's three-year-old serve again, as it had already served him very often.

Having at length equipped himself for country exercise, he broke cover and proceeded down stairs.

On the centre of a most bachelor-like little table in the middle of the parlour, conspicuous on the green baize cover, lay a note—pink paper with a blue seal, a woman's all over !—

" Why here's a letter from *her!* " exclaimed Tom, darting to where it lay.

He opened and read it.   Thus it ran :—

" MY DEAR MR. SCOTT,

   " *The kind, I may say fatherly, interest you have ever taken in my welfare makes me anxious to give you the earliest intelligence of a matter deeply affecting my future prospects.   My cousin, Harry Crow, to whom you doubtless know I have long been deeply attached, has at length made sufficient money to enable him to quit the sea, and we are about to be married forthwith.   I would not for the world that you should hear of this from any one but myself.   I have therefore sent the boy over on the young horse at exercise; and with the repeated expression of my sincere gratitude for all your kindness, believe me to remain, My dear Mr. Scott, ever yours most sincerely,*

" LYDIA CLIFTON.

   " *P.S.—Would you have the kindness to ask your housekeeper for her receipt for making gooseberry fool, and send it by post as the boy must not wait."*

   " *Curse those cousins!* " exclaimed Tom, dropping the note and sinking into his easy chair.

*   *   *   *   *

   " *No man's safe with them, I declare!* " continued he, thumping the stuffed arm as he rose.—"This young vagabond's been running about the house just like a domestic cat when he was ashore, for I don't know how many years, without ever raising the slightest suspicion, and now it turns out—

   " Fatherly interest, indeed," muttered he, eyeing himself in the glass,—" that's a precious piece of impudence too.—Not so old as all that comes to, either.—"*D—n all cousins, say I !* " exclaimed he, pacing hurriedly up and down the room, adding "*No man's safe where they are.*"——

"Gooseberry fool, indeed !" exclaimed he, tearing up the note and committing it to the flames. "I wonder who's been the fool in this business. Dare say she wants to feed that young water-rat upon it ; " adding, as he turned away, "I hope she'll make him sick if she does."

But we will not pursue the painful subject.—The old ladies will doubtless say—"sarved him right," while the young ones— to whom we now address ourself—will, we hope, take a kinder view of the case, especially as our friend Tom is now in the market. We alluded to the fortunate circumstance of "Phiz" having made a sketch of Hawbuck Grange, and the little dears will see why we thought it so. Addressing ourself personally to them we may say, it is all very well for you to give yourselves airs among other girls,—say "I wouldn't have this man,"—"I wouldn't *think* of that," and so on ; but when it comes to a downright case of tangible matrimony, few of you are such fools as to throw away a chance. Here then *is* a chance. Our young friend, and we are confident your mammas will tell you that all men are young till they are married, our young friend Tom Scott wants a wife, and, as we have shown, he is not imperative about money. That is putting the case we believe in its true light. He doesn't say, "No girl with money need apply ; " far from it. He would rather have one with money, but money is not a "sine quâ non"—which is French for indispensable.

"Up then and at him !" as the Duke of Wellington said to the Guards at Waterloo.

Of Hawbuck Grange we need not say much ; indeed Phiz has saved us the trouble of saying any thing, for as poor Hood sang of Tom Rounding the huntsman, when he exhibited him as a frontispiece to his Epping Hunt,

> Here shall the muse frame no excuse,
> But frame the man himself;

hiz serves up Hawbuck Grange in a similar way.

*   *   *   *   *
   *   *   *   *

N.B.—Only purchasers of this work will be entitled to view Hawbuck Grange. They must come, Hawbuck Grange in hand, in fact.

THE END.

List of Subscribers up to 31st January 1988

Michael J. Abberton
Miss Gloria Abbey
J. S. Abbott
Mrs I. M. Adamson
Robin Addison
H. W. Aidley MFH
D. B. Alexander-Sinclair
R. N. Alington Maguire
J. A. Allen
J. H. Allen
James Allen
O. J. R. Allen
D. W. Allen
P. M. S. Allen
P. H. B. Allsop
A. G. Amos
P. T. K. Anderson
Cecily Anderson
Dr Robert L. Andre
D. G. Andrew
Miss Diane Andrews
G. A. N. Andrews
Dr M. E. Anfilogoff
Miss I. R. Archibald
Mrs H. E. Armitage
C. J. Armstrong
J. H. Arnold
Lt Col R. M. Arnold
Mrs & Mrs P. Ashby
Peter R. Ashley
R. A. C. Ashworth
J. P. Asquith
Aurelian Books
Andrew C. Ayres

Colonel & Mrs G. O.
  Baker
W. J. Baker
G. D. N. Balderstone
H. A. S. Bancroft
A. Banfield MH
D. I. Barker
John Barker
Robert D. Barnard
David J. Barnes

Sir David Barran
F. J. Barratt
Henry L. Barrett
A. G. S. Barstow
D. S. Bass
Paul Bass
W. G. Bate
Anwer Bati
Peter Batty-Smith
Michael Baxandall
P. A. Beddows
A. F. L. Beeston
Nicholas John Belcher
Denis Bell
G. Bennett
Mrs M. D. Berger
Sigi R. Bergmann
Peregrine Bertie
M. Ide Betts
Lt Col R. T. Betts
T. J. Bigg
Major K. R. McK Biggs
D. Bilham
Dr R. J. Birts
L. C. Blaaberg
P. J. W. Black
Dr Bernard Black
The Rev F. A. Black
Mrs Jill Blackbourn
Peter Blacklock
E. C. Blake
M. D. Blake
Mrs P. Blake
The Reverend Michael
  Bland MA
A. H. Boddy
T. E. T. Bond
Col R. G. Borradaile
L. A. F. Borrett
Stanley W. Botterill
Colonel M. C. Bowden
A. G. Bowden
Miss Mary J. E. Bower
Dr J. R. Bowers
John G. Bowler
L. F. Bowyer

G. W. Brazendale CMG
Dr O. B. Brears CMG
The Lord Bridges
D. C. Bright
Frank Brightman
John E. Brindle
Sir Ronald Brockman
D. H. V. Brogan
R. J. Bromwich
Col J. M. Browell
J. F. Brown
David Brown B V SC
  MRCVS
P. M. Brown
R. C. Brown
M. G. Bruce-Squires
Mrs D. S. Bull
John S. Burgess
Lieut A. G. Burns RN
John D. C. Burridge
Dr J. D. K. Burton
W. G. Burton
Dermot S. L. Butler
Mrs M. C. Butler
Dr J. W. Butler
Mrs B. B. Buttenshaw
J. Byles
Brendan Byrne

A. J. Cairns
C. R. H. Caldow
A. J. C. Campbell
W. H. D. Campbell
L. R. Campfield
The Rev W. R. D. Capstick
A. R. P. Carden
Robert Carew
Major F. W. L. Carslaw
Brigadier Caruthers
A. G. Casewell
P. A. Cattermole
Mrs E. L. Catto
Mrs Eileen Cawkwell
E. S. Cazalet
Lord Charles Cecil

Philip Chadwick
Robert Chadwick
C. L. Chafer
W. T. Chaffer
Lt Col J. E. S.
  Chamberlayne
D. Chandler
Captain L. W. L. Chelton
  RN
Dr Max A. Chernesky
D. M. Child
Mrs G. S. Ching
Mrs J. Chisnall
Mrs M. W. Churchward
J. R. Clack
D. L. Clarke
A. M. Clarkson
W. Clunies-Ross
A. C. T. Cochrane
B. E. Cole
Christopher Newbury
  Coles
R. H. Collard
Edwin Collins
F. L. Collins
Ken Collins
Mrs S. P. Conan-Davies
M. L. Congdon
F. A. Connelly
P. P. Cooke
Richard G. Coomber
V. F. Cooper
W. H. Cooper
A. Cooper-Reade
John Cope MP
M. D. Corke
Lt Col J. N. Cormack
M. Cosgrove
G. W. Cottrell
M. H. Couchman
J. Cowen
Major W. D. Cox
T. J. L. Cox
Mrs C. A. F. Cox
S. R. Craddock
H. P. Craig
S. J. Crane
M. G. Cripps
Major J. S. Crisp
Lt Col R. N. R. Cross
J. P. O. Crowe
John J. Crown

Hugh Curling
Mrs M. Curtis
Geoffrey Cuttle

Mrs R. E. D'Arcy
Dennis D'Vigne
T. L. A. Daintith
Michael R. Dampier
M. R. M. Daniel
F. W. Daniel
Paul Daniell
John H. Daniels
Mrs & Mrs D. G. Daniels
Paul J. Daniels
Dr M. L. R. Davies
Mrs C. J. Davies
R. W. Howard Davies
Mrs C. A. Davis
Mrs E. J. Dawkes
Mrs H. L. R. Day
Robin de Wilde
G. R. Deacon
Geoffrey J. Dear
Martyn J. Dearden
E. Dearing
Rowland P. Dell
Capt. S. J. Dell
E. A. K. Denison
John Devaux
R. A. Dewhurst
J. J. Dingwall
Dr A. M. Dixon
Dr William Dodd
R. C. T. Dorsett
John E. S. Driver
Mrs G. Lloyd Drummond
Miss F. Duncombe
C. D. Dunstan
P. G. Durrans

A. C. Eaton
Lt Col W. R. Edgedale
R. C. Edgell
E. F. Edwards
P. S. A. Edwards
J. M. C. Elder
E. T. Eley
Mrs B. Ellington
Wray Ellis
T. J. Ellis

D. M. Ely-Brown
J. E. R. Emmet
M. G. Esther
David A. H. Evans
L. J. C. Evans
J. M. Evans
Mrs J. P. M. H. Evelyn

J. C. Fareham
T. C. Farmbrough
Paul Farnsworth
Major A. Farrant
J. E. Farrer
T. M. H. Fawcett
The Rev M. S. Feben STL
  PHL
The Reverend J. M.
  Fellows
Mrs M. R. Ferens
Dr J. B. Ferguson
D. H. Field
George Findley
R. A. J. Finn
Mrs Peter Fitzgerald
J. E. Fleeman
G. J. Fletcher
A. M. Florey
G. Ford
Mrs V. M. Foreman
Mrs B. J. Foster
Roy Foster
Mrs D. J. Foster
Lt J. G. Fountain 17/21
  Lancers
Kenneth Martyn Fox
Mrs R. Fremantle
Lt Col S. J. Furness
Dr M. J. P. Furniss

R. De V. Gaisford
Mrs Mary Gallop
Oliver Gardener
Mrs Audrey Gardham
W. J. Garforth
Peter Gargett
A. F. Garnett
C. J. Garnett
Professor J. C. A. Gaskin
Major R. H. C. Gates
Ivan Gault

N. George
Major Andrew A. Gibbs
  MBE TD
Dr Hugh Gibbs
Mrs R. I. Gilchrist
His Honour Judge S. S.
  Gill
Lt Col R. F. F. Gillespie
H. R. Gillespie
Prof R. W. Gilliatt
Richard Gilman MD
  FACS
W. A. Gilmour
Richard A. S. Gimson
J. M. Glaser
Anthony Goddard
John Godley
Capt. W. E. B. Godsal RN
C. A. Gold
Mrs Bronwen Goldsmid
C. R. Goodall
Paul Goodlet
M. P. Gordon-Jones
Capt J. E. Gorst
Mrs D. W. Gorton
C. A. J. Gosland
T. F. Gostling
Andrew H. Gould
Mr and Mrs J. H. Gould
G. B. Graham
David Granger
Guy D. Grasby
B. T. Gray
J. Michael Green
Robin E. Greenwood
Mrs E. Griffin
His Hon Judge B. Griffiths
  QC
Miss J. A. Groom
John D. Grossart
Mrs C. Guilding
A. D. Gunner
P. L. Guy MH

Mrs P. R. Hadfield
J. Hafok
C. Hagenbach
J. A. Hall
Richard Hall
N. K. Halliday
Clifford Halsall

J. A. L. Hamilton
W. S. Hamilton
R. M. Hannam
Dr G. H. de G. Hanson
J. I. Hardwick
G. M. Hardy
Dr B. J. Harrison
Edwin Harrison
Lt Col J. A. Harrison
Dr Nicholas Hart
Alan Hartnell
J. R. Havers-Strong
Joseph Hawes
Dr P. W. Hawkes
A. W. Hawkins
Derek Hayes
I. S. Haynes MFH
Jiro Hazama
John Heald
Wg Cdr N. V. O. P. Healey
John E. Heath
Mrs Irene Anstey
  Hebditch
John Hefford
Timothy Heneage
M. C. Henman
Sir James Henry Bt
Robin Herdman
Mrs A. M. Hesketh
M. D. Hewison
Ms Sylvia E. Heyworth
R. Hibbert
E. C. Hicks
Anthony Higgins
S. de Premorel Higgons
J. A. de C. Hill
Miss Sophie Hill
G. E. D. Hiller
Miss J. Hirschfeld
M. R. Hoare
James G. Hobden
A. R. A. Hobson
J. A. Hock
Miss Gillian Hodges
P. Hodgkinson
C. J. Hodgson
T. Hodson
J. W. Hoggard
Graham Holdsworth
Peter Hole MH
David C. Hollis
R. I. Holman-Baird

W. Holt
Barry Hook
R. W. J. Hopkins
H. L. Hoppe
Malcolm Hord
J. M. C. Horsfall
Capt M. A. Houghton
Mr & Mrs M. J. Howard
D. Howcroft
Mrs D. C. Howe
Miss Wendy Howes
The Lady Howick
Miss J. Hoyland
Mrs Denis Hulme
Mrs Gilbert W. Humphrey
Brigadier K. Hunt
P. B. Hunter
James Hunter Blair
I. W. M. Hurst MFH
Geoffrey Hutton
G. L. Hylands

A. F. Iliffe
Andrew Illius
Nigel Ince
Col F. J. Ingham
G. W. Iredell
C. Kenneth Irvine
J. G. Irving
Maj Gen D. E. Isles CB
  OBE

Mrs J. M. Jachim
His Honour Judge C. P.
  James
D. M. Jarvis
David Jeffcoat
Robin Jenkinson
C. P. Jenner MH
J. M. Jerram
George A. Jones
Terry Jones
W. D. Jones
P. K. Jordan
Malcolm D. Joslyn
Michael Leo Keane
Francis Kelly
J. E. Kelly
V. Kelly
Dr A. J. I. Kelynack
Edmund Kendall

Callum S. Kennedy
Miss P. Kennedy
Mrs M. B. Kent
HRH The Duke of Kent
David Kenward
Dr D. F. Kerr
T. W. Killick
A. E. Kindred
Jonathan G. N. King
Dr Mary Ellen Kitler
A. J. S. Knox

G. W. Laing
G. A. Lakin
R. E. Lambert
Miss A. Langdon
Mrs V. A. Langridge
N. Lanham-Cook
Philip Lattaway
M. A. Lavis
Richard Law
Mrs Mary G. Lawton
M. S. Ledger MOH
Owen Legg
G. C. M. Leggett
Frank Lehmann
L. P. F. L'Estrange OBE
  FRSA
Brian Lewis
J. W. P. Lewis
R. V. Lewis
G. M. Lilly
Sir Anthony Lincoln
  KCMG CVO
G. C. Lindsey-Smith
Dr Charles Lipp
C. S. Lippell
Robin J. Lipscombe
William Lister
The Earl Lloyd-George
J. W. Lockwood
Anthony D. Loehnis
Sir Gilbert Longden
H. C. R. Ludlow-Hewitt
  MBE
Oliver Lynas
A. N. Lyndon-Skeggs

J. MacFarlane
Lt Col C. H. T.
  MacFetridge

A. J. Mack
R. D. Mackay
The Rev Hugh Mackay of
  Talmine
Capt M. J. MacKinlay
  MacLeod
J. G. H. Mackrell
Brig P. R. Macnamara
D. G. Maddocks
Miss J. Mahony
Stephen Mahony
M. V. Malyon
R. D. Mann
A. Marchant
Brian Margetts
R. D. Marshall
D. Marshall Evans
J. W. Martin
Major H. D. G.
  Martindale
Peter I. Maslen
A. R. Mason
R. J. Mason LLB FCIARB
Stephen & Penny Mason
A. A. Mawby
Michael Maynard
John McCaig
Mrs M. McCormack
W/Cdr G. E. McCullagh
Peter O. McDougall
Dr Ewen McEwen
B. T. McGeough
D. J. McGlynn
Brian McGregor
Mrs Sheila McKinley
J. A. McNeish
W. J. B. Meakin
C. J. Mears
Mrs P. Megginson
David C. Mellors
Keith Messenger
The Lord Middleton
A. J. B. Mildmay-White
John Millar
Keith Miller
C. H. Millin
Mrs C. Millum
Dr C. J. Mitchell
N. H. Mitchell
Mrs G. M. Mitchell
A. Moger
E. G. H. Moody

Kenneth A. Moore
P. D. Moorhead
Neil A. Morres
G. E. Morris
P. A. Morton
John Murray QC
John F. Murray
R. C. Musetti RSH
John A. Mutimer
Andrew Mylius

Mrs S. J. Nash
P. Naylor
P. E. Neal
Malcolm G. Neesam
David Negus FRCS
Basil Newall
Mrs John Newcomb
D. A. Newton
M. J. Nicholas
Mark Nicholson
J. N. F. Norman
Cdr P. North Lewis
A. H. W. P. Norton
D. H. L. Nugent

Michael O'Donoghue
Mrs & Mrs P. J.
  O'Donoghue
Miss Roseanne O'Reilly
M. B. Ogle
R. J. Oliver
Mrs D. C. Osborn
Admiral Sir John Julian
  Oswald
C. D. Outred
R. Elwyn Owen

D. J. Palmer
G. H. Paris
Anthony V. Parker
H. M. Parker
Mrs P. H. Parker
Dr Miles Parkes MH
Mrs C. H. Parlby
Miss G. M. Partridge
K. G. Pates
David E. Pattenden
C. Payne

Dennis Pearl
Mrs N. F. K. Pearse
Jonathan R. H. Pearson
J. F. A. Peck
Jorn Pedersen
J. F. Penley TD
R. S. L. Penn
S. W. Percival
Robert Perfitt
Tony Perry
D. J. Peters JP MA
H. M. Peters
Mrs B. W. B. Pettifer
Edna Phelps
J. O. Phillips
Andrew G. Phillips
Sir Charles Pickthorn, Bt
C. M. Plumbe
Michael J. Plummer
Robert H. Plumridge
George Pocklington
The Hon Mrs R. W.
  Pomeroy
P. Potter
Michael Powell
S. J. B. Pratt
Col R. F. Preston
J. Maurice Price QC
Mrs Rosemary Price
Mrs A. T. Prince
Mrs Carolyn Probert
Miss S. Jasmine Profit
Brion Purdy
Anthony Pye

M. F. Race
M. Radakovic
R. S. C. Ralli
Mrs J. Randle
H. T. Randolph
Mrs J. F. Rankin
J. F. Rankin
A. E. Ranson
J. R. Stanley Raper
J. H. Ratcliff
Cyril Ray
Peter Read
P. F. Rednall
M. M. Reeve
Dr R. W. Reid
Bruce Reid

Dr R. E. Rewell
David Reynolds
W. S. C. Richards
William Richardson
  RIBA
Andrew W. G. Rickett
H. W. Riddolls
Mrs Susan Roberts
T. J. Roberts
R. F. Roberts
Brig A. Robertson
Wg/Cdr S. Robinson RAF
  (Retd.)
B. E. Robinson
T. A. Rogers
John Rolls
Mrs Laurence Rook
J. M. Rose
Mrs Genevieve Rose
Joseph Rosenblum
C. M. Ross
Pamela Rowe
The Rev A. G. B. Rowe
Dr A. C. Ruddle
Dr Josephine Rutter

C. G. C. Sayer
Philipp Schoeller
Richard Schutze
L. R. Scott
J. H. Scrutton
A. J. Sears
J. C. Sedgwick
Jonathan Selby
Mrs R. E. Selby
M. Shannon
Vernon K. Sharpington
Frank Sheardown
Mark Sheardown
A. J. Shears
Clive Shenton
A. G. Sherratt
N. E. C. Sherwood
G. M. Shipman
Mrs F. R. Short
Richard E. Silvey
Alfred Singer
A. L. Smith
N. L. H. Smith
Sergeant M. B. Smith
J. C. S. F. Smithies

Timothy Smyth
Dr H. M. Snow
Mrs I. J. Barclay Sole
Miss M. L. Solman
I. P. G. Southward
Sir John Sparrow
Major B. L. Speegle
I. D. Spencer
Mrs P. Spiller
J. A. Spooner
S. A. Springate
Simon Stacey
Mrs J. M. Stannah
Miss Lesley Stark
Peter Starr
E. W. Stearn
David Steeds
B. G. Steff
Jenni Stone
J. S. R. Storer
Mrs J. R. Strange
Dr F. S. Stych
D. Sullivan
Stephen Sumption
Mrs H. Sumption
Dr S. J. Surtees
Philip Alexander Surtees
R. V. N. Surtees
Sir Ronald Swayne
M. C. Swift
Mrs W. A. Swinerton
Hugo Swire
Mrs Annette Syder
Lt Col G. Symonds
A. Symonds

Miss M. Tait
B. V. Talbott
G. G. Tarlton
Alec I. Taylor
D. F. Taylor
Miss Anne Taylor
Maurice Taylor
Mrs M. E. Taylor
Irving L. Theaker
Hugh R. Thomas
L. C. Thomas
P. C. F. Thomas
G. Thompson
J. W. M. Thompson
Major A. F. P. Thomson

Capt Eric A. Tidy
C. H. Tinsley
H. J. Titley
A. G. Todd
Maj Gen D. A. H. Toler
C. M. L. Toll
P. B. Tompsett
J. P. L. Tory
Dennis Tracey
J. J. Trapp
Miss V. Travis
D. J. Tregidgo
Mrs Jennifer M. Trippier
R. W. Trollope MFH
Dr J. D. G. Troup
G. P. Tucker
David Tudor-Pole
I. M. Turner
Oscar Turnill
C. H. Tutton
Peter Thompson-Tweddle

F. A. Underwood
R. J. Unwin

D. B. Vale
George Vallance
S. van Praet D'Amerloo
D. J. Viveash
William von Raab

Michael Wace
C. Wagstaff

T. Wainwright
Michael Wake-Walker
D. Walker
J. H. Walker
Major M. P. Walker
Mrs P. M. Walker
P. B. Walker
B. J. Wallis
Miss T. M. Walsh
John H. Walton
Michael Ward-Thomas
A. T. Warwick CEng
   MIEE
R. F. Waterer
H. A. Waterson
P. S. Watson
Ian R. Watson
R. K. Watson
M. A. Watt
E. D. B. Way
M. J. R. Wear
Mrs H. D. Webb
Mrs A. J. Webb
W. R. B. Webb
P. Welford
Dr Paul Wellings
G. Westall
Mrs Mary Davan Wetton
M. Whitaker
Edmund H. White
Ralph White
A. P. Whitehead
D. Whiteley
Frank Whitmarsh
Michael A. Whittle
The Rev H. D. Wiard MA

Rodney W. J. Wild
John Williams
R. M. C. Williams
Major General E. A. W.
   Williams
Richard J. Wilne
Mrs R. E. Wilsdon
Steven N. Wilshire
B. R. Wilson
C. M. Wilson
Charles Wilson
Herbert Wilson
Patrick Wilson
John Winch
E. A. Windsor
K. R. Wing
Barone R. Winspeare
John Winter
Harry Wolton QC
Douglas J. Wood
Miss S. M. W. Woodman-
   Smith
J. G. Woodrow
J. G. Wooldridge
Mrs David Wright
H. W. Wright
Patrick G. Wright
M. A. Wright MRCVS
W. D. Wright
E. A. Wrighton-Edwards
C. P. Wykeham-Martin
Rhydain Wynn-Williams

G. Yates
Ian Yeaman
Nigel Yonge

PUBLICATIONS OF
THE R. S. SURTEES SOCIETY
R. S. SURTEES

Mr. Sponge's Sporting Tour. Facsimile of 1853 edition. 13 full-page coloured plates and 90 engravings by **John Leech.** Introduction by **Auberon Waugh.**

Mr. Facey Romford's Hounds. 24 coloured plates by **Leech** and **'Phiz'.** 50 engravings by **W. T. Maud.** Introduction by **Enoch Powell.**

"Ask Mamma". Facsimile of 1858 edition. 13 coloured plates and 70 engravings by **Leech.** Introduction by **Rebecca West.**

Handley Cross; or **Mr. Jorrocks' Hunt.** Facsimile of 1854 edition. 17 coloured plates and 100 engravings by **Leech.** Introduction by **Raymond Carr.**

Jorrocks' Jaunts and Jollities. Facsimile of 1874 edition. 31 coloured plates by **Henry Alken, 'Phiz'** and **W. Heath.** Introduction by **Michael Wharton** ('Peter Simple').

Hillingdon Hall or **The Cockney Squire** (Jorrocks). Facsimile of 1888 edition. 12 coloured plates by **Wildrake, W. Heath** and **Jellicoe.** Introduction by **Robert Blake.**

Plain or Ringlets? Facsimile of 1860 edition. 13 coloured plates and 45 engravings by **Leech.** Introduction by **Molly Keane.**

Young Tom Hall. 16 illustrations by **G. D. Armour.** Introduction by **Cyril Ray.**

Hawbuck Grange. 8 coloured plates by **'Phiz'.** 36 engravings by **W. T. Maud.** Introduction by **Michael Clayton.**

Price **£16.95** in each case, packing and postage included.

SOMERVILLE AND ROSS

Some Experiences of an Irish R.M., Further Experiences of an Irish R.M., In Mr. Knox's Country. Facsimiles of the first editions of the Irish R.M. trilogy, which include the illustrations by **Miss Somerville.** Introduction by **Molly Keane.**

Prices (including p. & p.) **£8.70** each, **£24** for set of three.

CAPTAIN GRONOW

Reminiscences and Recollections. 17 coloured plates.
Last Recollections. 12 coloured plates.

Price **£16.95** each or **£30** the pair (inc. p. & p.).

W. W. JACOBS

Ship's Company. 12 short stories. Facsimile of first (1908)
edition with 23 illustrations by **Will Owen.**

Price **£8.70** (including p. & p.).

RUDYARD KIPLING

**Soldiers Three, The Story of the Gadsbys, In Black and
White, Under the Deodars.** Near-facsimiles of first editions
in the Indian Railway Library series of 1888. Forewords by
Philip Mason, C.I.E.

Prices (including p. & p.) **£2.95** for each of *Soldiers Three* and
The Story of the Gadsbys, **£3.75** for each of *In Black and White*
and *Under the Deodars*. **£12.50** for set of 4 Kipling books.

First published in this edition in 1988 by
The R. S. Surtees Society

Rockfield House
Nunney, Nr Frome
Somerset

© This Edition and Compilation The R. S. Surtees Society, 1988

ISBN 0 948560 08 8

Printed in Great Britain by Butler & Tanner Ltd,
Frome and London